The Issue of Faerie

Emma Bradley

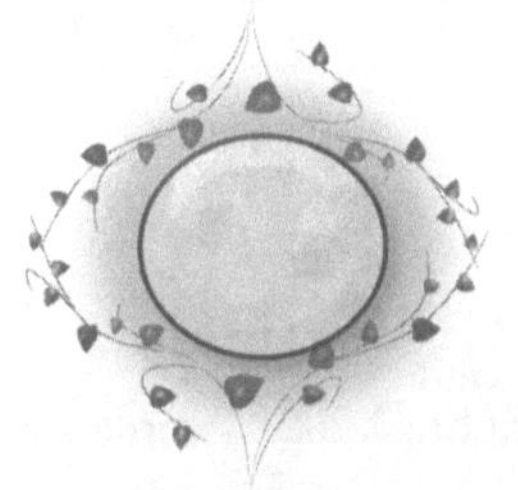

WATCH. LISTEN. LEARN.

DEDICATION

For those who dream of other worlds and want nothing more
than a place to belong – yours will come!

CONTENT WARNING

This book features imprisonment and also deals with some issues
of bereavement – every effort has been taken to deal with this in
a sensitive way, but please be aware that there are some near-
misses and also one full passing.

CHAPTER ONE
An Unexpected Return

Footsteps echoed through the long corridor, the thuds hurried and heavy on the blue carpet. I would have winced at the sound in the otherwise silent air, except it was my feet making the noise.

I rushed toward the classroom, almost knocking my arm against the wooden panelled wall. As a loud buzzing started up to signal the end of lessons, I skidded to a halt near one of the classroom doorways and pressed my back against the opposite wall. Unable to do anything about my flushed cheeks, I swept a dark lock of hair around my fingers and eyed the sheen of purple glinting amid the dark strands. While my hair was dark and curly, it had this weird habit of shining different colours, like an oil slick on tarmac.

Given that I'd been at Arcanium as a first-year Fairy Deity Person (or FDP if you were being quick about it) mentee for almost six months now, I was still learning pretty much every day. Today, the lesson was that finding new books in the library was guaranteed to distract you for longer than you planned.

I flinched as the nearest classroom door banged open and dropped my hand to my side. A stream of second-year trainees burst out, some nodding to me in recognition. The Eastwick sisters gave me smiles as they strode past, but I was glad they didn't stop to talk.

I tried to calm my smile as Kainen Hemlock ambled out of the classroom at the back of the group, but somehow I couldn't help it. While his short, brown hair showed off his angled cheekbones and made him look more like a male model, his grey eyes were full of shadows and whispered secrets. It's not like I had a massive crush on him or anything, but he'd been kind to me since we started training together over the past couple of months. Surprisingly so, considering that his family were supporters of the Forgotten, my mortal enemies, and how much his sister hated the mere sight of me.

He smoothed a hand over his hair and looked me up and down. It was impossible for me to look in any way attractive in my baggy black hoodie with the sleeves rolled up to the elbows and black cotton trousers, so I didn't hold onto any hope that he was going to ask me up to the surface world or to the canteen for a drink.

"Demi Darcy, you forgot about me again, didn't you?" he asked, no doubt noticing my flushed cheeks.

"I didn't forget." I flicked a glance up to his eyes, which were staring directly into mine. "I misappropriated my allocation of time."

Kainen laughed and started walking toward the large training hall at the end of the corridor. I followed, preparing myself for a brutal session. That was another good thing about Kainen, he didn't hold back.

As FDP mentees, we had to be ready for anything. Once we got thrown into assignments in the Faerie realms, we were mostly surviving on our own wit and ability. That was the sole reason my mentor Petra had singled Kainen out for me to train with, but I'd been worried at first because of his family connections to the Forgotten and the old ways of Faerie.

"You stick to that excuse," he said. "At least we know your word-tangling is getting better."

I gave him a look. "You're implying my fighting skills aren't?"

Kainen opened the training room door and stood aside to let

me pass. I led us into the hall, deserted now that most of Arcanium would be rushing to the canteen or to do their own thing for the rest of the evening.

"I wouldn't dare," he teased.

I turned in the middle of the room, folding my arms across my chest. This was generally how we started, him trying to annoy me before attacking, and me just about managing to keep up.

"I reckon you would." I shot back. "Don't forget, you've already told me the lying loophole."

Kainen's smile widened. There was something dark about him, not only the way his eyes seemed to go all charcoal and smoky when he was really close up, but he liked to test people, see what made them get within an inch of snapping before he backed off. I'd learned not to rise to it, but I guessed it was his family that had instilled the trait in him.

"And you swore you wouldn't tell a single soul for as long as you live, and never discuss it unless the person knows of it or finds out themselves," he countered.

"I haven't. But still, it's interesting to find out that the more something becomes a common phrase, the less it becomes a lie."

Fae and fairies couldn't lie, or each one would stick inside them like a thorn and slowly unravel their mind. So, I'd been both horrified and elated to find out that some lies could be less damaging depending on how common they were.

Telling someone you loved them when you didn't was a lie. Telling someone it was raining cats and dogs when it wasn't counted as an obviously incorrect saying, which technically could be overlooked.

I hadn't dared test any technicalities yet, but my best mates Ace and Milo spent most of their time in the library where Milo helped out, so I'd done my homework. The lie loophole was a thing. Kainen had forbidden me from telling anyone, but I kept leaving the page of the relevant book lying open, hoping Milo or Ace would see it so we could dissect its details. So far, Milo just kept tutting at me for leaving books lying around.

Kainen copied my folded arm stance and we stood in silence for several moments. I managed to hold his gaze, but his eyes looked extra smoky across the few metres between us.

What approach is it today? I wondered, tense with anticipation. *Will he attack out of nowhere, or try to word-tangle me into dropping my guard?*

I focused inside myself, digging for the thread of connection to my fairy side, which usually lingered near my left elbow. It tingled awake and travelled up my arm, filling my chest. I held myself ready, eager to do something physical after a day full of theory classes.

Kainen's finger twitched at his side. I threw up my hand and cast a protection warding over myself, a faint glow of rainbow like a soap bubble, visible only to me.

Whatever Fae gift Kainen had sent my way was also invisible, but I could feel it push against the warding, my protection linked right through me.

"What was that one meant to do?" I asked.

Kainen smiled. This was what he loved, baiting people and playing Fae games. It was in his blood and probably right down to his very marrow, given that he was part of the Hemlock family who were court Fae and related very distantly to the Queen of Faerie, and my best friend Taz.

"Where would be the fun in telling you? Lower your protection and you'll find out."

I snorted. "Yeah right. I've been practicing and I can hold this warding for ages now, so you might want to think of something else, or suggest it. Otherwise we're probably at a bit of a stalemate."

I eyed him up and down in the silence that followed. While I'd dressed for combat training, he was wearing black jeans and a *Demon Babies* t-shirt exactly like the one Taz often wore.

At least, I guess he still wears it.

Two months had passed since I'd seen Taz. Shortly after our last assignment into Faerie where we competed in a Puzzle Tower and almost got torn to pieces by a gang of Fae socialites, his mother, the Queen, had called him home to her court. We'd orbed a few times, but always with Ace and Milo as well.

Kainen tilted his head, the smile never wavering.

Without warning, his appearance rippled. The straight, dark strands hanging around his temples and ears curled and lightened to a honey brown. His face took a different shape, not as long but still Fae-like, with a sprinkling of freckles bursting across his nose and cheeks under turquoise eyes.

I managed to hold in a gasp of shock as Taz appeared right in front of me. It wasn't the actual Taz of course, only Kainen putting on a glamour of him, but that fact didn't translate to the confused excitement that jolted in my chest.

"You miss him. That's so charming," Kainen taunted.

"You're reading my mind?" I panicked and tried to think of nothing at all. "That should be off-limits."

He shrugged, splaying his hands out wide.

"We're Fae- oh, sorry, and fairies," he added, referring to the fact I had part-human blood. "Nothing is off-limits. And when we step into this room, the same applies."

The shock of seeing Taz, or an image of him at least, was fading. The fury woke up inside me, burning through my gut. Somehow, and I couldn't quite reason why to myself, Kainen had crossed a line.

I dug deep and summoned my gift, the one I tried not to use

unless I had to. I'd been training with it on my own, but now Kainen was toying with me and he deserved to be taken down.

I'd gotten my gift because Fae are spiteful, Kainen's sister specifically, but they can also be careless. Diana hadn't intended me to get the gift with quite this much control, but that's what she got for being lazy and sending a friend to dole out her cruelty instead of doing it herself.

I focused on the buzzing energy in my fingertips, growing stronger and building up the pressure. I eyed Kainen's mid-region and thrust my hand out.

The electrical energy of my gift crackled through the air, lethal without being visible. Usually it had a subtle white-blue glow, but I'd been teaching myself to concentrate on making it move unseen. It was either focus on practice or think about certain people who weren't around anymore.

Powered by vengeful fury, my gift tore through the air and hit Kainen square in the groin. I grinned as he doubled over with a loud grunt. I called the energy back after a moment, knowing it wasn't anywhere near enough to cause him damage, just a warning shot like a small electric shock.

Kainen raised his head moments after my gift left him, and the smile was gone.

I'd never used it on him before.

He muttered something under his breath, hoping to catch me off-guard. I barely had time to fix the gap in my protection that I'd made with my gift before glittering black smoke filled the air, doming above me as it hit my warding.

I breathed a sigh of relief, safe under my protection, but I knew Kainen would be attacking to fight rather than to practice now.

Good. About time he started treating me like a proper fairy.

I stood ready, wondering what he would do next. He trained

tough in hand-to-hand combat, but he'd always warned me before attacking before. Now he eyed me, his chest still rising rapidly after the shock.

"We won't get anywhere the way we're going," he said through gritted teeth. "Back to combat training."

"Only combat training? No Fae gifts or trickery?"

After a long pause, he nodded. I wasn't convinced.

"Swear it."

As he grimaced, I knew he'd been trying to catch me out. If he swore it, I'd be safe. Or as safe as someone who'd angered a court Fae about to fight them could be. My pulse began to pound.

"I swear it," he said. Just like that, his shoulders relaxed and he smiled again. "You're getting better. Good. Okay, combat training. Also, that zap really hurt, and it's still tingling."

I ignored the mention of his tingling gentleman regions. For one thing, there was nothing gentlemanly about him now, and I knew he was trying to unsettle me.

I lowered my hand to my side but kept my protection warding around me as I walked a few paces toward him. If he was fibbing somehow, or using another Fae loophole, now would be when he'd attack.

He didn't, so I quashed the warding when I got to the point of it almost touching him. Standing a few feet apart, I decided I could avoid the inevitable sparring beforehand and throw the first punch.

Placing my foot one in front of the other, I ducked and feinted forward. Kainen reached out to grab my wrists, but I was ready for that and swung them wide, twisting sideways so he stepped past me.

With one hand pressing the small of his back, I hooked my foot around his ankle from behind and pulled back.

He twisted with all but inhuman speed so that he was falling backwards instead of forwards. His fingers clamped around my arms, hauling me down on top of him. I struggled, but he was stronger. No amount of writhing or kicking would get him off, I knew from previous training sessions.

My cheeks flushed with frustration as he rolled so I was beneath him with his hands pressing my wrists into the wooden floor and his shins pinning my legs.

"Concede?" he asked, his eyes glittering.

I could say yes. Or I could do what I'd done to his sister several months ago. I blinked at him for a couple of moments, as if I was thinking, unsure. He stared without so much as twitching his eyelids.

"Demi? As fun as this is, I'm going to need an answer. Concede."

He locked eyes with me and leaned closer, no doubt with some inane idea of trying to make me think he was going to kiss me or some nonsense. Memories of the last time I'd let a Fae boy close enough like this flickered, and I pushed aside the sudden hint of nerves fluttering in my gut.

The original plan had been to spit at him, or mime it to distract him at least, but instinct drove me forward instead. With a grunt, I jerked my shoulders upward and headbutted him in the face.

It was a sloppy effort, and my forehead barely hit his cheek, but it was enough to stun him so I could pull one of my legs out and knee him in the unmentionables. I heard the tell-tale groan and wriggled backwards until I could get to my feet.

Petra, my mentor, was teaching me how to fight all these kinds of advances, but I'd failed every single attempt Kainen had made to pin me so far. The nerves turned to elation and I faced him with my warding strong and a broad grin on my face.

I leaned forward and bent my knees in preparation as Kainen staggered to his feet, but a shadow flickered in the doorway to the hall.

I thought for a moment the figure standing there was a distraction of Kainen's, some more of his black smoke sent to draw my attention.

But it wasn't.

Oh my god.

With his back to the door, Kainen took a couple of furious steps toward me, but even as he barrelled into me, he seemed to realise that I'd lost interest in him. He steadied himself and took a step back.

"Demi?" Kainen called my name, but I couldn't answer.

I stared at the figure in the hall doorway who stood glaring back at me. A wholly different kind of fizzling started rushing through my limbs as my heart started racing.

Not racing with adrenalin, survival or amusement. Not from the odd awkward quibble at the flirtation Kainen kept trying to use so I'd lower my guard.

All-encompassing relief.

CHAPTER TWO
A Reunion and Some New Appendages

I stared across the hall but Taz didn't move toward me. He didn't smile or open his arms enough to encourage me to rush across and hug him. Not that I was the huggy type in any way, but in all the imaginings I'd had about him returning to Arcanium, I'd expected something less hostile.

I recognised the irritated spark in his turquoise eyes, and the sulky press of his lips. The way he stood spoke volumes, arms folded with one hip slightly sideways so his whole body was doing the pouting. Even though he was my best friend, we hadn't seen each other for a few months now.

What if something's changed? What if he's changed?

Without a single thought for Kainen, or what he might do if he considered training not entirely over, I set off across the hall. Behind Taz I could make out Milo and Ace hovering. As I drew closer, they looked like they were having one of their silent arguments, all pulled faces and hand gestures, but I couldn't care about that now.

Taz watched me as I approached, but whatever had put him in a sour mood seemed to have made it a permanent thing.

Was I supposed to know he was coming back? I came to a halt just out of reaching distance. *We haven't talked in like three weeks, how could I have known? Have I done something wrong and not realised it? Or not done something? Oh God, did he see Kainen glamouring into him, or hear what he said?*

I gulped against a catch in my throat.

"Hi!" It came out as a strangled squeak.

Taz eyed me, not returning the greeting. Before my nerves

could bubble over and make me explode enough ask what the hell was wrong with him, Kainen appeared beside me.

"Hi Taz, welcome back," he said, all smiles. "That was better, Demi, but next time don't get so easily distracted, okay? See you later."

He squeezed past Taz who was still sending out hostile vibes and disappeared down the corridor. I noticed Milo shrinking, his hefty arms pinning to his sides and his broad shoulders rounding like they did whenever he sensed confrontation. I always imagined him like Paddington bear with his build, brown hair and soft nature, but it took all of my effort not to say it out loud sometimes. Ace didn't shrink away, easy-going and stoic in all situations, but even he ran a hand over his short black curls and grimaced at the back of Taz's head.

"Um, yeah, we'll, we've got-" Ace hesitated.

"-Library stuff," Milo offered.

They disappeared before I could beg them to stay, although why I should need them to stick around when my best friend had just returned, I couldn't fathom.

We should be happy about this, catching up and sharing stories, not glowering at each other.

"What's up with you?" I asked, folding my arms. "Aren't you happy to be back? You look like you're about to annihilate someone."

His eyes narrowed, the flashes of arctic-green colour in them deepening.

"I don't know," he replied. "Should I be happy or worried? You seem pretty friendly now with someone who's meant to be on the side of the Forgotten. I know we haven't talked much recently, but silly me I thought you were still my friend, on *our* side."

Ah. I should have considered that.

I should have found a way to tell him I was practicing with Kainen. Probably wasn't the best time to explain how Kainen didn't associate himself with his family's ideals either, as it'd only sound like I was sticking up for him.

The best I could do was aim for derisive indifference and hope it was enough to bring Taz down off his high horse. I relaxed my arms down by my sides and aimed for what I thought would reassure him the most. Or annoy him even more; with Taz I never could be sure.

"Oh, that." I shrugged and picked my best sarky tone. "Petra's been training me pretty hard, thanks for asking. She insisted I practice with Kainen. So I did. Why, are you jealous?"

I thought I saw the slightest hint of pink in his cheeks then, although it could have been there before. He didn't answer, his eyes roving over my face.

"I wasn't doing too badly either before you showed up," I added. "I even managed to catch him with my gift, but if you're scared of missing out, I can zap your bits as well if you really want?"

Taz stared at me, his eyes boring into mine for several seconds. I wished right then I had whatever mind-reading skill Kainen had used on me earlier. Taz wouldn't ever hurt me, but his ability to sulk was legendary so I was better warding it off now rather than dealing with it later on.

Before I could find some way of breaking the stand-off, Taz sagged and huffed out a breath. As his hostile expression calmed, my insides began to unknot.

He's probably over-reacting, emotional about finally getting home. Maybe he even had ideas about what it would be-

I squeaked in alarm as Taz folded his arms around my shoulders and all but strangled the life out of me.

Unnerved, both by the close contact which I wasn't great with at the best of times and the surprise of it, I wound my arms around his waist and settled for patting somewhere in the region of his shoulder blades. Even though the surprises, like his return and the random hug, were overwhelming, I couldn't fight the sheer, shoulder-sagging relief of having him home.

It took me a few moments to realise that he was still hugging me, and as the familiar scent of apple caught in my nose, I focused on holding my breath instead.

Probably weird to be caught smelling your best friend's shoulder.

He didn't say he'd missed me or anything, but he didn't have to. I kept up an awkward patting until my fingers skimmed something nestled between his shoulder blades.

I pulled back and stared at him, barely noticing his pink cheeks this time.

"You got wings?!"

He froze, then his face descended into a disagreeable frown, so familiar it was as if he'd never been away.

"Yeah. Some aunt or other came to visit and said I should at least look like I had some Fae blood."

I bit my lip, fighting the urge to forcibly turn him around so I could have a look. He didn't sound happy about the wings, but then this was Taz; he didn't see getting gifts the way most fairies and Fae would. It was technically rude to ask, but then we were still friends. He raised one eyebrow, the two hoop piercings there still the black rings I remembered.

"Go on." He sighed. "Step back a bit then. I can tell you're dying to see them."

I made a tiny shuffle backwards as Taz unfurled his wings. I'd seen a few FDPs with them around Arcanium, but wings were chosen as a serious gift so they weren't overly common. Some had bird-like ones with many feathers. Others had bright, colourful displays shaped more like a butterfly's.

Taz's wings extended outwards like an angel's with long, glossy feathers that brushed his hips, except they were a burnished hue of reddish-orange. I skipped over how beautifully powerful they looked as a thousand questions flitted through my head, like how the wings fitted with his clothes.

"Can you feel them?"

Without thinking, I reached forward and ran my fingertip along one of the ridges near the top. Taz shuddered and furled his wings back in place between his shoulders.

"Don't, that tickles."

"Sorry." I ignored his tetchiness. "But how does it work? Like, do you have to cut holes in all your favourite t-shirts in case you need to use them without taking your top off? Are they hard to reach, like if you need to wash or- do you have to pluck dead feathers out? Can you hold your own weight in the air with them?"

Taz's residual irritability cleared as he started to laugh. His entire face brightened up, his eyes picking up a determined sparkle. I squeaked as he threw an arm around my shoulders and pretended to throttle me. I shoved him off, fighting to hide my smile, and led the way out of the training room.

"You haven't changed, Sparky," he said as he followed me down the hall. "It's really good to be back. I've- I've missed you."

I gulped, uneasiness fluttering in my chest. I'd missed him too, so much. But he meant as his best friend, nothing more. Determined to re-establish the way we'd been before he left, I frowned back at him.

"So, you're not going to explain the wings?"

He rolled his eyes. "You're relentless. Okay, in short, my t-shirts are safe. I just usually throw them on and keep the wings tucked, but I have others for combat now, or I just don't use the wings unless I really have to. My washing and plucking habits are none of your business, nosy." He stuck his tongue out before continuing. "I can just about hold my own weight, but I haven't had them long so it'll take time to strengthen the muscles enough to do anything more than hover."

I nodded. "We learned the other week about gift differentiation. Guessing you know already, but it's the difference between gifts that are a part of you, gifts like wings that are embedded by bone or protections on a person, then attacking abilities like my zap power and your transmutation."

"Not heard it described like that before, but it's actually a really good way of putting it. What else have I missed?"

"Not much. Gnat dropped a book on his foot and we now know at least four new swearwords. Milo's redone the library's inventory and is horrified nobody's noticed. You could seriously get into his good books by doing that, but I'm not going to tell you what's changed. Leo- oh, wow yeah, you won't have seen him. He's, um, grown."

That was putting it mildly. Leo was my chameleon, or at least we assumed he was a chameleon in that he changed colour, but as he came from Faerie we couldn't be 100% sure. He'd done a lot of growing since Taz had gone to stay at the Queen's court.

"What like, you now share your room with an elephant kind of grown?" Taz asked with a grin.

Okay, slightly need to tone down how much I've missed him.

I pushed aside the fizzling excitement that bounded through me at having him back, desperate not to make things even more awkward by feeding his ego.

I couldn't stop myself from grinning back at him.

"Not quite, but he was about the size of a large squirrel when you left, and now he's more like a not-so-dainty cat. How he still manages to curl himself up in my satchel I don't know, but somehow he does."

Taz raised his eyebrow, the rings making a tiny clinking sound. Something about it, his complete similarity to how I remembered, made me feel calmer than I had in ages.

Before I could ask him how his time away had been, Ace was back. He ran a hand over his hair, his face quirked in anxious anticipation.

"Emil's asked to see you. Both of you."

Taz and I exchanged a dubious look.

"Oh, hell."

CHAPTER THREE
Off to Faerie

Taz, Ace and I hurried along the corridor toward the lift. My boots made no sound on the carpet, but I reached out my fingertips and brushed the wood panelling as we passed. Each hallway in Arcanium looked almost identical, but I couldn't imagine feeling at home anywhere else now.

Especially now Taz is finally back.

"Emil didn't say what I'm in for?" I asked.

Ace shook his head as we arrived at the golden grill that protected the lift's entrance. He pulled it aside and we stepped in.

"No, which is infuriating. He caught me going past at speed, and when I turned around to ask, he was halfway down the hall already. I'm sure it won't be anything too bad."

I caught his uncertain eye and grimaced. "Not in my experience."

We said no more as the lift shot downwards, the golden cage around us exposing the brickwork flashing by and sending air rushing against our faces. I was used to it now, but I don't think I'd ever forget my first day in one of these lifts.

I smiled to myself, remembering how I met Taz up in the arcade that linked Arcanium to the human world. Aside from being an actual prince of Faerie, he was both the grumpiest and the kindest person I knew. *And now he's back.*

I side-eyed him, but he was staring through the grill at the lift shaft whizzing by, caught up in some deep thought given the frown on his face.

The lift came to a stop and I pushed the grill aside, stepping out into the Ogle. Built to resemble an aircraft hangar or a military stronghold, vast rows of monitors filled the otherwise empty space with desks and chairs running underneath them. The Ogle showed a view into every realm of Faerie that Arcanium could reach, and I'd spent many a sneaky half hour roaming through to catch glimpses of different places when I should have been running errands.

I tensed when I saw Emil striding towards us. He looked his usual non-emotional self, a beanie hat covering his bald head and one of his trademark boilersuits zipped up to the neck, this one a dark red. Him summoning us could mean absolutely anything, but often it meant I was about to get sent to do something dangerous with zero idea how to do it.

"Right, Demi." He faced me and held out a slip of paper. "Very simple this one, more of an errand than an assignment. Taz, as you're only just back, I reckon you'll be safe to slip along with Demi. Old Tara knows you, but Demi will be a novelty so she might mention more with you both there."

I took the paper and read, even though Taz was already reaching out for it.

"Who's Old Tara?" I asked.

"She sometimes feeds us information from parts of Faerie," Emil explained. "It's just a simple task. You'll be out and back in an hour."

I nodded. I doubted I'd be back in an hour. My previous two assignments hadn't gone smoothly at all, but perhaps third time lucky.

"All you have to do is go and pick up the information and report back," Emil finished.

I blinked, confused. "That's it? No psychotic Fae clubs or demonic Forgotten people waiting to jump me?"

"A simple assignment for once." Emil chuckled. "Old Tara

has certain foibles of course, but it's straightforward. Flatter her and do not, under any circumstances, eat or drink anything she offers you. I've already sent your purple slips up top on your behalf."

I glanced at Taz. He wasn't meeting my eyes, and now that I looked closely, his usually tanned face was pale as if he'd not been sleeping.

I'll get this done, then find out what's got him so troubled.

"Get the information and don't eat or drink anything, got it," I confirmed. "So, will she give the info to me, or should I write it down?"

Emil scratched his chin. "Not sure, Taz usually just gives me a verbal report."

I nodded. That was Arcanium all over, a heaving mass of people doing different things and hopefully joining up in the middle before something exploded. It also sounded like Taz had done this before, so that was another plus.

"Right, off you go," Emil said, putting an end to my hesitation.

I took a step backwards as he disappeared into the nearest aisle of screens.

"I'll look after Leo until you get back," Ace offered. "Just in case. Have you got your room key? I'll take him down to the library for a run around."

I nodded and pulled my bedroom door-key out of my pocket, handing it over. I checked my other pocket to make sure my orb, the Arcanium equivalent of a mobile phone, was there and set off toward the lift. If Taz was in a mood, I'd be best off taking charge until I did something dim and he saw fit to turn into his usual grumpy, know-it-all self again.

I got into the lift with the others and pressed the top button for despatch along with the button for the residents' hall.

Curiosity and worry played tag in my head as the lift shot upwards, but it was only when it stopped that I realised Emil hadn't told me anything specific about where exactly I was going. Ace opened the gate when we reached the residents' hall and stepped out, shutting it behind him.

"Good luck!" he called as the lift shuttled on upwards.

Taz and I descended into awkward silence. I tapped my foot until I couldn't bear it any longer.

"How was it at home anyway?" I asked.

Taz shrugged. "Arcanium is home. But it could have been worse. I've been practicing with my transmutation gift, and one of my aunts gave me a conditional shifter gift."

He glanced at me. I blinked in confusion and his lips softened into a smile. I brushed aside the idea that my ignorance was a familiarity for him, but at least he was smiling.

"I'm almost afraid to ask," I admitted.

Taz put his hand on the gate as the lift came to a stop at the despatch floor, but didn't move to open it.

"I can change into an animal, but it's linked to my DNA or something, so I can't do it if I'm glamouring already or using my transmutation gift. Still, might come in handy one day, if I need to disguise myself as a cat."

He opened the gate and I followed him out, marvelling at his ability to be so blasé about a new gift.

The lift opened onto a wide metal walkway that led to a big circular platform. Over the edge of the platform and walkway were sharp drops into the atrium a long way below, with tiny people scurrying about like ants.

I focused on the platform and the vast stone wall of sparkling white quartz waiting at the far end of it. When I reached the platform and stood inside the circle of wooden rickshaws, I found Trevor already waiting for me.

"Hiya, Demi, Taz." Trevor beamed.

I smiled. "Hi Trevor, how are things? How's Moss?"

Trevor's head only came up to my torso, and he had the leathery skin and bat-like ears that all the trolls I'd met had. He was my personal realm-skipper, a shot of luck as he was the fastest one at Arcanium and unfailingly loyal. I'd met his daughter, Moss, only the once about a month ago. She was a small four-year-old terror who'd escaped and terrorised half of the atrium looking for sweets until Trevor managed to round her up.

"Good, thanks." Trevor wiped his face with a rueful laugh. "She's still a handful, but she soon shuts up if I wave the fairy bag at her."

"Fairy bag?"

Trevor grinned wider. "The Jelly Babies you send up each week, she's still addicted to them. Her mum says she's too young for sweets, but she somehow manages to find wherever I hide them."

"She'll be realm-skipping her own FDP before you know it," I teased.

Trevor pressed a hand over his chest. "Don't say that, I couldn't bear it. The trouble she'd cause!"

"Well, if they ever decide to warn me first when these assignments come in, you could bring her up with Moira and she can see us leave."

Trevor waved that away. "I wouldn't dare, she'd be in the rickshaw and your responsibility before you could open your eyes. Now, I've had your purple slips already. So you're going to Prime Realm two to see Old Tara?"

I nodded. "Do you know anything about the realm, or her? I'm going in a bit unknowing here."

Trevor tapped his hands in a short rhythm on the railing of

his rickshaw. I put my hands onto the side to pull myself in, Taz right behind me as Trevor clambered between the spokes for pulling and twisted back.

"Old Tara is friendly and she'll give you what you need. Be polite, call her ma'am and don't eat or drink anything. It's a safe realm and an easy assignment by all accounts."

I sat down with a jolt as Trevor set off at a blistering run. He wheeled us in a sharp ninety degree turn and dashed headfirst toward the quartz wall. I closed my eyes quickly, knowing I should have given Trevor clearer instructions over the speed of travel and the landing.

The sensation of falling flipped my stomach and the nether that made up the fabric of existence between realms of Faerie stroked against my skin.

A jolt forced my eyes open and my hands outward a moment later. My palms hit the railing and something bumped the top of my chest. I didn't dare look down as Taz withdrew his arm from in front of me, but I huffed a breath as we came to a stop.

Warmth beamed onto my face, the gentle tweeting of birds the only sound reaching my ears. I inhaled the scent of fresh, of greenery and sweetness, while sliding out of the rickshaw. The grass underfoot was wild-grown, the ground sloping gently downward. Trees created a forest around us, save for the glade we stood in and an avenue that led down the hill. In front of us stood an enormous weeping willow, gargantuan as it towered over all the other trees with its thick fronds trailing into a clear, burbling stream.

Trevor and the rickshaw disappeared, leaving us in the middle of the glade. Alone.

I bit my lip.

"Are we supposed to wait here?" I asked. "Is Old Tara coming to get us, or should we start walking?"

Why do I never ask proper questions when I get thrown into these things?

Taz grinned. "Just wait."

I tensed as a rustling noise started up and one of the willow fronds swept aside.

"Well now, the young prince I recognise, but who's this other morsel come a-visiting?"

The voice was the brisk rustle of the breeze among the leaves. The huge tree trunk was just visible under the lifted fronds, with roots the height of horses ridged above the ground.

I eyed the trunk, assessing the knots in the bark. Before I could orientate myself, another branch slid down in front of me of its own accord.

"There now," the voice crooned. "Come sit and talk to me."

"Um." I hesitated as the branch beckoned invitingly with one of its twigs.

Taz gave me a look. "Hello, Tara. It's lovely to see you again."

The leaves rustled like laughter. "Oh, Prince Oakthorn, always flattering me. You're not the chattiest, but you do listen, which at least is something for your kind. Still, nobody ever comes to see me unless they have to."

As the branch swept to one side, I took a step closer and dipped into the dim coolness of the willow's den. The knots in the bark were moving, the whorls creating eyes and a small mouth. I'd only seen that once before, on a wardrobe at the Queen of Faerie's court.

"Well, I'm here, if that means anything," I tried. "My name is Demi."

"A pretty name for a pretty young lady. I am Old Tara, come and talk with me a little. Are you surprised to be talking with a tree?"

"I'm not much used to any of this yet," I admitted honestly. "This is only my third assignment and I still think the first two were mostly by accident. But I've met a talking wardrobe before."

The leaves rustled again, and the bark mouth widened.

"You are supposed to humour me, dear, while I moan about changes in the various realms I inhabit. Then from that you glean information that you take back to your elders."

I took another step forward, hesitation forgotten. "You inhabit other realms? Can I ask how many?"

"You are enthusiastic at least. I inhabit too many to count. Have you heard of bees having a hive mind?" Old Tara paused until I nodded. "Well, I have a root-mind. My roots stretch through many different realms and my various trunks and sprouts are like the many hairs on your arms, so I can offer a lot of information."

I frowned. "What do you get out of it?"

Old Tara froze, leaves still despite a gentle breeze. I could hear Taz huffing behind me at my questioning, but I didn't bother looking back.

"I- Well, I suppose people visit occasionally. I get to teach them about caring for their realms. Sometimes I get to see the time-old stories retold anew as young lovers tryst beneath my branches."

I narrowly stopped myself from pulling a face at that and raced on, more intent on getting my own questions answered now than the ones for the assignment I'd been sent on.

"Sorry, I just find it interesting. So, is it like your different parts communicate with each other, or is it all you, I guess?"

The knot-eyes blinked. "You are actually interested, aren't you?"

I nodded. "Very much, this sort of thing, I mean- The world

of Faerie in general fascinates me."

I sat cross-legged by one of the gargantuan roots, hoping Old Tara would warm to me.

"Would you like something to eat, dear? Something to drink? You must be thirsty."

Don't accept. Emil's and Trevor's warnings rang in my head.

"I'm sorry, I ate and drank before I came, but thank you."

I took a breath, pulling it in deep to quell the grumbling noise my stomach threatened to make in protest. I couldn't imagine what might happen if I did agree to eat something Old Tara gave me, but warnings were warnings and rarely ever given lightly at Arcanium.

Mostly because if they remember to warn us at all, it means something awful happened to the last person who didn't listen.

I chose not to notice the somewhat disgruntled rustle from above me. Then I saw one of the roots winding up the trunk and realised that sitting down had put me in a really vulnerable position.

Taz dropped to sit cross-legged on the grass beside me. Aware he was letting me carry the whole conversation, I gave him a look, but he shot me a childish smirk in return and said nothing.

"So, what kind of realms do you inhabit?" I ploughed on.

"Too many to mention, dear." Old Tara sighed in the breeze. "Snow and ice, desert and drought, black sand and red water, white grass and golden water. Many of the realms are still in turmoil though. Sadistic devils hacking me down with no consciousness about where it might lead."

My bottom lip dropped. "You mean-"

"Oh, I don't feel it as such, any more than you would feel the flaking of skin cells. I don't begrudge the Fae-folk my bounty, but they go too far, clearing vast portions of my root structure which makes it harder for me to communicate, and I'm a chatty old soul. As to what you have been sent here for, nothing has changed. I still haven't sensed any massive shift, but the collective discomfort is growing as people whisper in corners."

I stayed silent, but moments passed and Old Tara said nothing further.

"Well, thank you for telling me," I said. "I don't know much at all about Faerie, but I want to learn everything I can."

The lower branches shivered then, sending a few leaves spiralling down around me.

"Perhaps I will tell you much more, if you return to visit me. I quite like talking to you."

"Okay." I clambered to my feet. "Um, is there anything else that we should know? I don't like asking because then you're going to think I'm only here because they made me. I mean, this time it's kind of true, but I'd like to learn more about your side of it, and Faerie. Knowledge is a great thing."

"Knowledge is a dangerous thing," Old Tara countered. "But it can have its uses. All I know is that there are rumblings. The Queen's control over Faerie seems to be weakening, and there will always be others waiting to take her place. Their ideals are different too, especially on how the Fae-folk co-exist with the humans."

I eyed Taz, but if the news of his mother's hold weakening had upset him, his expression was locked down too tight for it to be visible.

The slender tip of a branch dropped to hover a few feet from my face. I flinched as it stroked a scratchy path from my brow down the length of my nose, then tapped lightly.

"Now, I insist you take this with you." Another branch appeared, the end curled around an over-sized green acorn.

"Oh no, I couldn't possibly eat-"

I froze as the branch that had tapped my nose waved beside me.

"It's not for eating, dear, a small gift and nothing more. You must keep it with you until the time it is needed. Your lot will know what that is."

I took the nut, half-expecting it to explode in my hand. It didn't, so I slipped it into my pocket alongside my orb.

"Off you pop then." Old Tara sighed. "I won't go through the rigmarole of trying to keep you here with treats as you seem like such a nice girl."

I smiled, relieved. "And for that, I will come back and visit you if I can."

It was a small promise to make to a lonely tree, and by using 'if I can', there was no set timescale either. When I could visit, if I was allowed to and had time, I would. I'd learned quickly that most of Fae trickery was based around word-play and manipulation.

As I ran my hand over the orb in my pocket to get us our ride home, I caught sight of Taz's face. Wide-eyed and tight-lipped, something had seriously annoyed him.

"Ah, but of course, I'm being rude." Old Tara called our attention back to her. "I can't give one a gift and not the other. Come closer, both of you."

I eyed Taz, trying to judge from him whether this was some kind of trick or not. He didn't so much as glance at me as he moved close enough to touch Tara's trunk. I joined him. If it was the acorn he was so upset about, he could have it.

"Now, we know that a little hardship grows the strongest stems. *Whatever be not thee, with touch be set free, exchanged until Faerie hour, so that both may see.*"

Before I could even commit the words to memory, a willowy branch came down to tap us both on the forehead, Taz first, then me.

A fizzling sensation tingled over my skin, similar to the feel of my fairy connection waking inside me. I shook myself to get rid of the residual warmth, but given Taz's stony frown, he wasn't impressed by whatever had just happened.

"There," Old Tara said, sounding supremely satisfied with herself. "That's a little cantrip for you to puzzle over. Off you go now."

Taz's jaw was tense, but he wasn't looking at me and he wasn't suggesting we should stay.

I called Trevor's name, one hand on the cool orb in my pocket. He materialised almost immediately and I clambered into the rickshaw. Taz went all the way around to the other side to climb in and practically pinned himself against the opposite edge. Ignoring him being weird, I sat down and leaned around my side to wave to Old Tara.

"I will come back if I can," I insisted.

Old Tara fluttered a branch at me as Trevor shot forward. I closed my eyes, trying to smile while my insides were threatening to leap out of my mouth.

Third time lucky after all.

I hauled myself out onto the platform, my brain beginning to itch. Old Tara had given us a rhyme, a riddle of sorts, and I was determined to decipher it.

"Thanks, Trevor. That was a simple one for once!"

Taz scoffed. I flicked a look at him as Trevor grinned and hurried off with his rickshaw. Buoyed up by the success, I strode along the walkway and stepped into the lift. Taz stood sullen beside me as I pressed the button for the Ogle screens, but I let him be. I would report back to Emil then go for dinner. Perhaps Taz might brighten up with Ace and Milo around.

As the lift shot downward, I forgot my intention to leave Taz to his sulking, folding my arms instead and facing him.

"Go on then. I've obviously done something to piss you off."

Taz's frown deepened. "What makes you say that?"

"Oh, I don't know. The moment you saw me earlier, you're glaring at me like I've just disembowelled your favourite *Demolition Ducks* hoodie or something, then you're all huffy because Old Tara gave me an acorn. I'm guessing it does something?"

"You don't even know what it is," he said, his tone dredged in disbelief.

The lift came to a stop and I hauled open the gate. I thought I saw the dark shadow of someone disappearing into the vast expanse of Ogle screens, but another look proved the whole place was deserted. I'd hoped Emil would be at his Ogle desk like he often was, but perhaps he was in his office upstairs.

Instead of redirecting the lift, I strode out and came to a halt near the first row of screens. If Taz had something to say, we might as well get it out in the open now and it was best to do it away from prying eyes.

I pulled the nut from my pocket and held it up between us. Taz stood several feet away, his brow furrowed and his hands fidgeting at his sides.

"Come on then," I prompted. "Out with it."

For a moment I thought he'd refuse, or tell me I was being ridiculous. Then he huffed out a frustrated noise.

"She gives it to you, just like that, and you don't even know what it is," he said. "Honestly, sometimes I can't work out why Emil sends you to these things in the first place."

I blinked. He'd never said anything that mean before.

"I'm sure he thought I could handle at least a simple errand," I said, hating that my voice was wobbling.

My connection to my fairy-side lurched up at the worst

possible moment, reacting to my mood. I wasn't always great at controlling my energy gift, but I was trying my hardest to practice. Now, with Taz's barb sitting at the front of my mind, the screens nearest us started to buzz and whine. I shoved the acorn back into my pocket as Taz folded his arms and glared back at me.

"Taz-" I tried and got stuck.

"Don't, just don't. It's fine. Did I expect Emil to at least trust me with the menial jobs like he normally would when I got back? Yes. Does he? Apparently not. *Apparently*, he needs you to babysit me. *You*. You know what? I'm fine."

I bit back the temptation to say he clearly wasn't. My habit of stating the obvious often got me into trouble and clearly it wouldn't do any good now.

Taz sniffed. "So yeah, looks like I can't even be trusted to do a simple errand now. Even you're more desirable than I am."

"What do you mean, even me?" I glared back at him. "I get you're upset but-"

"You're damn right I'm upset. You wouldn't even be here now if I hadn't helped you since you arrived."

Taz gasped over the last words as if he was trying to claw them back in. I guessed he'd just run out of irate breath.

But there it is.

Taz had helped me, so much, but to have my inexperience thrown back in my face hurt a lot. I couldn't help it that he'd grown up surrounded by Faerie and Fae, while I'd been born to a wholly human family. A stream of cutting retorts filtered through my mind, a buffet of delectable comebacks, but I couldn't bring himself to say any of them.

"That's what you really think?" I clenched my fists at my sides, the hurt firing through me. "What, I'm just some useless half-human person who you've had to babysit through everything we've done?"

Taz's eyes widened along with his mouth. "Dem, wait, I didn't-"

"Thanks for the support, *mate*." I turned away and stormed toward the lift.

"Demi!" Taz's anguished voice floated after me.

I slammed the grill shut and fixed my gaze on the golden bars above my head. I kept my head tilted upward while jabbing the button for the floor that had Queenie and Emil's offices on it with a furious finger. Now that I wasn't on my assignment any more, I should report in to Emil, then I needed to get the hell away from everything Fae and Faerie for the rest of the evening.

The lift jolted and swept upwards.

He's upset and I get it, if Emil is passing him over on something he usually does, that sucks, but that doesn't mean he can use me as a verbal punch bag. Maybe Emil just thought we'd have time to catch up this way, given Petra's got me training every spare minute. But of course, Taz wouldn't know that, as he never bothered to find out!

My anger swelled, my chest feeling like it was about to burst. As the lift came to a halt, I had to force myself to slide the grill aside and step out. The temptation to go back and make Taz apologise raged, or to at least find out what was making him such a vicious grouch, but stubbornness drove my feet forward. I strode down the carpeted hall, my eyes glancing off the various paintings of Faerie.

As I reached the end of the hall, framed by the doors to Queenie's office, I heard voices. Not wanting to intrude, I slowed my pace and inched toward the corner, peeking around.

Diana, Kainen's sister, stood further down the next corridor with Emil. Her brown hair was straight and loose, a curtain hiding her face as her back was facing me, but I could tell it was her from the set of her shoulders and the impeccable jeans and shirt combo she wore.

"Your father has left a message asking to speak to you at the first opportunity." Emil said.

Diana stood tense, her arms sweeping behind her back with her fists clenching. Although Kainen discussed his family now and then, I'd never seen him have this kind of reaction when they were mentioned, more bored indifference.

"You can use my office," Emil offered. "No need for me to remind you of your family's expectations."

Diana turned enough that I could see her face, and I didn't want to hang around long enough for them to see me lurking. Diana would sneer and find some way to torment or threaten me, and I'd had enough of that from Taz today. I could brief Emil later.

As quick as my weary legs would carry me, I hurried back to the lift and closed the grill.

I tried to decipher the look on Diana's face though, a flash of trepidation maybe?

None of my business. I turned my attention to more pressing matters.

Everyone would be doing their own thing now that classes were over for the day, and I couldn't bear the thought of Ace and Milo wanting the four of us to hang out while Taz was being horrible. I could go down to the canteen for dinner, but Taz's behaviour had completely ruined my appetite. No, for now I needed solitude.

I pressed the button for the training floor. As the lift swept down, I focused on my breathing and trying to curb the stinging in my eyes.

Did I imagine what it'd be like to have Taz coming back? Yes. Did I imagine he'd have turned into some kind of awful Fae monster? No. Perhaps it's the effect of spending too much time around his mother's court.

The lift came to a stop, the dim silence in the corridor beyond blissful. The lamps were turned down low and the classrooms in darkness as I walked along to the training room.

Where it all went wrong earlier.

I couldn't be arrogant enough to believe that Taz was affected by seeing me with Kainen. In a friends way maybe, but not in the 'traditional' sense.

He all but accused me of turning traitor on his family when he saw me with Kainen.

I slipped into the training hall with a sigh and sat in the middle of the floor. If someone came along and found me, so be it. They could bloody well drag me out again.

CHAPTER FOUR
A Dubious Invitation

I barely had five minutes to mope before someone burst through the doorway.

I froze, anxiety crawling up my chest to squeeze the breath out of me.

"There you are." Taz approached at a hesitant pace, each step slow. "Dem, I'm so sorry. I shouldn't have shouted, or said such awful things, none of which are true."

I stared at the toes of my boots. "So you were lying then? How?"

"Well, I guess I thought, in the moment… I'm an idiot, okay? I've never thought anything like that about you before, I promise. I can't even remember what happened. I must have been in some weird mood, but that's no excuse. I'm an awful, despicable person."

I looked up, uncertain. The torment on his face as he stared at the floor told me he meant every word.

"You're not that bad," I offered. "Moody as sin, but you're a good person. We all say things we think in the moment but don't mean I guess."

The hurt still lingered, but at least he'd apologised. I stood and moved toward him as he rubbed both hands over his face. I got inches away and lifted my hand to do something comforting, although I had no idea what.

Taz shook his head, his stormy eyes startled and wide.

"No, don't!" He flinched away as my hand, destined for his shoulder, landed on his forearm instead.

A tremble rumbled through me, the sensation under my

fingertips shivering though Taz as well.

I stumbled back, my fairy connection bursting into life. Instead of rising through me, gaining strength like it usually did, the sensation dropped, fading, leaving my insides yawning like a void.

All too quickly, something slammed into me, through me. My connection latched greedily onto it, but the feeling stuck under my skin like a film of silk, soft but too cool and smooth.

"Now look what you've done!" Taz hissed. "Honestly, I thought you were at least half-smart!"

Okay, ouch.

I shivered, refusing to join in and let him goad me into another fight. Something felt wrong inside me, a layer of something not mine sticking like a veil of ice under my skin.

"You don't listen, do you?" Taz ranted. "Did you even think about what Tara said?"

I scanned back, remembering her suggestion of a gift and hardship. I might not be half-smart, but I at least had a good memory.

Whatever be not thee, with touch be set free, exchanged until Faerie hour, so that both may see. I froze. *Not thee, set free, exchanged.*

"Oh."

How stupid could I be? In all my worries about Taz returning and his weird behaviour, I'd not had time to assess the assignment, or report in to Emil. If I had, I could have worked out and prevented this.

"Oh?" He raged, his eyes flashing. "That's all you have to say? Our gifts have swapped, do you realise that? You've no idea how to use mine. It could be dangerous. Orbs alive, you're meant to be learning more here, not less."

So the apology was total bull then.

I gulped against the rising urge to cry, or possibly find something to throw at him. The temptation to taunt him that at least I was getting chosen for assignments and deemed worthy of responsibility despite my faults bubbled up. But I wouldn't descend to his level, even if all I wanted to do was scream at him and maybe shove him a bit.

"You're being mean again," I said instead. "Go away and leave me alone."

"The first sensible thing you've said." He bit back. "We shouldn't be anywhere near each other, at least until this wears off."

My frustration spilled over and it was all I could do to keep my tears inside.

"Fine, sod off then. Tonight and forever, see if I care."

Taz hesitated, his face scrunching. "Fine, I will then!"

"Fine!"

I forced myself to watch him stride toward the door, through it and out of sight. I half-expected him to come back, either for a second apology or a third argument. After a minute or two had passed, I sat back down on the floor with my knees to my chest, my eyes against my knees and my tears flowing freely.

He must truly believe all the horrible things he said after all then.

I didn't dare test any of the unfamiliar gifts now a part of me, but a quick wriggle of my shoulders suggested I didn't have his wings.

"Demi?"

I groaned into my knees and lifted my head, not caring anymore about blotchy cheeks or puffy eyes. Kainen stood framed in the doorway, a leather jacket thrown over his shoulders.

"Not now, Kainen, please."

"What's wrong?" he asked, his tone soft. "Oh, wow, you're crying. I promise, no sparring, just talking for now. What's happened? Is it bad news? Your family?"

I wiped my face with my sleeve as he appeared beside me in an instant and sat down, his knee brushing my thigh.

"Just Taz being an arse." I folded my arms over my legs, ignoring the feeling that I was betraying my friend by talking behind his back.

He started it.

Kainen sat back, his hands resting on the floor behind him as he twitched his head to flick his hair away from his eyes.

"I hear his family's having some issues," he said. "He's probably lashing out, but that's not fair on you."

Agreed. But even then, I couldn't settle the feeling inside me that I shouldn't be talking to Kainen about Taz behind his back.

I shrugged instead and went for my usual brand of blunt honesty.

"He wouldn't want me talking to you."

"About his family?" Kainen asked.

In general probably. I managed a faint smile.

"Yeah, Montagues and Capulets and all that."

Kainen chuckled. "Ah, Shakespeare, did you know he was-"

"-one of ours, yeah."

My momentary amusement faded. It was Taz who told me that. Everywhere I looked, all my Arcanium memories had Taz in them somehow. I huffed, letting anger swell up to swallow the sadness as Kainen leaned forward, a body of restless energy.

"I guess my side and his do go far back," he said. "But I don't set much by my family's more narrow-minded views. What were you arguing about? Don't feel you need to tell me if it's private."

I hesitated. "Emil gave me a mission after our sparring

earlier. Taz and I went to see- well, we went together and our gifts got switched."

"Oh, wow. That must be unnerving." Kainen frowned. "Do you want to sneak out and do some practice? If you're carrying someone else's gift you should test it, make sure nobody's going to come to any harm if it splurges out. I can show you a place where nothing would get damaged, and I'm more than capable of defending myself."

I didn't like the sound of Taz's gifts splurging out of me. I knew the switch wouldn't last long, the caveat Tara had added about Faerie hour meaning we would likely be back to normal by morning, like fairy gold. Using Taz's gift without his permission also felt wrong.

But a tiny part of me suggested that perhaps it was also kind of exciting to have a brand new gift coursing through me, something I could learn to wield even though having it was temporary. I didn't know whether all gifts had swapped either, like the natural voice mimicking I'd been born with, or just the ones we'd been gifted with by other Fae.

If Taz wasn't being such an arse, maybe we could have found out together, had some fun to celebrate him being back.

None of that was looking likely though.

"Wouldn't in here be better?" I asked.

He shook his head. "The FDPs use this place for evening practice. They'll probably be along in a minute. We don't have to practice if you don't want to, but we could talk somewhere more comfortable than this at least?"

The sensible thing would be to go up to my room, sulk in silence until the gift swap wore off, then start afresh tomorrow. Perhaps around Ace and Milo, Taz might at least be civil. But being reckless and following Kainen felt more tempting than brooding alone.

"Okay, although I don't think I want to talk about this, but sure. It's not in the human world though, is it? Won't be long until the lift shuts for mentee curfew and I don't want to get in trouble."

Kainen grinned and leapt to his feet with depressingly Fae-like agility. Before I could stand, he held out a hand. His skin was warm and his hold steady as he hauled me up, but he let go immediately after. I watched for signs of him trying to wipe his hand on his trousers or something embarrassing, but he just started toward the door, arms loose by his sides.

I followed him into the hall, stopping to shut the door behind me.

"I need to grab something from my room," he said. "Meet me in the library? I know a place on the second floor."

It was an odd place to meet. The second floor of the library was just a storage facility, but I guessed he must have carved himself a place there amid the dusty old relics. I knew some students had carved out parts of the library for themselves as study spots or hangouts, and Milo was doing his best to keep on top of all of them in case any of the books got damaged or parties started.

I nodded and watched Kainen for a moment as he walked away. He was tall and broad-shouldered, only a bit more so than Taz, but he was all dark and grey shadow, whereas Taz was all colour with the explosion of freckles, his curly honey hair, northern lights eyes and-

Stop it. Taz is being a right pain and you need to get moving before Kainen reaches the lift and sees you staring.

I hurried in the opposite direction toward the stairs that led down to the library. Milo had dimmed the lamps already, which meant he was either on or about to start his final rotation through the levels to close down for the night.

I found Milo sitting behind the front desk, frowning at a pile of books with a hand snarled in tangles of his shaggy blond hair.

"No Ace?" I asked, by way of greeting.

Milo and Ace were still trying to keep their relationship a secret, although I really didn't understand why when everyone else knew about them already. I'd thought about asking but guessed it was just a privacy thing and left them to it.

Milo looked up. "No Taz?"

I scowled. "Considering he's being an idiot, no. I'm just meeting Kainen and going down to the second level."

Milo's frown deepened and he got up from his chair.

"Are you sure that's a good idea? I thought you'd want to be hanging out with Taz after so long apart. If you've had an argument, you should sort it out between you straight away."

I shook my head, trying to quell the irritation rising up in my chest. Knowing Milo couldn't see my hands hidden behind the desk, I started tapping my thumb over my fingertips.

"He just keeps yelling at me for being useless. I don't know what's changed but something has and I'm done with it until he sorts himself out. Kainen only wants to talk so I won't be long anyway."

I folded my arms, aware I didn't need to justify myself but somehow doing it anyway. Milo pulled his glasses off and shrugged his teddy-bear shoulders. Kainen had mentioned talking, so it technically wasn't a lie. If we happened to do some gift-testing by and by, Milo didn't need to know that.

"Okay. But don't leave it too long with Taz, yeah? Never go to bed on a quarrel."

"Very wise, Yoda." I rolled my eyes.

He smiled then. "Oh, before I forget, Emil was wandering around and asked me if I'd seen you."

I groaned loudly. "Did he say why?"

"Yes, he wanted a report on your assignment and also your orb for cleaning. Apparently, you're overdue."

I blinked, guiltily remembering that we were meant to submit our orbs overnight every three weeks for cleansing. I always imagined it like a mobile phone or laptop memory needing backing up, but I think it was more that Arcanium didn't want any remnant of old visions left lurking. I had a note on the 'to learn' list pinned on my bedroom wall to find out more about how it all worked, but so far it wasn't one of the ones I'd ticked off.

"Do you want me to pop it up to him when I'm done here?" Milo offered. "Then you'll get it back by morning most likely. I'll tell Ace to check in on Leo as well, in case you get stuck 'talking'. I swear, Ace loves that lizard almost as much as you do."

I ignored his suggestive eyebrow wiggle at the mention of talking and grinned, all irritation swept away.

"You're an angel, Milo, thank you."

I unclipped my orb keychain from the belt loop of my jeans and handed it over. Milo took it and sat back down, but his gaze hovering near my head made me turn. Kainen stood behind us with a rucksack hanging from one shoulder.

"Ready, Dem?"

I nodded, gulping against a sudden catch in my throat. Only Taz called me Dem usually, or Sparky, but clearly things were shifting. Unwilling to focus on the pit of yawning sadness in my gut at the thought of that, I faced the present instead.

"Yeah, what's in the bag?"

Kainen smiled, his lips curving and his eyes sparking amid their darkness.

"A surprise. Come on."

I shrugged to Milo, who had his mouth open as if he wanted

to protest, and followed Kainen down the stairs to the second floor.

"You've made yourself one of the student dens down here then?" I asked.

Kainen strode across the main chamber of the library and into a corridor. Milo clearly hadn't finished dimming the lights yet as I could see all the way to the end still.

"A lot of students have," he said, speeding even faster ahead. *Wow, vague.*

My stomach rumbled, reminding me I'd not had dinner yet, but I had a sneaking suspicion that there might be food in Kainen's rucksack. It was a sweet idea if there was, and he could be the type to do nice gestures when he tried. Early on after we'd started training together, he brought me a pack of Skittles down from the human world because I'd said how I didn't get round to going up there much. At least, I assumed they'd come from the human world. I suppose the Braunees in the canteen could have gotten them for him, but it was still a thoughtful thing to do.

We hooked left at the end of the corridor, venturing between cases full of books and old junk. I'd never been this far in before, but it looked as though ancient paintings were still hanging in their original places given the dust on the frames, and the wooden panelling on the walls had given way to bare stone and concrete.

"So, how far is it?" I hastened to keep up.

"Not far. Almost there."

I glanced ahead to see the end of the corridor and no more turnings left to take. Anxiety thudded through me, beginning to crush on my chest. The pictures and cases were behind us now, the walls ahead bare except for a long mirror hanging in front of us.

"This is my favourite place in the world." Kainen reached back to grab my hand. "I've wanted to bring you here for ages."

I flinched at the sudden contact and tried to pull my hand away. Kainen gripped tighter, his fingers all but crunching mine. I dug my heels in, tipping all my weight back.

With astounding strength, Kainen hauled me in an arc so I stumbled past him. I closed my eyes as the mirror rushed up to meet me.

Instead of crashing into it, the tell-tale whisper of air brushed my face.

Oh no, no no no no no.

I focused on the tight grip around my fingers. Even though Kainen had just bounced me through a realm-skip, presumably into some unknown part of Faerie, at least he hadn't totally abandoned me.

CHAPTER FIVE
Demi Feels Like an Idiot, But Fights Back Anyway

I opened my eyes to darkness. There was still a chance that Kainen was testing me like he usually did, but my instinct told me now wasn't the time to be trusting. Knowing my luck, this was probably another one of his 'be prepared for anything' training methods.

I blinked as shadowed shapes started to appear, my vision clearing enough to make out a large room with a vaulted ceiling.

"Where are we?" I asked, staring around.

Kainen stalked toward the centre of the room, dim lighting flickering on as he passed. The walls were dark, separated at intervals with columns made from black marble. Even the floor glimmered.

Like a massive marble mausoleum. I shuddered.

The air felt hostile, chilly against my cheeks. I shrank into my hoodie and looked over my shoulder. If we'd come through a skip-way, I should be able to see a slight haze around wherever it was.

I couldn't see any sign of the skip-way and squinted through the shadowed darkness.

Nothing.

I folded my arms across my chest in a pathetic attempt to hide my shaking hands.

"Where are we?" I repeated.

Kainen loomed in front of me with a wide smile, the movement slow and frightening in the shadows.

"You are in my home. Don't worry, my family are away

visiting the King."

I froze. *Of course, his family are big supporters of the Old King, the enemy of Taz's family. My enemy too now.*

I inched backwards in the vain hope the skip-way might magically swallow me up and send me back. At least then I'd have a shot at running, or screaming for help. There still wasn't any absolute proof I had anything to worry about, but the foreboding was screaming inside me.

"It's, um-" I couldn't lie. "Big. Imposing."

Kainen laughed. "It's the seat of the Mage of Nightmares, so it's meant to be frightening."

"Mage of Nightmares?"

Kainen moved around the vast room, lighting candles in holders on the walls. Alongside the automatic lights which seemed to brighten whenever he was standing near them, the candle glow threw up ominous shadows that loomed like demons.

Okay, no more late night horror film marathons.

"My father is the current Mage," Kainen explained. "Our family has held the position since before the new Queen was born, bound to spread terror and discontent to balance the power of Faerie."

My insides twisted. Calling her the "new Queen" didn't sound like he was a supporter, and I'd never heard of a Mage of Nightmares.

"Imagine a world where Fae could play without conscience?" he continued. "Too messy, things would be utterly destroyed in mere weeks. The Mage forms that conscience, although there is some freedom to spill into the human world for amusement too. Since the rebellion and the King being deposed, there has been little that the Lords and Ladies of Faerie can do for true fun, with no access to run riot through the human world."

He moved around the room with his back to me, facing the wall to continue lighting the candles. Now wasn't the time to start thinking how it would be a brilliant place to stage a showing of Phantom of the Opera, so I searched frantically for the skip-way instead.

"I plan to be the next Mage," Kainen continued. "Oh, you won't find the skip-way. It's one way only. The way back to Arcanium for me is in another part of the house, one you will never see."

Oh, because that's not scary at all.

I clenched my fists, insides knotting with fear as I turned to face him.

"So, what am I doing here then? I don't think you actually want to talk to me?"

Kainen walked toward me with a predatory smile. I'd not noticed it on him before, but of course he was Fae, no doubt well-versed in manipulation and playing a part to get what he wanted. As he approached, I frantically assessed my options.

I have Taz's transmutation gift. I can't risk using it though, not until I know what to do with it. I might liquify Kainen's bones or something by mistake.

Kainen took a breath, but instead of speaking, he breathed out a harsh puff of glittering dark smoke. I raised my hand and threw up a protection, but too late.

Black bars of writhing shadow surrounded me, pressing in on my warding. I visualised the warding shrinking down to protect me inside the cage instead. I twitched my fingers at the thought of being confined, but I'd handled worse than this before. There was room enough to lie down flat and roll from side to side, and a metre of so between the top of my head and the top of the cage.

This isn't like being trapped in tunnels or locked in cupboards. It isn't.

The reassurance didn't help any, the sensation of my muscles trying to leap out of my bones rising up inside me.

"Is that necessary?" I asked, fighting to keep the tremble out of my voice.

He stopped within reaching distance and I held myself tense, refusing to back down. The recollection that he could apparently read my mind through my warding occurred to me, so I forced myself to think the same thing over and over, the first thought that came to my mind.

Don't eat yellow snow. Don't eat yellow snow. Don't eat-

"Why would you think I don't want to talk to you?" he asked. "On the contrary, I want to know everything you know. I want to know everything you've got that will help me. And you will help me."

I scowled back at him. "You're being really creepy. While I accept that Fae like to play games and chase and all that, you're clearly using me for something more than whatever you think I know."

Kainen shrugged, sliding his hands in his pockets.

"The fact that my family want to use you to lure Taz out of Arcanium is irrelevant. I'm more interes-"

"That's what I'm here for?" I gasped.

I should have known. Should have thought this through.

Taz is right, I'm not smart at all.

As the realisation dawned, a burst of humiliation burned through me. Kainen was popular among his second-year peers and respected as a competent trainee with a well-established Fae family. I was a first-year fairy mentee who'd lucked out on a couple of early assignments. I didn't even have any Fae family lineage to trade on, while he clearly had loads. Of course he was using me as a way to get to the prince of Faerie.

During the last assignment, I'd stumbled on a plot to kidnap the Queen's children in an attempt to destabilise her. I'd even been there at Taz's birthday party where the Forgotten tried to storm the castle. But the fact that Kainen might be using me hadn't once occurred to my ridiculous excuse for a brain.

Taz's words shot back into my head, that I wouldn't have got anywhere if he hadn't been helping me.

Perhaps he was right after all.

Kainen frowned. "It's not the only reason you're here. I can ask you questions, or I can take the information from you. The latter is more fun, but takes longer. I've decided I want to do this nicely."

I dropped my arms to my sides, preparing myself. If his family wanted to use me to lure Taz out in search of me, they were probably going to be disappointed given the way he behaved earlier. My best bet now was to find a way of striking a deal for my safe return to Arcanium.

"What do you want to know then?" I asked. "Taz and I had an argument anyway, so I doubt he'll be coming to find me. If you have questions, ask them and I can get back to Arcanium. The whole Old King and Queen thing isn't to do with me."

Kainen laughed. "I can read your heart and your feelings, not just your thoughts. I can see the very depths of your fears and what drives you. There's no trickery you can think of that I can't sense you planning. All you have against me are your gifts, which you don't even have any more. You have Taz's gifts, but the beautiful part of it is that you won't risk using them to hurt me, because your human blood makes you good."

Crud.

He had me there. But I couldn't concede that easily. Summoning every shred of my irritable charm, I shrugged my shoulders.

"Okay. I'm tired and I haven't eaten, so just do whatever and get on with it."

My pulse thudded faster as Kainen approached the bars, peering in like I was some kind of interesting insect. I wanted to reach out and throttle him, but that would probably leave a chink in my protection and I needed to conserve my energy.

"I intend to achieve both goals," he said. "Taz must come to find you, which I really do think he will. But until then we have time and I need you to tell me things. First though, I'll bring you some food."

I raised my eyebrows as he turned toward a door in the far wall.

"Oh, I get treated like a person at least?" I asked, gasping in pretend shock. "Wow, aren't you wonderful."

Kainen hesitated, twisting to look back at me. "I may need to utilise your skills, but you will still get fed. I'm not a monster."

I bit my tongue to stop the words flowing out on exactly what I now thought he was. I glared at his back as he disappeared through the door at the other end of the room, then sagged until I had to sit down.

Great going, idiot.

I eyed the room, scoping out my surroundings. I may have been naïve, but now the self-preservation was gearing up. The room had very little in it, save for a few dark grey sofas at the far end near the door to the left of my cage, and a pile of boxes in the opposite corner to my right. I decided not to try touching the bars or lowering my warding to rest yet. Kainen would need to return to Arcanium if he was to keep up his pretence there.

Then I remembered the rucksack he'd brought with him. For all I knew, he'd told everyone that he'd been called home or similar and taken some days off.

When he returned a few minutes later, I forced myself to stay seated even though every inch of me was desperate to jump to my feet, ready for an attack.

He approached with a plate of food on a tray and knelt down in front of me. He pushed the tray through the bars, coming perilously close to pushing it into my warding. I couldn't imagine him going and fetching more if my protection bounced the plate across the room and sent the food flying.

"Okay, you stand over there please." I pointed to the other end of the room.

Kainen grinned, delighted as if we were playing a game.

"What, you think I'm going to do something to you?"

"Yes, absolutely you would, if it suited you."

Kainen sat cross-legged opposite me and shrugged off his jacket, leaving it in a heap behind him.

"Fair point, but I swear not to hurt, trick or use my gifts against you while you're eating," he said.

I narrowed my eyes at him, searching his face and his words for trickery. He sat with an immeasurably wide-eyed innocence but I could see the sharp lines of his face beneath, the watchful calculation as he tried to decipher the same deeper intentions behind my expression in return.

Without thinking, or giving him time to react, I whipped my hand out. Careful not to touch the bars just in case, I grabbed the tray and pulled it toward me, mindful to visualise my protection closing after it.

Kainen didn't so much as flinch, but his smile widened. It freaked me out that he was apparently going to just sit and watch me eat, but I was hungry and his opinion of me was beyond worthless now. I looked down at the plate then hesitated.

"You swear as well that the food's not been tainted, or

tricked, or in any way meant to deceive me?"

Kainen laughed. "You are deliciously suspicious. I swear there's nothing wrong with the food, no taints, tricks or deceptions. It's just food, human food at that. My cook was most offended."

I noticed he referred to the cook as his, rather than 'ours' in a familial way, and that he seemed delighted by his cleverness of thinking to bring me 'human' food.

I can probably use these little character traits of his against him at some point if I'm smart. Take that, Taz.

My insides ached with homesickness as I thought of him, back at Arcanium and probably sulking in his room. Right now I'd rather be sulking in mine than stuck here. Even another round of arguing would be better than this.

Ignoring the swoop of anxiety in my gut at the thought of Taz, I took a bite of the cheese sandwich in front of me, but nothing strange happened. Not entirely reassured, I devoured the rest anyway and shoved the plate and tray to the side.

"Cheers. Now what do you need to ask me? The quicker we do this, the quicker I can go home."

And the less chance he has to wear me down for ways to use me and draw Taz out.

Kainen frowned, one side of his mouth quirking as though I'd actually hurt his feelings.

"That's not nice. Like I said, I'm trying to do this the human way. I could just take what I need from you, but I'm not. I'm giving you a chance to cooperate."

This time it was my turn to smile. He might even believe what he was saying, but he was born for trickery. I leaned as close to him and the shadowy bars as my warding would allow me.

"No, you can't. My protection would stop you. That's why

you're still playing nice. If I couldn't cast one then you'd have taken what you wanted already. Kindness and charm only work if you mean it."

Kainen's frown deepened, and this close I could see the shadowed whirls of his pupils writhing.

"I am trying to be nice." He didn't sound entirely sure, as though he'd only learned the theory of what nice was supposed to be. "I got you those human candies from the Braunees. I taught you to fight properly."

I brushed aside the niggling idea that he was actually serious about this, holding his gaze even though my adrenalin was pounding on pure fear.

Kainen was powerful for his age and gifted to the hilt. He'd been charming for the past few months, but of course that was an act to keep me on side until Taz returned. And like an idiot, I'd fallen for it.

Would he actually hurt me if he had to?

I pressed my hands into the gap between my knees to hide the shaking.

"Well your grand efforts have backfired," I snapped. "Now I can hold my protection for as long as it takes. Sucks to be you."

His face twisted and he shot to his feet.

"I could have made you unconscious and carted you here the moment Taz arrived," he said, his tone wounded. "I didn't do that."

I stayed seated, taking enough strength from my protection to issue my parting shot.

"But where would be the fun in that? Either ask me your questions or leave me alone."

His mouth pressed in fury, his fists bunching at his sides.

First Taz, now Kainen. I'm winning at this whole pissing people off thing today.

"I will let you get used to your cage," Kainen said, the attempt to keep his voice calm clearly an effort as he didn't remember to unclench his teeth first. "Then we'll talk about you being more reasonable."

He was off across the hall before I could ask why he didn't just give me the questions and be done with it.

"Don't count on it," I shouted after him instead.

He disappeared through the door. Seconds later, a loud clanging filled the air, like several metal objects being flung against a wall.

I shook my head in disbelief. He seemed determined for me to *want* to help him, but even if Taz and I were fighting for the rest of our lives, I'd never do anything to betray him or his family. Even if that weren't a loyalty for me, I believed in what the Queen stood for. The Old King and his band of Forgotten followers with their anti-human mania, not so much. If Kainen aligned with them in any way, then he was my enemy too.

I took another look at my surroundings, but unless I could get out of the cage, they were useless to me. I couldn't risk using Taz's gifts either. I didn't know how they worked or how best to wield them, and the bars of my cage might have rebounding properties that would backfire if I tried anything.

I delved in my pocket, feeling for my orb. If I could at least get a message to Petra or Emil-

My fingers skimmed fabric, but no cool smoothness.

Crud. Of course, I'd given orb to Milo so he could take it up to Emil for cleaning. *Taz is definitely onto something. Why would you follow Kainen into the unknown if you didn't even have your orb on you?*

Because I'd thought Kainen was my friend.

I ignored the shame curdling inside me and eyed the plate and tray. Neither of them would do much damage or be much use. The plate might give someone a knock if I threw it, but my hand-eye coordination was sketchy at the best of times. The tray was wooden and unlikely to do much more than potentially stun someone if whacked directly in their face.

I pinched my thumbnail into the flesh of my forefinger to keep my mind sharp and closed my eyes. I could rest and keep the protection above me without actually falling asleep, so at least I'd last a bit longer. But if Kainen intended to keep me here for days, I'd have to sleep eventually.

I'll hear his questions and answer in riddles. Perhaps I can work out when he's going to be elsewhere and use that time to sleep, or escape somehow.

With my eyes closed, I heard the quiet shuffle nearby. I stayed as I was and reinforced the visualisation of my protection.

"If you're back to ask your questions, just get it over with," I said.

Moments of silence drifted, but I refused to look, until a familiar voice that was definitely not Kainen's filled the room.

"Actually, I came to gloat."

CHAPTER SIX
<u>An Ill-Advised Escape Attempt</u>

My eyes snapped open at the sound of Diana's voice. Kainen's sister stood a respectful distance from the bars, but her face was lit with vicious delight. In her shirt and blue jeans she was the only colour in the room but considering she hated me, I wasn't glad to see her. She flicked her brown hair over one shoulder and smirked down at me, waiting.

"Oh, well done," I retorted. "Riding high on your brother's accomplishments suits you."

Her eyes narrowed but the smirk remained.

"Kainen has some misguided belief that you know things," she said in a bored tone. "So he finds you interesting. He's weird like that. But once Taz is here, he'll break you down to pieces, probably literally once he's got what he wants."

I shrugged, trying with all my might to keep the anxious urge to jitter and fidget from showing. I'd been doing so well up until now trapped in this cage, mainly because I could see outside of it, but the itches of anxiety at being confined were beginning to crawl over my skin.

"Not much incentive for me to give him what he wants then. I know that's why he's being kind, although I wouldn't call tricking me and locking me in here very nice."

Diana laughed. "Oh, he's convinced if he gets information from you without force it'll mean more. I don't pay much attention to his nonsense."

I couldn't bring myself to ask her what kind of information, not wanting to give her the satisfaction. There wasn't anything much I could tell them either, other than Taz's weaknesses

55

which I'd rather die than offer up. Instead, I went for the longer game.

"So, you came through the skip-way? Does anyone else know that it's there?"

She folded her arms, hip jutted to one side as she flicked a dismissive gaze over me, no doubt debating whether I was worth telling. I hoped she'd see me as no threat considering I was caged, and she sure did like to taunt me, so her arrogance could work in my favour.

"Only family. It serves us to have a link to home, but of course we have to be careful. Kainen was rash to bring you down here, but then I suppose he thought your little friends would run straight to Taz and that would lure him out."

"Oh. Well, I don't know about that. Kainen said the entrance is elsewhere."

Diana nodded. "Yes, in the far wing of the house, near the kitchens."

"Where does the entrance come out then?" I aimed for polite curiosity, but her gaze sharpened on me.

"Why am I even talking to you?"

A memory was already dusting itself off, giving me the perfect opportunity to taunt her back.

"To gloat, you said. I'll bet the entrance comes out in the library as well. Remember when you stole the Book of Faerie?"

Although it had been months ago now, I hadn't forgotten. The fabled Book of Faerie had vanished from the library, and I'd accused Diana of taking it. Mere minutes later, it was mysteriously returned. She'd also taken the opportunity to pin me to a wall and threaten me because of it. I hadn't forgotten that either.

"I reckon that's how you did it," I added. "Spirit the book away down here through the second floor skip-way, then return it through your kitchen. I already know you have a speed skill, so it would have been simple for you. Not exactly a grand achievement if people found out, huh?"

Her eyes glimmered with dangerous intent, and I saw her fingers twitch at her sides. Somewhere on her person, I had no doubt, was her jewel-encrusted, monogrammed penknife. I had my protection around me, but every strike I had to defend against would weaken me more.

Conserve your strength, don't bait her.

"Why does the Old King want Taz anyway?" I moved swiftly on. "Like, what's the point in taking the children?"

Diana seemed almost relieved to move on as well, so much so she answered me without hesitation.

"The King has his reasons, and he wants to destroy the Queen in every possible way, mentally then physically."

"And that's your thing is it, go where the cruelty is? No matter the carnage left behind?"

She frowned. "My family is one of the oldest lineages in Faerie. We have always supported the King. We do as we're bidden. He wants Taz, and Taz won't leave Arcanium or the Queen's court, so Kainen was ordered to bring you here to draw him out. Then again, I have my own orders to follow, in case my brother fails."

Her smile curved wider as she stared back at me. I wasn't sure why she was telling me this, but the sound of her 'orders' didn't sound like it would work out well for anyone I cared about.

I snorted. "To be fair, you do make a good mindless minion. March off the Old King's cliff for all I care, sure you'll be happy for him to use you any way he sees fit."

Diana froze. I thought for a moment that my feeble attempt to taunt her had hit a mark, but then I heard the footsteps in the hall.

Kainen came into view before she could answer me. He'd changed his jeans from blue to black, and his t-shirt for a midnight grey polo-neck. It made him look older and if I hadn't known what he was like, I'd have thought he was disarmingly charming.

"What are you doing here, Di?" he asked, his tone tipped with notes of warning.

Diana gave him a carefully constructed, non-committal glance. I remembered her almost nervous expression earlier in Emil's hallway, like a spoilt child still hoping to play grown-up games.

"I came to gloat. I'll drop a few hints to Taz about her if you like, everyone's saying he's returned now."

"He's stubborn." I jumped in before Kainen could consider it. "We had an argument and I'm pretty sure he's really anti-me at the moment."

I wanted to say he wouldn't be coming for me, that he clearly didn't care that much after everything he'd said. But the depressing reality was that Taz probably would come to rescue me, out of duty if nothing else, so I had to mind my words while trying to convince them.

Kainen and Diana exchanged a glance and both burst into laughter.

"She has no idea," Diana said. "So sweet, so naïve. I pity you. Sometimes being the good one is a curse all of its own, it keeps you totally blind to the weaknesses of other people."

She swished out of the room and I watched her go, wondering how it was possible to hate her the most when it was Kainen keeping me confined here.

"Are you ready to be more amenable?" he asked.

I heard the tinge of hope in his tone, the curious attention in his dark eyes as he watched me.

"Your sister thinks that you believe I have something special about me." I left that there, but Kainen didn't answer. "Look, you want to ask me questions, and I've told you several times to ask them. I'm confused why you're not doing it."

Kainen folded his arms. "I can't tell you that."

"Can't or won't?"

A slight hesitation. "Won't. For now."

"Well that's infuriating. So what, you're waiting for me to give up information willingly, is that it? Without telling me what exactly you want to know? Okay, a shrimp's heart is inside its head. Venus is the only planet to spin clockwise. Feet bones don't fully harden until-"

Kainen huffed loudly and I stopped.

"You know that's not what I mean," he said.

I raised my eyebrows. "You're not expecting me to change my mind and choose you and your side instead surely, and betray Taz? Why would I support a group that thinks I should be treated like filth for my blood, for something I can't even help?"

A shiver of discomfort crossed his face and his shoulders hunched. Still he didn't answer, and there was a scary possibility that I might never get out the way we were going.

"Tell me the parts you can tell me then," I suggested. "Convince me without trickery."

Kainen cocked his head to the side. I wondered if he was listening to my thoughts and reverted to my 'don't eat yellow snow' routine.

"While Taz is in the Queen's court or Arcanium, they can't get him out without making him step outside himself," he explained. "Even if they bodily dragged him, it wouldn't work. Apparently, Taz doesn't know it, but Arcanium is partially linked to his will. That's one thing I'll concede the Queen has been clever with."

I filed this away in my mind. If Taz stayed in Arcanium, he would apparently be safe forever. No wonder they'd resorted to using his friends to lure him out.

That's assuming we're still even friends, but I can't let anything happen to him.

"But I guess Taz's safety in Arcanium isn't what you wanted to ask me about."

Kainen shook his head.

"I can't use compulsions on you," he said, his tone quiet almost in wonder. "Even back at Arcanium, I couldn't compel you to do anything. It's laughably easy normally. Even with all Taz's royal blood and the protections around him, I compelled him to be cruel to you."

I gasped, my insides leaping with hope.

"What do you mean?"

I wedged my hands between my legs as my thumb began to tap back and forth across my fingers. My connection reacted to my mood, a little tingle near my left elbow, but I willed it to stay calm.

Kainen seemed swamped in his own thoughts, clearly a family trait. He would have usually pounced on the opportunity to make my desperation for info a game, a trade, but he kept talking without realising that I was pressing him.

"I have special strength with compulsions. Not many can compel members of royalty, but I can. When Taz returned earlier, I compelled him to think you and I were together. He was furious, I could feel it swamping the entire hall immediately. Then I waited around in the Ogle for you to report in and compelled him say mean things to you. It wasn't difficult to imagine what he might say and put the words in his head. I followed him straight to you later on in the training room."

I ignored Kainen's gleeful laughter, settling on the one thought that consumed me.

It wasn't Taz saying those things, not really.

My heart lifted. It took all my effort to keep the smile off my face as Kainen's expression darkened.

"Even when he fears he's hurting you, he can't stay away. I heard you both arguing about your gift swap and it was easy to compel him to call you stupid again. But you, even before he returned you were astoundingly oblivious to it. I'd compel you to follow me and you'd say, 'okay, bye' and wander off in the other direction."

So people can be compelled to say stuff they don't mean. Interesting. But what does he mean by not being able to compel me? Is that a 'him' defect or a 'me' thing I wonder?

I realised Kainen was watching me now with dedicated intensity, waiting for an answer.

"I don't know what to tell you." I could at least be honest about that. "You know I only have the one gift, and the normal ability to protect myself that all Fae and fairies learn."

Kainen frowned. "It's almost like you've been blessed, but who'd bother blessing you?"

Ouch. One point to him for arrogance. But of course, I have been blessed.

The memory of Taz's birthday a few months back came screeching into my head. My old mentor from junior fairy classes had arrived mid-fight and given me his blessing. I had no idea what it meant, but perhaps-

If I could distract Kainen from mind-reading me, I might be able to keep this one to myself.

"What's a blessing?" I asked, feigning confusion.

"Oh, it's a ritual of protection from the older days of Faerie.

Potent magic that only court Fae can cast."

Xavio's court Fae? I thought back. *I guess he did warrant an invite to Taz's party that was nothing to do with him knowing me.*

"Well, as you said, who'd bother blessing me?" I posed it as a question to get around the lie and skipped quickly on. "Anyway, I'll admit that you compelling Taz has put my mind at rest, but he still thinks I'm furious with him, as he is with me. Do you really think he'll bother to come looking for me?"

Kainen nodded. "Yes, but he'd probably come for Ace or Milo, just as you would. That's not why I chose to bring you."

"What, my winning charm then? I doubt that."

Kainen laughed, his attention focusing back on me, his dark eyes sparking with determination.

"You don't need to hide behind being flippant," he said, his smile curling softly at the corners. "We both know we've gotten on well lately. It surprised me, but as I said, I'm not as bothered by the narrow views my family hold. You having human blood doesn't bother me, your power does. Taz, Queenie and even Emil all see something in you. Why else would they have kept sending you on assignments?"

Ah.

I tried to hold in my smile, beginning to realise what was motivating him. He thought there was something special about me that he could use. Perhaps he thought I had a secret link to royal lineage or a powerful Fae somewhere in my family, or that I'd been born unnaturally gifted somehow. He was drawn to the mysticism of what he thought I was capable of.

I assessed my options, not sure whether I should let him keep thinking it and lead him on until I could escape, or insist otherwise and hope he soon lost interest in me.

"I don't know about that." I took the cautious route. "I think they send me on assignments because they need a body to send, that has to be at least part of it."

He leaned closer, his eyes narrowing. "Part of it? And the other part would be?"

I shrugged and said nothing. No words = no lies.

He grimaced and sank down into a crouch, the fingers of one hand pressing to the floor.

"I want you to trust me, Demi. It's important that you trust me and tell me things. Can you see that this is important to me?"

I nodded. "Do you care what's important to me though? Doesn't seem like you do. Do you even know what's important to me?"

I thought about Taz and my friends. Better me here and them safe. *Especially Taz.*

Kainen launched upward with a growl. I bashed the sandwich plate with my knee and almost sent it flying as I flinched away. He didn't notice as he started pacing in front of the cage.

"Of course I know. I can read your emotions through your protection. I can't get your thoughts, but I can feel you. I'm getting absolutely nothing other than cloying anxiety, except every time we mention him your emotional aura shivers."

Okay, weird, and creepy. Also very inconvenient.

"Can't help the way I feel, clearly." I shrugged.

Kainen scowled. "You will. I'll be back with something that will make you happy. Then you will tell me things instead of leading me around in circles."

I had no idea what he thought he could bring me that would make up for kidnapping me. I couldn't think of any object I might want, and the Queen had assured me that my family were safe under the highest level of protection she could give them a visitor was unlikely.

The only thing he might be able to sway me with were my friends, or Leo, but all of them were safe in Arcanium. Even if Taz never spoke to me ever again, or never got the chance to the way Kainen was behaving, he was safe.

Kainen huffed at my silence and stormed out of the room. No doubt my emotional aura had told him exactly what I was feeling, or rather who I was thinking about.

Even though I was in serious trouble here, I couldn't help the relief buzzing through me when I remembered what Kainen had admitted.

It wasn't Taz being horrible, it was him being compelled.

It baffled me though that Kainen was so intent on getting me on his side. He thought there was something powerful about me, and he wanted me to tell him things willingly so he wasn't asking any questions, but I wondered then if there was something deeper. Not actual emotions like him having feelings for me, but curiosity perhaps. He definitely didn't seem like the type who was content doing a movie and snacks evening, so maybe he had mad visions of us conquering the world together or something.

I sighed. There was only one option left, and I really didn't want to have to resort to it.

My connection had been sitting patiently inside me, the protection warding almost a second nature now, like tapping your foot or breathing. I let the protection fade and visualised inside of me, scanning across my limbs and torso for any sign of where Taz's gifts might be hiding. I wasn't sure if anyone else saw their gifts like I did, located somewhere physical inside the body, but it helped me to visualise and I always chickened out of asking people in case they thought I was bonkers.

I didn't have Taz's wings, but they were innate to him. I'd felt my energy gift leave me during the exchange, which meant

I most likely had his transmutation gift, and his ability to turn into animals. Out of the two gifts, I guessed transmutation was the safest one to start small with, as I might end up half a fly or something if I used his shifter gift wrong.

My brain ached with tiredness and I didn't have my orb to tell the time either. It would probably be the early hours in Arcanium now, assuming Kainen's part of Faerie kept the same time.

After a full day of classes, training with Kainen, then the assignment, gift exchange and all the upheaval around Taz's return, I was exhausted. My eyelids drooped but I forced myself to focus. A moment later, a subtle tingle spread out from below my left shoulder, right above my heart.

Aha, there you are. Come on, Taz is my friend, or at least I hope he still is. I just want to make sure you won't hurt me.

I knew it was silly to be talking to a Fae gift as if it had thoughts and feelings, but the positive, welcoming emotion I put out encouraged the gift to grow.

It felt warmer than my own energy gift, which tingled like frozen fingers burning after coming inside out of the cold. This was enveloping, smooth and rich, like balmy summer days and crashing seashore waters. It reminded me of the beach Taz had taken me to in Faerie a few months ago, before he left me at Arcanium and returned to the Queen's court.

I took hold of the nearby food tray with Taz's gift thrumming through me. Using the wood, I tapped the shadow bars. I flinched as the tray made contact but, while the bars were solid, there was no defensive rebounding, no explosion, nothing.

When Taz used his transmutation gift, he simply had to concentrate. I decided to try that. Worst case, it wouldn't work.

I can do this. The bars are liquid like water. Plain cold water, like you'd get from a tap.

I imagined the edges beginning to dribble, the shadow glinting and the darkness rolling down like a waterfall.

Dribbles appeared and the darkness of the bars began to thin. I forgot about the rest of the cage and focused my effort on just enough of them to create a Demi-sized gap to walk through.

I could feel the exhaustion clawing at me as I pushed the bars thinner and thinner, the smoke dripping down and away. I wasn't used to Taz's gift like I was my own, so the concentration took more effort. One day, I might be able to wield gifts as easy as breathing like Xavio could, but for now, I had to keep all my focus fixed on those few bars.

After countless ages, I had a gap big enough to squeeze through. I grabbed the sandwich plate and waved it through the gap to be safe.

My insides writhed in knots as it inched into the space between the bars.

And straight through without any reaction.

Phew. I put the plate back on the floor. *Here goes.*

I clambered to my feet and inched forward, petrified that my wobbling limbs would throw me against the bars and make something awful happen.

I huffed a relieved breath the moment I was out of the cage, the sensation of being trapped fading. I twisted in a circle to survey the room. If I left, I'd probably get caught in the halls. I also didn't know the way to the kitchens, let alone have much chance of finding the actual skip-way when I got there. I hadn't learned how to glamour into anyone else yet either to disguise myself. Then I remembered Taz's new gift, the ability to shapeshift into animals.

I really could do with turning into a fly right about now. Should I risk it?

Footsteps echoed in the hall, making my decision for me. I

darted behind the pile of boxes as quickly as I could on uncoordinated feet and crouched low. My legs screamed at the extra effort, but it took all my strength to keep my breathing quiet. As footsteps echoed on the marble floor, my insides pounded with sickening fear.

CHAPTER SEVEN
A Rescue Gone Wrong

"Ah, Demi." Kainen sounded disappointed. "This isn't what I had in mind. You won't have escaped, because there's only one exit to the hall outside and there are guards there."

Crud.

I stayed crouched down in case this was a ploy to flush me out. I didn't know the guard's voices either, so I couldn't even throw mine and impersonate them to draw Kainen away.

I found a gap in the boxes and peered through. Kainen was standing by the cage, his arms folded and his face irritable. He was staring at it like he expected me to materialise back inside it, concentrating his effort right there.

"I'm going to give you a chance to make this right," he snapped. "I want you to trust me. It's important to me. I will close my eyes and you'll get back in the cage. Otherwise, I will have to hurt you."

I tried to keep my breathing silent, but my entire body was shaking. I had no doubt he would hurt me if he had to, and knew he wouldn't be shutting his eyes for me to get back in the cage either. He'd want to see every second of what I'd done, where I'd been, in case I tried to escape again if he got called away.

I noticed something colourful hanging from his hand, and a stab of unexpected confusion shot through me.

He thought a massive bag of Skittles would be enough to make up for kidnapping me?

I shook my head and tried to find my connection. It sputtered, barely there after the effort of using Taz's gift. Knowing I needed to rest it at least a few more minutes before trying for a protection warding, the only option I had was pretend to play nice.

As I bit my lip, frantically assessing my non-existent options, I saw a flash of something totally unexpected. A creature the size of a cat but with scales the colour of shadow that matched the room darted past where the skip-way in had been.

Leo! My heart leapt. Then realisation see-sawed, tearing away any joy. *What the hell is he doing here?*

If Leo was here, that might mean Taz, Ace or Milo had followed him. They might even be here already, although none of them could turn invisible that I knew of.

But Milo has his secret realm-skipping skills. If they're coming for me, I need to play for time and pretending to go along with Kainen is better than him finding me hiding and punishing me.

I stood up, having to press my hands against the boxes for support as my legs almost refused to go through any more physical torment.

I walked toward Kainen, keeping my steps as steady as I could, even though every element of my being was screaming at me to run for it. No doubt if I did run, someone would be waiting to grab me in the hall, or he would be right behind me the moment I moved.

"Are those for me?" I asked.

As I got closer, I saw he actually did have his eyes closed. Again, a strain of discomfort squeezed me tight. He really did think we were playing by some kind of 'rules of nicety' that he'd invented.

He never bothered to share the rules with me though, or give me any kind of choice other than his.

I glanced over my shoulder to see if Leo was still visible, but couldn't see a single flicker in the shadowed room.

As I turned back, glittering black smoke clouded around my head. I raised a hand but I couldn't even find my connection in time to raise a protection warding.

The smoke blocked my vision and I could feel it creeping against my skin, slick like drying sweat. I had to close my eyes as it filled my nose, the sensation of choking filling my head. I tried to huff a breath but the feeling coated the inside of my mouth like a film of washing-up liquid, oozing bitter across my tongue like earwax and sour lemons.

"I warned you." Kainen's voice was the only thing I could focus on as I struggled to breathe.

I wanted to remind him that he'd said he would only hurt me if I didn't get back in the cage, and I'd been walking toward him already when he attacked.

Foolish. Idiot. Stupid. Taz was right.

"Ah yeah, he probably was. I put those thoughts in his head because I knew it would hurt you the most, drive you away from him toward me. But you're still irritatingly loyal. I'm digging around in your mind right now that your protection is down, and I've got some wonderful things to show you. Do you want to see?"

I tried to scream no, but the sensation of not being able to breathe was fogging my mind. Or was that the smoke? All I could see was darkness, and all I could feel, and smell, and taste was the awful sour film of nightmares.

Through the darkness came noises, the familiar rumble of the boiler in our airing cupboard at Mum's house.

"So, this first one is what started off your fears, wasn't it?" he said, his voice all sharp edges and malice. "Locked in there with a monster that was going to eat you and drag you away somewhere unknown. It's the unknown that frightens us, isn't it, but what if that monster were real?"

Through the darkness came dark shapes. Tentacles wrapped tight around my arms, dragging and yanking. A vast pit of black yawned beneath my feet, darker than the shadow around me as the rumbling grew louder and louder from behind.

I tried to open my eyes but they wouldn't respond. I couldn't even force out the scream that was building inside me, pressing, punching, bursting. I flailed against nothingness, panic clawing at me.

"What about some embarrassment?" Kainen continued. "Oh, hmm, no that won't work. Ah, your gift, yes. What a nice boy Jack seemed, didn't he? Spending time with you, laughing with you. And you thought when he told you to close your eyes that he was going to kiss you."

I cringed as mortification burned hot over my skin. The tightness stayed around my arms but without the vision of tentacles creating it. Instead, the image of a memory sprung into life right before my eyes, not something to watch from afar but something to take part in, to relive in all its excruciating glory.

I did think Jack Harmony was going to kiss me, along with all the anxious anticipation that brought.

The lifelike image of Jack solidified in front of me, all soft blond hair and wide blue eyes, lips curved in a smile as he mouthed at me to close my eyes. He'd given me my gift, not out of kindness but out of spite, because Diana told him to give me one that would make life horrible for me.

"Ah, but what's this?" Kainen hesitated. "Shame? Obligation? You didn't think you liked him after all. And fear. Too afraid to say no because you thought you should have liked someone like him and you didn't. My sister was wrong then. Jack was wrong too. He was so convinced you were totally smitten over him. He's my cousin, you know."

Through the crashing torment of emotions that Kainen was

no doubt heightening to torture me, I found my voice.

"You and he are very much alike."

The vision wavered before darkness engulfed me again.

"How so?"

"Both arrogant." I fought against the urge to vomit at the sour magic in my mouth. "Both assume your gifts make who you are. What are you without them though? Spoilt boys playing at being important."

Light burned my eyes as the smoke plumed away from me. I blinked savagely several times, able to make out the room and the candles still burning. Even though the sight of the room wasn't much better than the darkness of my fears, the sheer relief brought tears to my eyes.

I twisted to face Kainen, amazed I was somehow still on my feet.

Not for long. Even as I lifted a hand, trying for a warding despite weakness zapping every part of me, Kainen grabbed me. He caught my wrist in one hand and my shoulder in the other, spinning me so I was standing facing the door with my back to him.

With perfect balance, he had his foot across my ankles and swept me to my knees. I winced as I landed, but pinned my lips together so I couldn't cry out more than a squeak. I wouldn't give him the satisfaction of knowing he'd hurt me.

He pulled my arms tight behind me and upward, the angle shooting pain across my chest and the front of my shoulders. I flinched away as he leaned over me and his mouth brushed my ear.

"I'm stronger than you. I'm the one holding all the power. I tried to be nice to you, to give you a chance to give me what I want willingly. Usually, I wouldn't ask. What is it? Why are you so loyal to him?"

Guessing he meant Taz, I lifted my head, ready to headbutt him and try to break free. If I could get out of his grip, I could at least throw up my protection for as long as my strength would hold.

I considered his question, and realised with ruthless glee that the truth would be the perfect thing to upset him the most.

"Because he always asks. What I think is important to him. If *he* wanted to convince me to play nice, he'd be offering me things I wanted, not hurting me."

Kainen twisted me around and threw me so I was lying on my back. It was no worse than facing sparring practice with him or Petra, but I was exhausted. He put a foot onto my stomach before I could try and get up, but the touch was featherlight, as if he only needed to keep the connection between us so I couldn't protect myself rather than to hurt me.

As if he's trying to listen to what I'm saying and go against his natural instincts to impress me.

"Is this better?" he snarled. "Is this what you want?"

His entire body rippled until I was staring up at a perfect likeness of Taz, right down to the damn *Demon Babies* t-shirt. I couldn't help the wave of relief, even though I knew it wasn't really him. Kainen sensed it and his face twisted.

"I meant things I wanted in general, not a person or anything." I ignored the flush blooming across my face. "Anyone can glamour once they've learned how. Cheap party trick, even for you."

Kainen clenched his fists. "Perhaps I will torment you until all that are left are the nightmares."

Behind his back, I saw the impossible flash across the room a second time. I'd learned early on to recognise Leo when he was camouflaging and now my mind had become attuned to picking up those visual ripples. While this could be a completely different lizard, it was a big coincidence if it was. I almost cried out as he disappeared through the door to the hall and the rest of the house.

Kainen reached down and hauled me to my feet. I tried to twist away from him but he had me in a chokehold this time. His hand pressed into the small of my back and his other arm wound tight like a python around my neck.

"Let her go."

The familiar voice echoed through the hall and I whimpered, not caring if Kainen thought I was pathetic. He twisted us both to face the door again, and I had to sniff a couple of times to keep the tears of sheer relief inside.

Taz strode across the marble floor, no doubt with his protection firm around him. He didn't hold his hand out to keep it going, but then he'd never needed to.

I eyed the darkness around his eyes, the ruffled honey-blond curls of hair sticking up and the same t-shirt he'd been wearing earlier. He didn't look like he'd had a moment's peace since we parted.

"Get out while you still can," I shouted, struggling and managing to get a kick back against Kainen's shin. "It's a trap for you!"

Taz rolled his eyes. "Well, obviously. Are you okay?"

I blinked, baffled by the idea he was concerned for me when he was the one in the real danger.

"What? No, not exactly, but you have to get of here now!"

"So, Kainen." Of course, Taz ignored me completely. "I hear your lot have managed to capture all my full-blood Fae sisters, but not me, the half-blood. Good going. Really proving the pro-Fae point there."

Kainen still had a tight hold on me, but I could feel his muscles tense against my back. This wasn't going how he'd expected it to go.

I wriggled with all my strength against him but still couldn't get free.

"Ah, Demi." His voice suddenly crooned in my ear. "How do you know that's actually him though? I can read everything in your mind, all your memories. You told me to charm you with things you wanted, right? So I can conjure them up for you. What do you want him to say? I suppose, if we were doing this realistically, he'd tell you to ignore me."

"Don't listen to him, Dem." Taz caught my eye.

I froze. *Is this more mind trickery? But then, would Kainen have known to conjure Leo? How much of my mind does he have access to?*

"Shall I remind you of what he did last time?" Kainen taunted. "You'd rather see him yell at you again? I can show you that. He's my creation standing there, I can make him do it right in front of you."

I clung onto the thought of Leo, needing to believe that Kainen was lying frantically now to keep me confused and fearful.

His smoke clouded my eyes before I could react and plunged me back into darkness, but I knew the worst of it now. I choked over a breath and forced the words out.

"How far are you willing to go to convince me then? What if I promise I'll never believe you, that every effort you make to torment me just proves there's something more than me at stake? Why would you bother otherwise? You told me you're using me to get him here, so if he's not here, then I don't have to give you anything."

I gritted my teeth, my hands tugging with no success against Kainen's arm around my throat.

"Because you must have something else about you," Kainen

said, his voice quiet enough now to convince me that he didn't want anyone to overhear.

That must mean Taz is really here. It has to.

"Must I?" I sucked in another sour breath. "What, because of Queenie and Emil? Because the prince of Faerie wants to be my friend? Because Petra chose me out of all the other potential mentees?"

It was hard to talk into the darkness, to force the words out past the taint of his magic now back on my tongue, but I could feel my connection lurking, ready for when I had a chance to use it. I might not be special like Kainen assumed, but I was still part-fairy.

I don't have my gift though. An idea came to me, sparkling in its awful recklessness. *But Taz does.*

I lifted my voice, shouting into the dark.

"Taz, if you're there, if you're definitely you, do what I would normally do."

A moment of silence, then the smoke receded. Kainen appeared to be concentrating, his head nestling beside mine.

"He's not really there, Demi. This is your last chance. If you defy me now, I'll have to hurt you. Don't think I'll have a moment of last-minute chivalry and spare you any pain. I'll even play along and make you imagine him doing it, if you like."

I heard the angry bite in his tone, the sound of someone who was on their last desperate thread of losing control. I stopped clawing at Kainen's arms and fell still, clenching my hands into fists at my side instead.

"Oh, what is it then?" I taunted. "Teach the poor little fairy a lesson? I wouldn't dream of your affection in my worst nightmares."

I turned my head to look at him. He was still wearing his Taz glamour, both identical down to the very last freckle and piece of clothing.

I wonder if Kainen knows what underpants to glamour?

I shook the thought from my head even though it gave me another dangerous and extremely stupid idea.

I dug deep and found my natural skill, the one that I'd been born with rather than gifted.

"Guards!" I yelled in a perfect mimicry of Kainen's voice. "The prince is here!"

The sound of hefty feet charging down the corridor filled the room. I stared at the potentially real Taz.

If he's really him, he'll know what I'm doing. He'll understand. He has to understand.

Seconds before two men filled the doorway, the Taz standing opposite me shivered and turned into Kainen. Relief blossomed into my chest, expanding with a surge of adrenalin that giggled through my limbs.

Taz pointed at Kainen and I. The moment the men looked our way, I threw my voice to sound like Kainen's.

"There! Seize him!"

I couldn't imagine even Kainen saying 'seize him' like some pantomime villain, but it was the first thing that came to mind. It also meant that the natural gift for voice mimicking I'd been born with had remained with me during the switch. Taz had been gifted with conditional imperviousness to my energy gift by his mother, but there was no knowing if that protection had passed to me in the gift exchange, or if him using it on the rest of us would hurt me as well.

But I couldn't worry about that now. Kainen kept hold of me and I tilted my head sideways in time to see him take his normal form.

"Neat trick," he told me. "But you can't keep doing that forever. Sagar, Eldrich, he's the real prince."

The guards hesitated at the sight of two Kainens, and now I looked at them properly. Both were bulky and tall with bushy beards, either of them probably more likely to throw Taz over one shoulder like a ragdoll than need to manhandle him anywhere. One had red hair burgeoning from his head in messy straggles and an alarmingly cheerful looking face. The other stood frowning and dour, with dark hair.

They were there at Gallows Oak, back when Taz and I were last on assignment. They were guards to the Old King.

This wasn't good. Clearly, the Old King had sent them ready for when Taz walked into the trap which, like an idiot, he'd done on schedule.

I caught Taz's eye, hating that he still looked like Kainen. Even now though, I could see the slight sideways tilt of his hip, one knee bent and his eyebrows raised in a way that was so him.

I squinted until I was almost certain I could make out two tiny black hoops. My heart leapt.

He's forgotten to glamour his eyebrow piercings to get rid of them.

Finally confident that Taz really was here, I bit my lip. I had a scary premonition that the next plan of mine wouldn't go the way we wanted it to.

But this plan would be enough to get him to safety. He had to come first.

"Do what you need to do," I said. "Do my thing as strong as you can, while you still can."

Taz shook his head. "No, what if-"

"It's okay, *Sparky*." I glared meaningfully at him in case he didn't understand the instruction. "Do. What. You. NEED. To. Do. It's okay."

The guards were still caught in hesitation, looking back and forth between us. Kainen tightened his hold on me, his arm wrapping around my middle while the other one continued pressing against my throat. Perhaps he thought Taz was going to try and pull me away with the sheer power of mind or something.

"This is all very dramatic," he said. "But we should probably just-"

Taz's eyes fixed on mine, wide and panicked as he threw out a hand. A jet of white-blue light blazed across the room, fracturing in all directions until it dazzled me, brighter than I'd ever seen. It illuminated the walls of the vast room, sending sparkles of light bouncing off the black marble and casting Taz's petrified face into my memory as the last thing I'd ever see.

I screamed when the energy hit, the feeling of my own gift alien as it attacked me, burning and scraping white-hot pain against every single cell of my being.

I had the vague notion that I'd never use it on a single living person ever again.

Then the realisation that I'd probably never use it again anyway.

Without a single clever quip or final word, I died.

CHAPTER EIGHT
It's Not Just a Nut

Ouch.

My first thought was that something extremely pointy was poking one of my hips. Usually Taz would snigger when I made some kind of accidental innuendo, but I couldn't hear anything. I couldn't see anything either, which was weird.

Eyes. I should have eyes to open.

"Let yourself rest a while, dear."

The voice was familiar, but I had no idea who I was meant to be, let alone who someone else was. But weirdly I remembered someone called Taz, which was something.

I had a name, I knew that much, but what was it? Half something? Quarter?

Demi. My name's Demi.

Agony splintered through me and I cried out as every single memory, feeling and thought burst back into being. Words flowed out of my lips, but there was no chance of knowing what the words were.

"Now, there's no need for that sort of language," the familiar voice said. "That should be about the worst of it, so sit up when you're ready."

Was I ready? I had aches in every single part of me. I had a head, which was pounding in a sickening, lumbering dance around and around. I had a chest, which was aching in a different way. Feelings. Those were feelings. I recognised anxiety, my old friend who I sometimes thought really hated me. Pity. Where did that come from? Anger, love, confusion, fear.

Ah, I can't be doing with this.

I found my way to my eyes and remembered how to open them.

Green filled the air around me, lines beginning to form. I levered myself up onto one elbow, my head so alarmingly heavy that I had to slump back down.

"It takes a while. Still, you'll be in no worse shape for it I dare say."

I blinked. Either it was my sideways view because I was lying down, or the knots in the tree were moving. Not moving, talking.

Old Tara.

I tried to sit up again, managing to get there this time but having to lean forward and support my head on my hands and my elbows on my knees.

"What am I doing here?" I asked.

"Oh, my dear. Do you remember what I gave you?"

I scanned the aching area between my ears. "A nut."

"An acorn, yes. Do you know why I gave you that acorn?"

I shook my head slowly.

"I gave you that acorn as a temporary anchor, to only be used once. When you return, it will just be an acorn, but if you plant it maybe one day a talking tree might sprout."

I blinked. "You gave me a nut as an anchor, but now it's just a talking nut I have to plant?"

I had a vague memory of the word anchor; we'd learned about it in class, but I couldn't recall what exactly had been said. I could also remember my family now, and that I loved my mum but my sisters didn't like me much at all. No, my family was Arcanium, Ace and Milo, Petra. *Taz.*

I tried to stand up in one lumbering rush, like a baby elephant on a slip'n'slide. I fell flat on my face, only just managing to get my arms out in time to stop me breaking my nose.

"Well now, that was silly," Old Tara said. "You needed a temporary anchor to keep you tied to Faerie, otherwise things may have ended in a rather more final way than people would have liked. There are those who have placed certain levels of protection on you. The acorn did that, but now it's just an acorn."

"Thank you." I had to ask even though it might sound a bit abrupt. "Do I owe you a favour now or something?"

Old Tara's leaves rustled above me. "No, dear, but I'd say my dues are more than paid."

"Um, okay. What is an anchor though?"

"An anchor is something that ties you to keeping going. Rarely it could be your family, a goal or achievement you're working toward, but often it's a loved one. Not everyone finds an anchor, but they tend to keep you standing up when everything knocks you down. You are somewhat of a closed book, by all accounts, so I gave you the acorn to be on the safe side. I would suggest finding your anchor and guarding that knowledge closely. Remember I told you knowledge is a dangerous thing? It can be used against you."

I didn't like the sound of that at all. I pulled the acorn from my pocket with sensitive, aching fingers.

"Where do you want me to plant it?"

Old Tara's leaves chuckled in the breeze. "Somewhere light and bright in the natural earth. The human world, or Faerie, it doesn't matter."

I couldn't imagine planting a possibly talking tree in the human world, and Arcanium had no direct earth that I knew of. But I did have one idea.

I had to crawl on my hands and knees, but after a few moments I found a suitable patch of soft earth.

"What about here?" I called over my shoulder as twisting

around hurt too much.

"Why there, dear?" Old Tara asked, bemused.

"I might not be able to come to chat as often as I'd like. I thought it might give you someone to talk to. I can choose somewhere else if you don't like that?"

A branch appeared in front of me, as if straining out to reach. The tip of it settled on my shoulder.

"You are very kind." I almost thought I heard a sniff somewhere amid the rustling. "That would be lovely, such a generous thought. You may be part-human, my dear, but you are a good one, the sort anyone would be proud to have as kin. I think we'll keep you."

"Er, thanks." Weird, but kind of sweet if I skipped over whatever the mention of 'keeping me' meant. I guessed querying or arguing about it wouldn't do any good right now, and I had to get back to Taz somehow.

It took all my strength to dig my fingers past the grass and into the earth, but with Old Tara's not so gentle instructions, I managed to bury the acorn. I patted the earth back on top of it, desperate to get the gesture over with and get moving.

"Thank you, my love," Old Tara said. "Now, rest a few moments more before you go back. The Old King is getting stronger and the Queen is ailing, what with the disappearance of so many of her children. We need to find a way of restoring her because Faerie senses the young prince doesn't want to become king."

I sat slumped over my crossed legs, eyes hazy and half-closed as I sorted through that in my head. It took me more than a couple of moments to come up with an answer.

"I thought Taz couldn't be king anyway because he's half-fairy, not fully Fae-blooded."

Tara's leaves rustled. "He is *technically* half-Fae, but

entirely court-blooded. There's not as much human in him as some would lead others to believe. Perhaps the Queen told him that to give him some freedom. But still, he is a good boy."

"He's a pain in the arse more like," I muttered. "But then, I suppose that's to be expected when you're a prince and your friend doesn't have a clue what she's doing most of the time. He's always there, saving me when he should be thinking about the bigger picture and keeping himself safe."

Old Tara laughed. "He's a pain to you because you're his anchor, silly girl. Anyone with life can see it."

I flinched and the enormity of that statement almost took out my elbows and sent me face first into the dirt.

Orbs alive. If I'm Taz's anchor, anything I do is going to put him in danger. He'll always be trying to save me or help me.

Another thought occurred to me then, one slightly less daunting.

"What's the Queen's anchor?" I asked.

The knot in Old Tara's trunk smiled sadly.

"Clever girl. It used to be Faerie, but perhaps if you follow that thread, we may yet come out of this. Now, I will give you a gift."

"Oh, you don't need to, you already gave me the-"

"Don't be rude, dear." Old Tara tutted with clacking branches. "You have a good heart, and Faerie rewards those who defend it. That is something the Old King has forgotten in his bitterness and cruelty, among other things. I will give you the gift of translocation within reason. You may translocate within environments but only in those you have already visited."

I raced through the potential pitfalls. Translocation gifts were unbelievably rare.

"Um, can you do that?" I bit my lips together the moment the words were out, aware how insulting that sounded.

Old Tara laughed. "I am formed of Faerie, my dear, of course I can. No tricks, no leaving part of you behind when you translocate, no gradual chipping away of any parts of you. Just the ability to move yourself from one part of your environment to the other."

I couldn't help myself now. "So, if I'm in Arcanium, like in the library say, I could translocate to a different room like Queenie does?"

"I daresay you could with practice. But you wouldn't be able to translocate from Arcanium to Faerie, or from one realm of Faerie to another, or one village to the next, close spaces only. And remember, only once you've visited a place previously can you translocate through it. Your body will need that knowledge to travel through."

I scrolled back through my memories and lit on one of the more nightmarish ones that sometimes woke me at night. Tight spaces crushing in. Translocation might just come in handy for escapes in future, if I could learn to wield it.

"How does it work?" I asked. "Do I need to enter a room and then leave it and enter it again before the gift will work there? Are there words or- sorry, I'm so new to this, and I don't want to get it wrong."

"Oh you are precious. I don't know these things, they are Fae and fairy affairs, but you will have many books and brains to guide you I'm sure. Close your eyes."

I obeyed, my heart leaping in my chest.

A translocation gift. Everyone else is going to be so jealous!

I flinched as something brushed my forehead, feeling like a kiss from the cool, soft surface of a leaf. A warm fizzle sparked though the contact before turning cold like a breath of air similar to realm-skipping, filling my entire body with a sensation of lightness.

"There," Old Tara said. "You are gifted. Now I must send you back. There are rumblings your young man is getting very fussy."

I skated over the mention of my young man, guessing she meant Taz and not having the energy to correct her.

"How do we do that?"

Old Tara's leaves chuckled. "Why, just stamp your feet three times and say 'Quacks away', of course."

"Really?"

"Of course not. Don't you watch *Demolition Ducks*? Now, eyes closed would be best. You'll feel a slight disassembling."

I closed my eyes and a rolling sensation swooped bubbling warmth through every single part of me, like the lurch you get that tingles all over when you're in a big drop on a rollercoaster.

The moment I focused on the tingling, it vanished, leaving a void.

A savage ache spasmed across my shoulders and my hips, hard ground reappearing underneath me, as if I'd been flipped over onto my back with a slam. Thrums of sensitivity jolted into my skin like bad sunburn, and I could smell the faintest whiff of apple.

"I'll sacrifice my gift then!" Taz's voice splintered whatever was left in my ears. "That'll bring her back surely, or her gift, or whatever the hell one I've got at the moment. All of them. I can't lose her."

"Sacrifices don't work like that." I recognised Ace replying, although he sounded like he was standing a good punching distance away from Taz. "She's breathing again now, and you have to think of Faerie. Demi wouldn't want you-"

"Don't you dare tell me what she'd want! You have no idea. What have I done?"

The sensation of having sunburn crackled all over me, but

when I grinned my lips felt unscathed.

"You've made a complete mess of everything," I croaked. "That's what you've done."

Something hot and firm pressed against my forehead. A similar heated weight crushed my fingers seconds later.

"You're alive!"

I opened my eyes, blinking to find Taz's wide turquoise ones swimming inches from my face.

I huffed. "Of course I'm alive."

"Why didn't you tell me that would happen, that you'd get hurt?"

"Because if I had, you wouldn't have done what you did, then we'd both be dead or you'd be captured and off to join your sisters, and Kainen would have carved me into bits or something. But Tara's gift switch thing didn't work, not completely. You got my power but I didn't get your immunity to it, must have been part of the 'conditional' imperviousness your mum gave you when I got the gift. It didn't transfer over, like your wings didn't."

"What?"

I merrily skipped past the dangerous quietness in Taz's tone.

"Luckily Tara gave me this nut thing, which I planted to keep her company now that it's just a nut. I think."

"You knew you'd likely die?" he asked, his voice eerily calm. "Your pulse disappeared for a moment and you stopped breathing. You knew that would happen?"

"I guessed something like it could have been a potential possibility. But also that it might have been totally fine. I had to give you a chance to get yourself out either way."

"Can you stand?" His teeth were clenched.

I shook my head. "Not well."

Taz pushed his arms under my shoulders and I squeaked as

he gathered me against him. In one swoop and a slight fiery orange flutter from behind him, we were standing.

Kainen's hall rushed into view, him and his two guards unconscious nearby. Whatever Taz had done with my gift, it was something huge.

"Are they, um…" I couldn't bring myself to say it, taking the coward's way out and succumbing as he hugged me tight and my face landed on his shoulder.

"No, just unconscious," Taz muttered. "Ace insisted on checking on them for some reason."

I heard Ace grumble somewhere nearby.

"I wanted to make sure they weren't going to get up any time soon," he said reproachfully. "Besides, 'Prince of Faerie in enemy family murder saga' isn't the kind of publicity you need right now."

I clung onto Taz, but lifted my head to look him right in the eyes, forcing him to acknowledge me. The eye contact sent jolts of anxiety bolting through my system, but I had to face this, no matter how awkward it was.

"Old Tara said I'm your anchor."

I waited, my insides roiling. The urge to throw up wasn't entirely ruled out either.

I had no idea what anchoring meant in a person-to-person sense, only that in a Faerie sense I'd be in danger if he was, and that he'd likely keep putting himself in danger to protect me.

I quelled a squeak of alarm as his forehead dropped to rest against mine. With all these new revelations around us, I had to fight the urge to close my eyes to avoid eye contact and focused on our feet instead.

"Of course you are," he murmured. "That's not anything to worry about now, but if you do something like this again I'm going to kill you."

I bypassed the threat, an empty suggestion rather than a lie considering he didn't mean it. Most likely.

Desperate to avoid the awkwardness settling around us, I turned my head to see Kainen a metre away, unconscious on the marble with a huge bag of Skittles near his feet. Pushing aside the stab of revulsion, I decided he wasn't my biggest problem right now.

"I wonder if Tara knew this would happen," I said. "And I wonder how. She must have known, or why give me the nut in the first place? Argh, I didn't ask her any sensible questions. We need to find your mother's as well though, her anchor, Old Tara said. She said she used to be anchored to Faerie, but apparently not now by the sounds of it. So I guess we either need to re-anchor her, or find something else."

Okay, perhaps the impromptu shocking and my projecting through Faerie experience had flipped my auto-babble switch. Taz slid an arm around my waist to keep me secure.

Like an anchor holds a ship. I shook the thought away. *So not the time right now.*

"But how?" Ace asked.

I glanced at him and saw Milo standing close beside him, both of them still a wary distance from Taz and I.

"We need her to see what's happened to Faerie," I said. "Find a way to make her realise what's going on without her. Or rescue her daughters so she goes back to normal if she won't listen."

Taz groaned. "Simple then. Since my sisters have been going missing, she's lost the plot. Won't eat, won't talk to anyone, just keeps sulking and saying, 'what have I done' like some over-dramatic diva."

"I think losing your kids is kind of a justified reason for losing the plot," I suggested, resisting the urge to compare mother to son on the dramatic scale.

He stuck his tongue out at me and I opened my mouth to retaliate, but only managed a startled squeak.

A fizzling sensation shot over my skin and through to the very core of my bones. I was still clinging onto Taz, who seemed to also be standing straighter and stronger next to me all of a sudden. I tapped a finger on his bare arm.

"Nothing?" I asked.

He shook his head. "It must be Faerie hour."

Ace stepped forward and extended an arm to me, wordlessly offering. No doubt Taz had explained to them about our gift exchange. I dug deep and found my connection, just a little fizzle, and tapped the back of Ace's hand. He flinched.

"Ouch, yeah, you're sparking again."

Despite still being stuck in the house of the enemy with the potential peril of Faerie now hanging over us, Taz pulled me against his chest again and spun me round with a loud cheer.

I met his gaze. He smiled, one side crooked like he was thinking of other things, although I had no hope of knowing what those might be. My insides started the most inappropriate fluttering and I looked away even as a smile still tugged at my lips.

"We should go before this lot come around." Ace was trying not to laugh. "We have a realm to save still and worse, reports to make."

"What about Leo?" I asked, more memories and worries returning by the second.

Taz shook his head. "He's safe at home, don't worry."

"But I saw him!"

"You did." He held up a hand when I started to interrupt. "I'll explain when we're back home. Trust me?" I frowned but nodded agreement. "We'll skip into the Ogle so we have a few minutes before going to see Queenie."

Milo nodded and took Ace's hand moments before they disappeared. Taz held me close as the air rushed and the landscape blurred around us. I sagged as the brush of air from realm-skipping faded to reveal a familiar wall of screens.

Taz propped me against him in the main aisle of the Ogle, a little way down from the open space that separated the screens from the lift. I twisted to face him, my strength beginning to return at the sheer relief of being home again.

Now we were back in relative safety, Taz's eyes were storming. I found the courage to look up into his furious face.

"What the hell were you thinking?" he asked.

I bit my lip. I hadn't been thinking, not really. He had his own questions to answer, like how he'd found me, and what he had been thinking bringing Leo into it. And how did he get him home again so quickly?

"I wasn't," I admitted. "You were being mean, or at least I thought you were, before I knew Kainen had been compelling you-"

"He what?" Taz straightened up, but caught me again as I wobbled sideways.

"He told me he'd compelled you to be horrible to me, when you got back and again when we argued in the training hall."

Taz frowned. "I thought that was weird. The minute I got out of the room I was furious, but couldn't understand why I'd said those things. I figured I'd leave you to cool off and try again in a better mood, but then you disappeared. Milo came crashing into my room saying you'd disappeared with Kainen down to the second floor, which has absolutely nothing in it other than junk, and I knew something wasn't right."

"Not quite nothing," I muttered, remembering the skip-way. "But why in the name of Faerie did you bring Leo?"

"I didn't." Taz hesitated. "Remember I told you I got a new

gift?”

I wracked my brains. “Oh, the animal shifting? That was you all along?”

He might have answered me, but heavy footsteps filled the air. I pushed against Taz’s shoulders in case anyone should see us and jump to conclusions. Taz clung to me with way more strength than I could dredge up.

Stubborn arse.

I had no energy left to struggle, but folded my arms to show him I wasn’t impressed with the manhandling. Even though the weight of his arms pinning me to him were the most comforting thing I could have ever imagined, even scarier for the fact I didn’t go in for hugging at all.

I grimaced helplessly as Emil appeared, a thunderous scowl on his face.

“Demi, my office, now.”

CHAPTER NINE
A Revelation and an Unexpected Ally

I nodded but Emil held up a hand the moment we took our first step.

"Not you, Taz."

Taz started towing me along beside him. "She can barely stand. Unless you want to carry her?"

Emil grimaced and strode off toward the lift. My gut sank. He had always turned a blind eye to the odd misdemeanour, but I had no hope that this would end well for me now.

I left Arcanium without any warning, without signing out, no orb to call in on. My natural instinct to assume the worst warred with rising anger. *No, he has no right to be angry with me. Okay, I shouldn't have gone with Kainen, but then he's another mentee and a second-year. Why wouldn't I trust him?*

We got into the lift and I glossed over the innate mortification of Taz holding me up. I could have supported myself now, but if they kicked me out after all this, it would probably be the last time I ever saw him.

Emil slid the grill aside the second we appeared on the floor with his and Queenie's offices. He set off but even though I straightened up, forcing myself to prepare to take my punishment with some measure of dignity amid the shame, Taz wouldn't let me go.

If I'm truly his anchor, what will he do if they make me leave?

Emil was already turning into the side corridor to his office while we were still lagging halfway behind.

"Don't worry," Taz muttered, his breath tickling my ear. "Explain exactly what happened, and that I came to get you.

None of this is your fault."

I nodded, even though the embarrassment of being foolish enough to trust Kainen was swamping around me in thick waves.

Emil's office was a lot smaller than Queenie's grand, imposing one next door. He had a desk piled high with papers, a couple of filing cabinets and a door in the right wall.

I stood in front of the desk, leaning against Taz and awaiting my fate as Emil sat down in his chair.

"We're going to have to ask you to leave, Demi."

The words knocked all hope of talking out of me.

I'd assumed any punishment would be minimal, a lecture on realm-skipping without permission maybe, or some kind of awful extra duties to regain favour.

Given that Faerie rules meant I couldn't accuse Kainen of anything without actual proof, my hands were tied. I could explain what happened, but unless I actually proved that he'd kidnapped me, it wouldn't make any difference.

Stupid, stupid rule. I sniffed.

"You can't do that-" Taz started.

"Demi realm-skipped out of Arcanium without permission. She didn't even take an orb with her. She refused to report in. There are also certain rumours about high court Fae going missing around the same time, and the families are starting to lodge enquiries."

That was fast. Kainen must have woken up and got his father involved or something to do a cover-up of his absence.

I ignored the traitorous flare of relief that Kainen was at least still alive, but the sensation felt far away, as though it was a distant memory rather than one happening inside me.

I bit my lip hard, my entire body shaking from combined shame and exhaustion. I opened my mouth and managed to force out a word.

"I-"

"Demi, don't say another word." Taz growled as he let go of me. "None of this is her fault. If she goes, I go."

Emil rolled his eyes. "You're the prince of Faerie, we can't kick you out, and you can't leave. Unless you walked out of here into the human world with her, and you'd be unprotected then, defenceless and weak."

I couldn't meet Emil's eyes as Taz growled something defensive in reply, couldn't say any more without bursting into noisy, snotty tears. The wet began to drip down my cheeks but I didn't care anymore.

Only the sound of the office door banging open was enough to lift my head. In my fatigued slowness, I noticed a wariness leap into Emil's eyes.

"Taz, out."

I rotated to see Queenie framed in the doorway, decked in her vampiric black velvet dress with bright red talons twitching at her sides. I quickly wiped my eyes with my sleeve.

"I'm not-"

Taz barely got a breath out before Queenie grabbed the back of his t-shirt and was bodily forcing him out of the door, shutting it behind him.

"I don't believe you're in full awareness of the facts, Emil," Queenie said, giving him a dismissive look. "You can't be, as you of all people know the rules and by-laws of both the Queen's command in Faerie and the rules set forth by the Arcanium council."

Emil shrugged, his shoulders never quite descending back down from his ears.

"Clearly, Demi was not to blame," Queenie continued. "I have two accounts that confirm she was all but abducted by someone older and much more experienced than she is herself."

Two accounts. Ace and Milo must have gone straight to Queenie on my behalf.

Emil sighed. "Unless she has proof, we have to take this seriously. Kainen's father is insisting she be dismissed, as it was her gift that left him with a serious case of what looked like sunburn."

Queenie eyed him for a long, silent moment. I wondered if I should offer to wait outside. At least then I'd probably be passed out in a nice, carpeted corner by time they decided my fate.

"I would consider Ogle footage, two individual accounts of the situation and her testimony to me proof enough."

"Footage?" Emil asked.

"Yes." Queenie eyed her nails as though she wasn't pinning my entire future between them. "Strangely, there seems to be a blind spot in that exact section, but there is enough to suggest that Demi was dragged *mostly* against her will."

Queenie gave me a look, the disapproval in her dark eyes somewhat watered down by the tears in mine.

"Anyway," she continued. "Arcanium law insists that any dismissal should be taken under advisement before a decision is made. You should be aware of that, Emil."

Astonished, I clung to the tiny ray of hope she'd just given me.

Queenie, of all people, fighting my corner.

"I need to learn the absolute truth of this." Her stern gaze fixed on me next. "Leave nothing out."

So I explained everything I had learned from start to finish in one rambling, breathless monologue. I told them about the plot to abduct Taz, and also the role Kainen and Diana had played. I told them about Old Tara and stopped just short of what she'd said about the Queen. I didn't mention Ace or Milo either.

Even if they had gone straight to Queenie, I couldn't risk dropping them in anything until I knew what they'd said. But Taz's part was unavoidable and, like Emil had said, he was the sole prince of Faerie; they couldn't kick him out.

"I will alert the necessary people," Queenie said, once I'd managing to halt my rambling. "If Kainen returns, he will be questioned."

Emil huffed. "Kainen booked his time off to sort out a family matter, all approved. I wouldn't expect him back any time soon."

"Hmm." Queenie pursed her black-painted lips as she regarded him for a moment. Then she turned to me. "Come to my office. I have something I believe you may be able to assist me with. Not you, Emil. I'm sure you have work to do."

I tried not to focus on Emil's scandalised expression. He'd been halfway out of his seat, no doubt to follow us, but had to sink down with a scowl.

Queenie flung the door open to reveal Taz pressed against it, his indignant expression exactly the same as it had been when she shut it in his face a few minutes ago. He almost tumbled against her but caught either side of the doorframe just in time to avoid faceplanting right into her rather sizeable chest.

Queenie swept past him and I didn't dare tell him I could support myself this time as his arm pinned around my waist again. If he wanted to come and keep me company, I wasn't going to argue.

I should probably stop blushing and avoiding looking at him every time he does it though.

As Queenie opened her office door and turned to face us, she noted the tight hold Taz had on me and rolled her eyes.

"I'm serious, Taz, go away." She pointed to the corridor. "Demi has nothing to fear from speaking to me, and I'm sure she'll update you with anything she feels you need to be aware of. You're not her keeper."

No, but I'm his anchor.

I half expected Taz to argue or refuse, but he huffed and slid away from me. As Queenie swept into her office, he gave me a weary look.

"Come find me when you're done," he murmured. "They're holding a revel in the atrium tonight apparently, but we need to talk first."

I nodded and followed Queenie into her office, watching Taz's departing back as he made his way to the lift.

He came to save me, even though we argued. I smiled, the happiness fizzling inside my chest. *Kainen was compelling him to be mean, but he didn't know that. And he still came for me.*

Queenie clearing her throat with pointed impatience brought an abrupt halt to my ogling. I closed the door behind me and faced her, no less fearsome as she sat in her huge wing-backed chair behind her imposing ash-grey desk with spiky carvings.

I averted my gaze to the nearest patch of plum-purple wall over her shoulder, determined not to cry this time. Whatever punishment she decided to give me, anything beat being asked to leave.

"I won't skip around the necessary," she began. "I'm sure you're exhausted and will want to be clean in time for the revel. There is a task to be done, and not an easy one, but I get the feeling that you are loyal to the family."

I hesitated. "The family?"

Queenie pressed her fingers to the arms of her chair and sat back. I remained standing, although given the plushness of the purple carpet, I could have quite happily gone for a lie down while we had our 'chat'.

"Taz and I don't confess it, but I am sister to the Queen. Taz is my nephew."

I blinked.

Wow, okay, I really didn't see that one coming.

When I didn't reply, possibly because my mouth was too busy flapping open, her lips twitched upwards.

"I chose the name Queenie to intimate that I have ideas above my station but, in reality, I protect the family. When Taz was born and we decided Arcanium would be the safest place for him, my sister would trust nobody else to run it."

"Okay, um, that's your business." I decided to skip over that particular revelation, for now. "But I am loyal to Taz, for what it's worth. What's the task?"

Queenie sighed. "My sister is missing all but one of her children. This is secret knowledge known only to a few, other than the rumours now circulating, but every one of them except for Taz has been captured by the Old King. She is becoming unhinged without them, and has given up caring about what happens to Faerie because she thinks she's already failed. A regent who has lost faith in her own rule loses her kingdom. Above all, a leader must show confidence and self-belief."

I kept silent and focused on staying upright, glad I didn't have to be a queen as the exhaustion of merely being an FDP trainee was currently threatening to topple me.

"I've since learned the location of the Old King's lair," she continued. "It's a castle, hidden in plain sight in one of the Arcanium realms. It was the first realm that you visited, which I'm now starting to believe is no coincidence. We also know that there is a traitor in our midst who has been pulling the strings for far too long."

I gulped.

She can't think it's me, can she? I mean, I'm close to Taz, and I've met the Queen, but I fought with them against the

Forgotten twice already. Unless she thinks I'm being used by someone, like Kainen maybe?

"Who?"

Queenie eyed me like a hawk for several moments until sweat started to bead over my forehead. Although not generally a sweaty person, she seemed to have this effect on me whenever I had to stand in front of her for too long.

"That's not your concern," Queenie said. "Where do you think the Old King would have hidden my nieces?"

I frowned. "Well, I'm guessing he'd want to keep them close to his court. He'll be the most heavily guarded so there's less chance of anyone springing the princesses free if they're also there."

"Exactly." Queenie sat up. "Now, we've lost a few FDPs who have gone off-radar, but there is only one person who links Arcanium and that particular realm from your first assignment."

I had to ask. "Wait, you don't mean me?"

"No of course not." Queenie scoffed. "Are you an FDP yet?"

Mortified at making the assumption, I thought quickly back to the realm I'd spent a short few minutes in on my first assignment.

"Oh. Alannah." I remembered meeting Alannah in passing not too long ago, and that Petra had almost come to blows with her before. "She told me when she got back from her assignment there that the prince of that realm met a sticky end, and her chosen charge had made it to queen."

"The Old King has likely had minions hidden in place for a long time. Alannah is from an old Forgotten family, cousin to the Hemlocks and the Old King's own lineage of Belarin. She most likely found or even orchestrated a suitable realm for the Old King to set his new court in. I wouldn't be surprised if the Queen now installed there is one of the Old King's court, perhaps even his next intended bride."

I let my soup-like brain spoon through the information for several moments. Alannah had always been nice to me, even keeping Leo for me when I wasn't supposed to have him at Arcanium.

But now she's the enemy. I frowned, sadness sinking in my gut. *I can't let that distract me though. If she supports the Old King, she's on the opposing side.*

"So, you're what, asking me to somehow storm the Old King's court, find Taz's siblings and rescue them?" I asked, fully expecting Queenie to laugh.

"Yes, essentially that's it." She ignored me gawping at her. "They won't expect mentees. But I will allow you to take a team of people with you. Not too many though, maximum of six. You should choose wisely-"

"The Eastwick sisters, if they'll go." I didn't need to tell her I'd had many self-indulgent daydreams already about who I'd invite on my dream FDP team. "I want Milo and Ace as well. And Taz. I doubt his sisters would make things easy for me so having him there might help smooth things along. I didn't exactly get on well with them the one very quick moment we met. Plus, he can skip them straight to the Queen's court, and it's the last place the enemy will expect him to turn up if they're hunting him."

Queenie frowned. "I meant actual qualified FDPs, but you're sure those are the people you choose?"

I thought about Milo's secret ability to realm-skip at will, Ace's smarts and speed, the way the Eastwick sisters worked as a team to intimidate anyone they came across. There was also Taz's complete inability to back down over anything. Ever.

"Absolutely, I need people I can trust."

Queenie sighed. "So be it. You should stay for the revel this evening, take time to rest so you can leave fresh in the morning."

I stared at her, until she waved her hand at the door to dismiss me. I turned to go, but just kept spinning until I was facing her again.

"Um, Faerie's all but at war these days. Is now really the time to be having a revel?"

Queenie started to laugh. "That's exactly the time to have one. Hope is a funny thing, and we could all do with a bit more of it. Especially now."

I decided that was my cue to exit.

I half-expected Taz to be lurking in the hall or hiding in the lift, but no joy. As I eyed the lift buttons, I considered going to find him, but now I needed to rest and check Leo was really okay. I pressed the button for the residents' floor, determined to make the most of some peace and quiet in the common area up there once everyone was in the atrium revelling.

Might as well enjoy my last night before everything inevitably goes belly up again.

CHAPTER TEN
The Prince of Moodsville Makes a Confession

I needn't have worried about finding Taz. The moment I reached the residents' floor, my thoughts only on checking Leo and having a long shower, he was lounging outside my door.

"Well?" he asked.

I frowned. "Hi to you too. She gave me an assignment, and said I could take a team. I need to ask people though."

Taz folded his arms, blocking my way into my room by leaning back against the door.

"Who you going to take then?" he pressed.

He kept his gaze fixed on the floor beside me, no doubt trying to downplay how desperate he was for me to invite him so he didn't have to insist he come along. Perhaps he even thought I'd start telling him to stay here, keep safe, which I probably should be doing.

The few months apart had changed several things that I was too exhausted to face right now, but he was still the same, still stubborn. And if I didn't let him come with us, he'd find his own way to cause trouble instead, probably all in the name of the anchoring or however it worked.

I bit down a smile, beyond tempted to tease him.

"The Eastwick sisters, if they'll go. Ace and Milo. Are you going to let me in my room or what?"

Taz looked up at me then, his turquoise eyes wide like I'd just kicked a puppy. He stepped aside and unlocked my door. When he caught me staring he rolled his eyes.

"Ace gave me your key, here." He held it out.

I took the key and pushed my door open.

"Are you sure that's who you want to take though?" he pressed. "It's clearly going to be dangerous and you need people you can trust around you."

"You're saying I can't trust the Eastwicks? Or Ace and Milo?" It took all my effort not to grin as I glanced back at him. "Well, I believe in them. You don't have to come along if you don't want, if it's going to be too dangerous for you. Sorry, I should have asked your permission first. I just assumed you'd be up for it, but you don't have to."

After so many mind-games with Kainen and the exhaustion of being in danger, it was a relief to tease someone who I knew would take it as harmless banter, and who wouldn't use it against me. Kainen was the enemy, no matter how nice he'd pretended to be, but Taz I could trust with my life.

Taz pulled a weary face and slumped in the doorway as I rushed across to Leo, who was fast asleep under my covers with his head poking out. I wondered if he was casually taking liberties or if Ace had actually gone to the trouble of tucking him in. Either version was entirely possible.

"Hi, lizard," I murmured, smiling as he opened his eyes and crooned at me. "Has Ace been feeding you too much again? I'll stay here and hang out with you tonight I think, much less drama."

"You don't want to go down to the revel?" Taz asked. "It would do you good to have some proper fun after everything."

I hauled Leo up and settled him on my shoulder, sagging under the weight so much I had to sit on the bed. There weren't any rules about mentees being in each other's rooms, but Taz stayed in the doorway all the same.

"Ah, you know me," I said. "I've not been to one before, but I was hoping for some peace and quiet. Queenie said we should rest and start the assignment fresh tomorrow. She also said something about the revel being what everyone needs because of hope, but I think that was just to get me out of her office."

"She's got a point."

I grinned at him.

"What, you mean your aunt?"

His jaw dropped. "She told you?"

"Yeah. Shortly before she gave me the assignment. Maybe she thinks I'll never come back so a bit of fun is the least I can have."

"Wow, she must really trust you. When do we leave then, and what do we have to do?"

I smiled as he stood there, his shoulder propped against the doorframe and his fingers playing idly with one of my scarves hanging on the side of my clothing unit. There was absolutely no existence in his head where he wasn't coming with me.

"How much do you know about the state of things?" I asked. "Like um, your sisters?"

Taz grimaced. "I know they've all been captured by the Old King now. My mother's gone a bit dippy about it."

I gave him a disapproving look.

"She's lost her children, and her rule is unravelling. I imagine that's more than enough reason to 'go a bit dippy' as you put it."

Taz grunted. "What's that got to do with you though?"

A moment later, realisation dawned on his face. I bit my lip and aimed for a sheepish smile.

"That's the assignment," I admitted. "Go to the Old King's lair, rescue your sisters and take them back to your mum. Simple."

Taz thought for a minute, a multitude of emotions shivering across his face. He was no doubt debating whether to revolt and say we weren't doing it or assessing how we'd achieve it. I busied myself scratching under Leo's chin.

"That's even more reason to go down to the revel then," he said eventually. "You can ask the Eastwicks, Milo and Ace there. I reckon they'll all join you though. We can also relax a bit before we go."

I sighed. "I dunno. I'd rather hang out up here."

Again Taz's face descended into that kicked puppy look that tugged on my heartstrings. He'd done so much for me, more than I could ever repay.

Oh orbs alive. I huffed out a breath. *I guess it would be nice to spend some time with him finally without arguments or stupid Fae idiots trying to kidnap us.*

"Fine, I'll go down for like one cherry bubble juice and a couple of songs. Okay?"

Taz's expression cleared like the Braunees' buffet counter on Sundae Sunday.

"Okay." He grinned. "It starts in an hour so I'd be quick. I'll come by for you and we can go down together. It's not dress up or anything, but you might want to wash the dirt off at least, look somewhat presentable."

I scanned the room for something to throw at him, but he was off and the door was shut before I could.

I spent half of the next hour in the bathroom, getting rid of accumulated grime and trying to do something with my hair that wasn't 'here's a bunch of electrical cables'. The bathroom was like a pre-school play dressing room, everyone swarming into each other as they primped and preened. I'd never bothered with make-up before, and even if I had my sisters would have just nicked it anyway, but Meryl threw me some tinted strawberry lip-balm as she ran past in a towel.

"You'll thank me later, considering you've got your royal fancy man back now!"

I decided not to dwell on that, already worried about what the rest of Arcanium were assuming about Taz and I.

Dodging people racing about in the hall, I retreated to the sanctuary of my room and found some lace-style ballet flats in the very bottom of my clothes unit, which I paired with black jeans and a dark green velvet top.

Considering the Arcanium uniform was usually 'clothes you can be comfortable and move easily in', I now looked like I'd made an effort for once. I even managed a small smile.

"Not too shabby?" I asked Leo.

He blinked at me and took refuge under my covers.

Thanks for the support, reptile.

Knowing this was as good as I was going to get, I opened the door and almost walked my face right into Taz's fist before he could knock. I swept the quickest gaze up and down, amused to see he'd conceded to putting on an actual dark grey shirt instead of the uniform slogan t-shirts, and his black jeans looked smarter than I'd ever seen. Even his boots were shiny.

"Hey." I shut the door behind me.

He nodded, but in the space of an hour he seemed to have lost some good mood vibes, his brow furrowed and his gaze distracted.

I started walking toward the lift, well aware of him walking alongside me but not acknowledging me.

Weird. Perhaps he's having second thoughts about the assignment.

It was the kind of thing he'd do, charge in with determination then actually start thinking of all the potential pitfalls. Or more likely, he'd had time to think about just how easily I'd skipped into Kainen's clutches, and how it was always me getting these assignments. I knew that was Kainen compelling him to be mean, but the taunts about me being useless had cut deeper than

I'd realised.

I left Taz to his brooding as we got in the lift and pressed the button for the atrium. I listened instead to the air rustling past as we shot downwards, determined not to be the first to speak. If he wanted to go all introspective after making me come to this thing, then fine. I pushed the grill aside the moment we stopped, but only made it a couple of steps.

"Oh, wow."

A lot of other people had already arrived and the vast space of the atrium was cluttered. The back half was clear and reserved for dancing with groups already swaying together to a raucous *Demon Babies* song while others drifted around in couples.

Ribbons in the dark Arcanium red had been woven around the tables and chairs at the front end nearest the lift to the human world. The only sign left that this was a professional place was the reception desk still in place, with Call Me Henry standing sentinel behind it. I squinted.

"He's letting someone use the desk as a DJ booth!" I nudged Taz.

"Yeah." His tone was flat and he pointed to the table full of cups and pitchers at the other side of the atrium. "Let's get a drink."

I refused to let his mood dampen this for me, even though he'd been the one who wanted to come originally. When he started across the hall toward the table, I went off in the other direction to where the Eastwick sisters were dancing. They wore identical dresses to match their wild hair colours, Beryl in purple, Cheryl in green and Meryl in blue. They looked up at me as I approached, expressions neutral.

"Alright, Demi?" Beryl nodded to me.

I nodded back. "I have something to ask you, all of you."

Cheryl grinned before I could explain.

"Yeah, your assignment," she said. "Queenie sent our purple slips through, so we were a bit surprised, but of course you'd choose us, shows good sense. We'll be there, and we'll follow your lead, other than like to the death or anything."

Meryl smiled at me, although her gaze seemed to be drifting off into a far corner with dedicated intensity. Beryl bumped my shoulder rather too hard.

Meryl mumbled something about speaking to someone, and I noticed the beady-eyed glances her sisters sent after her as she walked away. She sat down next to Petra, both of them somewhat hesitant as they started to talk.

"Finally," Beryl muttered.

As much as I liked to join in with the Arcanium gossip occasionally, especially when it wasn't about me, I scanned the room once more to find Ace and Milo. I couldn't see them in the crowd yet, but turned when Beryl and Cheryl both focused on something behind me.

"Want to dance, Taz?" Beryl asked with a wolfish grin.

He appeared at my side with the same disagreeable frown on his face. I guessed Beryl was only winding him up anyway, but he shrugged.

"Don't dance. Sorry."

I pressed my lips together to hold in a smile. *Liar.*

Beryl laughed. "Shame. Oh no, Harvey and Hutch have spotted us. Alright Demi, let us know what time to meet you at despatch and we'll be there ready."

She and Cheryl shot across the room with alarming speed, and I noticed the Hutchinson brothers following them with identical grins of intent. Then I realised that left me with the Prince of Moodsville.

Taz scuffed the sole of his boot across the floor. The marble underfoot was pale ivory, but a flash of shining black shot through my mind and I shivered at the memory.

I shook the thought off as Taz handed me a cup, and I gave him a pointed look as I took it. Any distraction was better than remembering right now, even his sulking.

"Thanks, I think."

He frowned. "You think? Something on your mind?"

Should I bring it up now? Here?

"Yeah, you've been really off with me lately." I shrugged, not meeting his eyes. "Even after I explained about the whole 'you getting compelled' thing. Is that it? Because he's not here now and you're still sulking."

I didn't dare mention Kainen's name, but Taz's expression twisted at the mere suggestion of him. I expected him to say something cutting, or to walk off. Instead, he surprised me yet again.

"Do you want to dance?" he asked.

I blinked. "Er… What?"

"Dance, move feet about in time to music."

"With you?"

His brow furrowed deeper. "Yeah, who else?"

"You literally just told Beryl you don't dance."

Before I could press him on it, knowing full well from previous experience that he did dance and not too badly either, he grabbed my hand and pulled me into the crowd. My pulse started to thud as he dumped our cups on the floor beside us and pressed an arm around my waist.

With a nervous gulp, I settled my arms around his neck with my insides churning enough to make me queasy. I forced myself to insist on an answer, because it was either that or risk staring at each other. Or worse, not staring at each other and not talking until I couldn't face him ever again.

"So, are you going to tell me what the moody routine is about or not?" I asked.

Taz stiffened. "I wasn't the one running around with the Dimwit of Darkness and getting myself caught. He's the enemy, what's not to be grumpy about?"

So this is about Kainen. The sudden urge to smile tugged at my lips. *I guess we never actually discussed it properly, or him. Never had time to.*

"I told you it was Petra's idea for us to train together originally. It's not like he ever replaced you as my friend. What's the big problem? I only went with him to the library because he said he wanted to talk and I was upset already because you and I argued. I didn't expect him to fling me through a skip-way."

I focused on my wrists resting on Taz's shoulders and both of his arms now around my waist as I found it a bit more difficult to breathe. But this was perfectly normal, friendly behaviour. Just two friends dancing.

The butterflies are just nerves about dancing, definitely nothing else. I'd be like this with anyone.

"I don't want to see people like Kainen smiling at you," he said. "Hate it. Ace is okay, and Milo."

I frowned. "So people can't smile at me?"

"No, that's not it. You were smiling back like you used to smile at me. Killed me."

I took a shaky breath, glad of the loud music, although I couldn't do anything about my arms shaking against his shoulders.

"No smiling at Kainen, got it. I'm more likely to punch him next time anyway. I just don't get why it bothers you so much."

Taz grumbled something inarticulate.

"What was that?"

He pulled back so I could see his face, the wide

expressiveness of his stormy eyes startling me. I wanted to take a step away, the intensity making my pulse leap, but I couldn't get my brain to speak to my feet or move my arms away from him.

"I said I like you. A lot."

CHAPTER ELEVEN
It Was All Going So Well

Taz bit his lip, hesitating after he made his life-changing statement. I stood there staring back at him, so stunned I couldn't even sway or move or speak.

"Demi? I wasn't going to tell you until I was sure how you'd feel about it, but you're mysterious as hell and I have no idea what you're thinking half the time."

Oh. What do I do with that?

Had I thought about Taz in that way? Okay, maybe more often than I'd ever want to admit. But we were friends, so I just kept reminding myself that it was fine to drift over the boundaries occasionally in my own head, as long as I never let it stray into the realms of reality.

Okay, breathe. Use words now.

"That's not helpful." I played for time, my insides pinging about as I tried to work out exactly what he was saying. "There are a million different ways you can like someone. As a friend, romantically, in a mutual acquaintance kind of way, as a fun, good time kind of thing, as someone to rely-"

I squeaked as Taz leaned forward so his head was beside mine, his mouth by my ear as the song hit a loud part.

"As in I really want to kiss you, or strangle you half the time, but you're hard to read. I don't want to push you into anything you're not ready for, or risk you freaking out and never speaking to me again. I'd rather die than lose you, even if it's just as a friend."

"I'd rather die than lose you", who the hell says things like that?!

I tried to breathe as I pushed aside the suggestion that I was emotionally flighty and thought instead about what Old Tara had said, about me being Taz's anchor. Kainen's words filled my head straight after, that all he could feel from me was anxiety until I thought about Taz.

Given the unbearable fluttering in my everything at the mere mention of him kissing me, glossing over the hopefully empty threat of strangulation, I apparently wanted to give whatever this was a try.

Taz took a step back, his arms disappearing from around me. He looked so crestfallen that I didn't even hesitate, my only thought to erase any sadness on his face.

Because, in reality, this is actually so, so simple.

I curled my fingers around the front of his shirt before he could turn away and leaned forward to brush a featherlight kiss between his dimple and his mouth.

"I think that's all I'm ready for right now," I added.

Taz blinked. Then a smile of sheer sunshine spread across his face so suddenly I almost flinched.

"It's probably more than I deserve," he said, his grin thawing the last chilled remnants between us. "Especially after the way I've behaved since I've been back."

"Oh, no, you're-" I couldn't force the lie out and started laughing. "You're generally alright most of the time."

He chuckled, stepping close and resuming dancing. As I pressed my arms back around his neck, I realised the fluttering sensation spreading through me was happiness.

"If you say so," he said. "But I'm happy if you're happy, so whatever you're comfortable with is fine with me, as slow as you need. I just hated seeing you with him. That moment I got back and saw you lying underneath him, I was one step away from turning his bones to liquid."

I guessed in the moment he probably meant it, but now wouldn't be the best time for some kind of lecture on ethics of gift use and morality.

"You're a big softy really, aren't you?"

He shrugged and I laid my head on his shoulder, not needing anything more. The song changed to a faster one, but we stayed as we were, swaying soft from side to side.

I tried not to catch Milo's gaze across the atrium, or Ace's, but they were standing side by side with identical Cheshire cat grins pointed in our direction. I couldn't help it; I grinned back.

We danced until the crowd thinned and the drinks table was a mess of empty cups. Milo and Ace had joined us for the faster songs, all of us jumping about like kangaroos, as if we didn't have a dangerous assignment hanging over us come morning. I didn't even mention the assignment to them, not wanting to ruin the evening although they had no doubt received their purple slips already. Only as the party started winding down did the songs slow and the remaining groups separate into couples.

"We should get some sleep in before tomorrow," Taz said. "Do you want to go and double check with Ace and Milo quick?"

I nodded, taking a step back. Something had shifted after I kissed him, an unspoken agreement between us that it was officially now me and him against the world, not just a couple of friends hanging out slightly more often than we did with other friends. But I didn't feel like labelling it immediately and apparently neither did he.

Taz squeezed my hand and disappeared through the crowd of stragglers. I watched him go toward the lift, knowing that I wouldn't have to go looking for Milo or Ace. They would be on me like jackals in three... two...

Milo's head appeared beside mine, his face radiating

absolute joy as he beamed right into mine.

"You and Taz!" he squeaked. "I saw you kiss him! It was like Carrie and Malachi outside the Toppled Turrets, except *real*."

I glossed over the mention of *Carrie's Castle*, our favourite fiction series, still all warm and fluffy inside. At that point, I was possibly even less excited about the whole thing than Milo, who was now trying really hard not to clap in his excitement.

"It's not-" I tried again. "It's- We're just, seeing where things go. I think. We didn't discuss it much or anything."

Ace gave Milo a sideways smirk as I rushed on.

"Besides, I have something to ask you. Queenie gave me an assignment and I leave tomorrow. It's a bit of a dangerous one, but I'd like you two with me, but you can say no obviously."

Ace grinned. "We know, Cheryl came up and asked what time we were leaving. I've already thinned the books Milo wants to take down to one rucksack-full."

I blinked. "You're both coming?"

I'd asked for them, but somewhere in the back of my mind I assumed Milo might decide not to go. He wasn't technically an FDP mentee, or a mentor, and he didn't have much outside-realm experience. He had braved Gallow's Oak some months ago with me, but now he shied away from any mention of jumping straight into danger. His lack of experience and rank clearly didn't matter to Queenie, but I'd asked for him to be a part of the team to avoid him feeling left out, although his ability to realm-skip at will and the cavernous contents of his brain would be so useful on assignment.

"Of course," Milo said, although I could see nervousness twitching the corner of his smile up and down. "I won't say it's because I owe you, although I do for getting me out of Gallows Oak and finding me a place here, but we're friends. We're with you the whole way."

Already low-key emotional from everything else, not to mention about to drop with exhaustion, I had to sniff to hold back sudden tears.

"Thanks, that means the world. Okay, we start early, like 9am."

Ace snorted. "9am isn't early, Demi."

"Is in my book." I shrugged. "The enemy won't care what time we rock up, but we'll need to spend the first day surveying what we're up against anyway, then probably move in at night-time for cover. Can you tell Beryl or one of them for me?"

Milo nodded and Ace placed a hand on my shoulder to turn me toward the lift.

"Go, sleep. If you're not up and about in the halls by 8.30, we'll come and get you."

I set off toward the lift, dodging the lingering revellers. Nobody got into the lift with me, and I sagged in relief the moment the atrium disappeared out of sight.

So, Taz and I are friends again, or whatever we are. I escaped the Forgotten yet again, or Kainen at least. Taz is safe, for now. We just have to go into the enemy's lair, steal a couple of really uncooperative Fae princesses and get back to the Queen.

I put a hand on the grill to slide it aside, but froze when I saw the residents' hallway occupied. My insides twisted, squeezing out a soft gasp of shock.

Diana leaned close to Taz, whispering something in his ear. He had his back slightly to me, so I couldn't see his expression, but he wasn't shoving her off or anything.

Before I could do anything, like press the button to run screaming to a different floor, Diana looked over Taz's shoulder right into my eyes. Her smile stretched with malice.

Rumbled, I pushed the grill open and strode forward.

Taz flinched at the noise and turned around, his eyes wide.

Diana winked at him and approached me. I thought she might issue a parting shot, some kind of quip about me being too naive or too trusting, but she only gave me a cruel grin and swept into the lift.

I kept my steps measured as I walked toward Taz. His family and Diana's were firm enemies, so this would be something completely innocent.

As I came to a stop in front of him, he wouldn't quite meet my eyes, but I waited until I heard the rushing of the lift departing before I asked.

"What was that about?"

He hesitated. "Nothing, don't worry. Just her being her."

If it's so innocent, why is he being shifty?

"Go on, tell me." Icy doubt stabbed my insides. "What's she looking so self-satisfied about?"

Taz grimaced. "Trust me, you don't need to know." When I glared at him, he reached for my face and brushed a strand of my hair back with his fingertips. "You do trust me, don't you?"

He was asking the impossible. I couldn't lie, couldn't say yes when every element of me was now screaming that I'd trusted people before. Jack Harmony, Kainen, a brief brush with one of the Fae boys during my assignment at Gallows Oak. I seemed to have an idiot switch flicked around Fae boys that made me too trusting.

This is Taz though.

But he'd been at his mother's court for months. I'd trusted before and it never did me much good.

"I want to." I bit my lip.

He sighed. "I'd never do anything to hurt you, Dem. This just isn't something I can tell you, but you're safe now and that's what matters."

He couldn't promise never to hurt me; accidents could always happen. And how safe could I be if we were going into the enemy's lair in the morning? Had Diana sworn him to secrecy about something?

I shook my head.

You're worn out. Get some sleep. Get the assignment done. Then you can torture Diana or something until she tells you.

"I'm going to bed," I decided. "We're meeting up at despatch at 9am to realm-skip."

I went to move past him, but he caught my hand, his expression beseeching me to believe him.

"You're literally the most important person to me in the world, in all of the realms. Okay, this looks dodgy so get why you can't trust me outright, but at least believe me when I say that?"

I couldn't promise to do that, but right now I needed sleep. I pulled my hand free and aimed for a hopeful smile.

"I'll try."

I left him standing there and walked to my room. Safe inside, I pulled off my shoes and slumped on the bed.

Leo was busy winding around the branches I'd managed to get dragged in for him as a mini playground, so I sank into the lulling sound of his claws scratching away. Despite my misophonia causing a reaction to certain sounds, the rhythmic noise of Leo ambling around soothed rather than irritated me.

I sighed, getting ready for bed.

This wasn't the blissful ending I'd hoped for after Taz's confession and all the dancing, but then how often did I get blissful endings?

Tomorrow we'd be straight back into the mayhem, and I had to be ready not only to do the assignment, but also to lead the others.

I set my alarm for 8am on the Arcanium issue clock and faced the wall with my eyes shut tight.

Stupid Taz, making me like him.

CHAPTER TWELVE
Into the Enemy Realm

I stood in despatch the next morning at 08.57 Arcanium time with Trevor, who was more than eager to use the multi-seater rickshaw to transport all of us. I'd been determined to arrive first after Ace's quip about my timekeeping, and I'd also had to find Petra to retrieve my orb and ask her to look after Leo while we were away.

I thought about taking him with me but, while I could openly admit it wasn't safe, the idea of taking him back to the realm he came from also worried me on a selfish level. He seemed happy with me, but I couldn't be sure he wouldn't run off into the wilderness because he recognised it and get squashed. Guilt forced me to promise myself that I'd find a way to take him back at our leisure, so I could give him the opportunity, but not now. Not just yet.

I left him snoozing in my room, and didn't even hear him wake when I had to dash back in to pick up my almost forgotten satchel, rather too heavy with packets of Jelly Babies and a change of clothes for all weathers.

I wouldn't have forgotten something as vital as my satchel normally, but my mind was plagued with thoughts of having to face Taz after our hallway talk last night. Unfortunately, he was the next one up to despatch. We stood in silence, although he kept shooting me anxious side-glances while I chatted with Trevor about where to drop us off. I didn't want to be awkward with him, but the Diana issue had kept me up most of the night worrying.

My mind flashed back to the recent months I'd spent without

him and I couldn't bear the silence any longer. If he said I had nothing to worry about, I needed to trust him.

"Do you think if someone fell off the edge, they'd just go splat?" I asked, peering at the drop over the platform. "Or would there be some kind of protection?"

Taz looked up, startled. He inched toward me, as if scared I might bite if he got too close. A quick look at him suggested he'd not managed to get much sleep either, his honey-brown curls lacking some bounce and his eyes ringed dark.

"You know, I've never thought to check. I guess there must be something supportive on the way down, or they'd probably have put railings in by now."

I raised one eyebrow. "What, like a huge magic net?"

Taz beamed with relief at the normality in my tone, but anything he might have said was swept away by the arrival of the others.

"Nice day for it!" Cheryl called, staring up at the overcast sky above the domed glass ceiling. "What's the plan?"

I straightened my satchel strap across my chest as everyone turned to face me, fanning out into a horseshoe shape. With six pairs of eyes fixed on me, my insides wrapped into knots.

"We're going to arrive in the forest and find a suitable vantage point to watch the castle and the village. No heroics, but we'll get as close as we can. When night falls, we sneak in. Use gifts to defend, but if we're in a spot you can stun people or whatever. If all goes wrong, Milo will be the one to come back for help."

The Eastwick sisters eyed Milo with varying expressions of doubt and curiosity. Perhaps they were wondering why I wanted to bring the mild-mannered trainee librarian, who I suspected had filled both his bulky rucksack and Ace's with books.

"Milo? You okay with that?" I asked. "If you call Trevor-"

Milo shook his head and lifted his chin, a determined expression on his face.

"I don't mind people here knowing, although I don't want it spread outside of this group please." He glanced around and bit his lip. "I can realm-skip."

Cheryl frowned. "As in you've been assigned to a troll? Is that a library privilege?"

"No, as in I can realm-skip at will. No trolls, no crystals like Taz has to get him to the Queen's court and back. I've been used for it a lot before, so I don't tend to tell anyone."

The three sisters stared at him for a long moment. Then at each other. After a moment, Beryl shrugged.

"Fair enough," she said. "We won't use it against you or tell anyone, don't worry."

Meryl and Cheryl nodded their agreement and relief spread over Milo's face, his hefty shoulders inching down away from his ears. I gave him a reassuring smile and focused back on the assignment.

"So, Milo will be responsible for getting people out if all goes wrong and we can't all get picked up by Trevor. Now, is everyone wearing sensible footwear?" I asked, eying everyone's boots and trainers.

It was more for a sense of sounding in charge than because I actually needed to check, but everyone stuck out a foot as if on command.

Well, that's something at least. I took a deep breath and ploughed on with the plan.

"We'll have a bit of a walk through the woods, but I'm hoping that'll keep us more covered than if we suddenly materialise out of nowhere and cause mayhem. Last time I was there the prince thought I was a witch, and we want to avoid that this time round. Okay, in we get."

I stepped up to the rickshaw, ignoring Taz's hand appearing beside me as if to help me in. Talking to him was one thing, but handholding was on- well, on hold until he was honest about what he and Diana had been discussing all cosy-like.

That resolution was spoiled by him sliding in right next to me, his leg pressed against mine to allow Ace and Milo to fit in after him, with the Eastwick sisters in the back.

I flinched as Taz's arm looped around my shoulders, but he refused to remove it, staring ahead with rigid stubbornness. Butterflies exploded in the pit of my stomach. Short of starting a wrestling match, he had me cornered and I needed to keep my dignity so that everyone would continue to follow my lead. I ignored the traitorous urge to lean into him and focused on the assignment instead.

"Okay, Trevor," I called up. "As we discussed please, and easy on the landing."

Trevor grinned over his shoulder from between the shafts.

"Absolutely!"

I closed my eyes tight as he wheeled the rickshaw around and set off at alarming speed toward the towering wall of glittering white quartz. The familiar brush of air that accompanied the realm-skip wafted over my face, and I was glad of Taz's arm clutching me tight as we whooshed to a halt.

"Here we are," Trevor said.

I opened my eyes. Woodland surrounded us, familiar in that it was a forest with trees of white, brown and green, but otherwise completely unrecognisable in terms of actual location.

Everyone clambered out and I joined them before turning back.

"Thanks, Trevor. I'm hoping this will be a simple extraction once we're done, but there's no knowing what'll happen."

Trevor tapped his head with both hands. "No worries. I'll be ready when you call for me."

He jogged on the spot moments before the air shivered around him and he disappeared with the rickshaw. I twisted around, looking left and right, as Beryl asked the inevitable question.

"Which way?"

I bit my lip. I had checked the Ogle screen after finding Petra this morning, and was sure the time followed similar in this realm to the human world. She'd also returned my orb to me with the promise that it had been cleansed, and I'd never felt more elated to have it hanging back on my belt loop, the grey crystal sphere tucked safe inside my pocket.

The orb wouldn't help me with the directions though, so I squinted up at the pale pink morning sky to work out how to orientate us. Luckily, Ace beat me to it.

"Given the location of the sun, if this is a 'normal' realm, left is east and right is west-ish."

Relieved, I turned in a west-ish direction. "I asked Trevor to drop us east of the castle, as that looked like the least treacherous path through the woods without sacrificing tree cover for spying."

I soaked in the impressed looks travelling around the group, proud that they trusted me to lead them. Ignoring the inevitable stab of anxiety that followed at the thought of everything possibly going wrong, I set off at the head of the pack.

Taz was beside me in an instant, but he didn't move to hold my hand or anything bold. My fingers twitched at the thought but I kept my hand pinned to my side. As we all started walking, mostly in silence, my arm occasionally brushed his. Deep down, I was glad to have him beside me.

I couldn't count how long we walked, following the narrow

paths made by animals between the trees. Now and then we dodged close enough to see a main dirt track, but I wanted to keep away from civilisation as much as possible.

The sky grew white as the day wore on, warm enough that most of us took off sweatshirts and started perspiring. My feet were beginning to ache and I tried not to give Ace and Meryl dirty looks, both of them striding along with broad smiles on their faces and not a single sign of ever tiring.

I risked a look to find Beryl as red-faced as I felt, and even Taz's cheeks were slightly flushed. Although Ace was carrying both his and Milo's backpacks now, Milo looked like he was about to keel over, so the moment we reached a stream running alongside the path we were on, I suggested a rest.

"We'll stop here for a rest. Shouldn't be too far now," I said hopefully.

Beryl frowned. "Assuming we are going in the right direction."

"Trevor dropped us east so we're following the sun west." I shrugged to hide my own doubt. "The ground is starting to slope down, so with any luck it isn't far at all."

Leaving the others sharing out the snacks that Meryl was in charge of, I walked to the bank of the stream and flicked a cautious finger through the ripples on the surface.

A fair few scare stories had done the rounds about various realms of Faerie, enough to make me mindful of fish that might eat my toes or water that might turn to acid against my skin.

What if I'm completely wrong about this? What if we walk in the wrong direction and have to go back on ourselves for ages, or the intel is wrong and this is just a castle, no Forgotten or Old King at all?

I was so absorbed in my own thoughts, I almost missed the steady thud of hooves on the track. The others drew close together and Taz was already turning to find me. I joined the group.

"Protection wardings up," I murmured, keeping my voice low.

I flinched as Taz appeared beside me and grabbed my hand. I let my protection warding spool out of me as Taz did the same. We'd practiced sharing wardings before, so I let my imagined rainbow strands of protection knit with his invisible ones. It reinforced our strength together, but I tried not to read anything into the delighted smile that flickered briefly on his face.

A middle-aged man with a spotless white waistcoat appeared a moment later, leading a stocky black pony. He eyed us as he came to a halt and raised a hand as if to touch the tip of a hat that wasn't there.

"Greetings, young ones." The man nodded to us. "Anything to interest you today?"

He pulled a string hanging down from the pony's back which unleashed two boxes attached to the saddle. They opened to form two thin tables on either side of the pony's back, full of wares such as rocks, crystals and potion bottles.

"This is clever," Ace said. "You can keep the contents safe with the boxes closed, but they open into show cases."

My mind raced over the potential dangers, but Ace was already approaching the horse's side without hesitation. I started after him, but Taz had my sleeve tight in his fingers before I could get there. We joined Ace, along with Milo, but the Eastwick sisters hung back and moved into a tight huddle.

Both Ace and Milo busied themselves assessing the numerous pots of different shapes, sizes and colours and other random items like stones, crystals or string.

I eyed a row of vials full of mysterious colours, the sight of them tugging at a memory as the man hurried to Taz's side.

"Can I interest you in a new micro-blade?" he asked. "Best quality and sharpest points in all of the land. Here, test that sharpness. Just a quick dab with your finger and tell me I am wrong."

Taz hesitated, then stepped outside the warding, one hand out behind him to leave it covering me.

I wondered why everything felt so familiar, like a fairy tale-

"Taz, stop!"

CHAPTER THIRTEEN
A Fight With an Old "Friend"

I darted forward in time to see the pad of Taz's forefinger press the thin metal point. He blinked in surprise and froze.

As he collapsed to the ground with a hefty thud, the strands of his protection left me. I rushed forward while reinforcing my own warding, panic and fury twisting inside my chest.

Something slammed into me before I could reach him, no doubt the man's protection meeting mine. I bounced and hit the ground with a bone-jarring thud, lifting my jangling head in time to see the air begin to shiver.

The man became a dark blur. The darkness elongated and took the form of a tall, thin woman. Her black hair had been curled and piled up onto her head like a Marie Antoinette-style wig, highlighting a large, pale forehead.

"You!" I screamed. "Get away from him!"

Anger fired through me as she kneeled on one knee next to Taz and passed a long fingertip over his forehead.

She looked different to when I'd properly met her last during the Forgotten's attempt to invade Arcanium. Back then, Elvira had been wearing a wide, white pantsuit with flouncy edging and lace. Now she was decked in a gothic, bare-shouldered gown of purple velvet, Queenie-style except for the huge skirts.

The chance that she'd randomly been the one person in this whole realm to find us was slim.

But how could she have found us by choice?

I scrambled to my feet, my protection firm around me as I started forward again, but I could feel my warding pushing against hers, refusing to allow us any closer. I snarled as she peered down at Taz.

"Oh dear. Such a trusting young man, what a pity it is."

Anguished and completely stuck, I sent my gift firing through my warding, aiming straight for her chest while the fear pounded dizzying sickness through mine.

The crackle of energy flew through the air, bounced off her warding and zapped a nearby tree, one of the branches cracking along its length.

"Now, that's not nice," she trilled. "It is very concerning to find the young prince travelling so far from home, but the King will be delighted he has been found. Sadly, I don't have time to deal with you, but your time will come, filth."

She spat in my direction, but it didn't travel far enough to hit her warding and bounce back in her face. Worse luck.

I wracked my panicked brain, wondering if I could use my voice projection to scare her off with something, but she'd probably try and turn me into a bug. Or worse.

Ace and Milo appeared on my left. The Eastwick sisters appeared on my right. We joined hands. Elvira laughed and turned her back on us, gathering Taz into her arms and clutching him to her chest.

This was why Queenie told me to take a team, I realised. *Not because she doesn't believe in me, but she knows exactly what strength the enemy has.*

"I can lower the ground to make a gap," Beryl muttered. "Only for about fifteen seconds though. Demi, plan?"

I eyed Milo. "Take me in under her warding. I'll distract her, you get Taz out. The rest of you, do what you can to keep her from getting the warding up, whatever you've got."

Elvira stood with Taz in her arms. I would have marvelled at her strength had it not been resolutely against me. I only had my energy gift and my skill with voices, but I had to hope those plus the confusion would be enough.

With a wave of her hand, Elvira's horse and cart shivered and became a black coach with purple plumes, the horse growing from a modest, stocky pony to a large, snorting beast.

"No tricks, children?" Elvira gloated. "You may have caught me off guard last time, but none of you are any match for me."

I squeezed Beryl's fingers. "Now!"

The ground began to shake, a sheen of sweat sweeping across Beryl's forehead from the effort. Elvira only had a moment to look surprised before the ground disappeared around the edge of her warding, leaving a gap underneath.

Air rushed past my face as Milo skipped me underneath the protection barrier. Elvira gasped as Milo dropped my hand and grabbed Taz's arms, dragging him away from her before disappearing.

I threw up my hands and sent a bolt of energy sizzling toward Elvira. It caught her on the shoulder, not enough to do much damage, maybe some burnt skin at the very most, but she yelped in surprise and flicked out her fingers.

Without waiting for Milo to come back for me, I dropped onto my front and rolled under the warding that was tumbling down.

I kept rolling until I hit resistance and looked up to see Ace towering above me, his hand held out. I scrambled to my feet and confronted Elvira, her face stuck in horror like a startled chicken.

"We can hold the warding all day," I taunted, victory flaring now that we had Taz back. "We'll take turns. Power in numbers."

There was nothing else I could say. We were at a stalemate. She couldn't attack us easily, but she didn't seem to be in a hurry to leave either, so we couldn't get moving toward the castle.

Besides, our cover was also blown now she knew we were here.

"What are you doing here, anyway? Hiding out?" I asked.

Elvira's lip curled, perhaps at the thought that a part-blooded fairy was talking back to her, let alone daring to question her.

"I serve the rightful King. You can hold your silly wardings, but once I return with him, he will unravel your protections and your gifts. All he needs is the last child of the Queen to push her over the edge and take his rightful throne."

Elvira blinked seconds after she finished speaking. Her face expanded in outrage, the gargantuan hair wobbling.

"Who *dares* cast a compulsion on me?"

I eyed the group. I didn't know anyone had the ability to cast compulsions. Kainen had a particular talent in that area, but he wasn't here. Luckily. Taz had once told me that some Fae sworn to the Queen's court could compel people, but nobody here was sworn into her service that I knew of, and Taz was still unconscious next to Milo. My chest squeezed tight, but I had to eliminate the threat before I checked on him.

There must have been a gap left under her warding as well for the compulsion to get through.

Whoever the compeller was, nobody else as much as flinched their gaze away from Elvira, so I followed their lead.

"Where are the Queen's children?" I asked, hoping we could get the same result.

"In the Egloriem castle dungeons, behind bars that cannot be opened or broken by magic."

Elvira clapped a shaking hand to her mouth, eyes wide with rage. I resisted the urge to look at everyone else this time. Before I could ask any more questions, she glared pure acid at all of us and backed up to her coach.

"You'll regret that. When the King rises to his rightful throne, you will be given to me, all of you, for permanent torture. I will make you wish you'd never been born."

I heard the sound of groaning behind me. Worry for Taz made me reckless and I dragged the line of us forward.

"How many guards watching them?" I pressed.

"Two, most have been sent away to prepare for the attack on Arcanium- aahh!" She scrambled up onto the driving seat of the carriage and grabbed the reins. "Hyah!"

The coach went clattering down the road, leaving us in a cloud of dust. I glanced over my shoulder at Taz, now on his side and struggling to sit up.

"Keep the warding for a bit, if you can please?" I asked Meryl.

She nodded and I dropped her hand, stumbling across the tufty grass to kneel beside Taz. Milo launched to his feet and stepped away to give us privacy, although I would have put money on the others eavesdropping all the same.

"What did you go and leave the bloody warding for?" I gave Taz's shoulders a gentle shove.

He winced. "Ow. At least I know you care what happens to me. What was it you said about your outing with Kainen? You didn't think? Well, neither did I. There, we're even."

"Not quite." I frowned. "I told you everything, but you haven't told me what Diana was whispering in your ear about."

Taz sat up, hunching over his bent legs as a breathless smirk crept across his face.

"Jealous?"

I rolled my eyes. "Worried."

He took my hand and the anxiety in my chest faded as the colour started returning to his cheeks.

"Don't be. Honestly, Sparky, it's nothing you need worry about, not now."

I froze. "Not now? What, were you secretly dating her before or something?"

"Urgh." Taz grinned. "Why, would you be jealous if I had been?"

I couldn't answer that without lying, but I could tell he knew the answer, his smile widening even further.

"Cosy as this is you two, we should get moving." Cheryl called over. "The hag will be looking for us now, no doubt with other guards."

He's not going to tell me anything about Diana. I groaned to my feet and held out a hand to help Taz up. *One problem at a time.*

"We go through the woodland and skirt around the edge of the castle." I decided. "At least we know we're going in the right direction now, if she's headed that way as well."

We continued on, following the path but sticking between the trees. Before long, we came to a hillside where the trees dropped away and the land rolled down toward a very familiar castle, turrets and towers of grey that would be suitable for the most traditional of *Disney* princesses.

I pointed, a grin of relief spreading across my face.

"That's the one. If we follow this line of trees around the valley, we can get up behind it. When the sun goes down, we'll creep through the gardens and go through a side door. Once inside though I don't know what'll happen, or where the dungeons will be."

We continued walking but kept the pace slow, moving close together so we could all hear one another without having to raise voices and draw attention.

"One of us could glamour as one of the guards if we see one?" Meryl suggested. "Although, that would be a bit weird if we accidentally came across them."

"And we don't want to risk having to hurt innocent people to keep them out of the way if we can help it," I added.

We reached a crop of rock jutting out from the hillside overlooking the back of the castle and the village.

"Here's as good as any," Ace said, dropping his rucksack with a weighty thud.

I eyed the group. Milo looked anxious now that we were close, gnawing at his lip and clutching the straps of his rucksack. Taz and Beryl were still weary from their tangle with Elvira. We needed to rest a while before anything else, so I waved a hand at the ground.

"We'll take turns to keep watch, two at a time," I suggested. "Cheryl, Meryl, you okay to go first?"

They nodded and moved to the edge of the rocks, sitting on lower ones to keep out of sight. Beryl slumped on the ground beside them, and Ace wandered a short distance away with Milo. I dropped to sit cross-legged on the grass and smiled to see Ace squeeze Milo's hand briefly, not sure why they insisted on pretending they were just friends. I'd considered telling them that everyone knew already, but it was too cute watching them sneaking around.

"You okay?" Taz asked, sitting beside me.

"Mostly." I nodded. "We're at a serious disadvantage now Elvira knows we're here. They'll be waiting for us with traps, and I wouldn't put it past them to move your sisters before we can get to them."

Taz shook his head. "Never underestimate the arrogance of Fae. The Old King will assume he's untouchable in his court, and we're mentees. Not even pure-blood ones at that. He won't see us as a threat."

"Oh come on." I snorted. "You're the prince of freaking Faerie. If anyone's going to challenge him other than your mother, it'd be you."

He grinned then, his face brightening despite the waning daylight around us.

"I'm so claiming that as my new official title, 'Prince of Freaking Faerie'. But I actually meant are you okay with us. I know stuff's' outstanding-"

"You could say that."

"-but I meant everything I've said. Don't you think I'd tell you if I could?"

I wasn't sure how to answer that, but luckily a loud rustling noise in the bushes nearby saved me from having to. Unluckily, the only people in the realm who knew we were here were enemies.

Everyone drew together, holding hands, and this time we managed to pull a communal warding around us. I wondered if there would be enough strength for someone to glamour all of us, but that probably wouldn't last long even if we did.

The rustling in the bushes grew louder until two dark shapes, vast and bulky, burst from the trees like a pair of ginger and black bulls.

CHAPTER FOURTEEN
New Recruits and an Attempted Jailbreak

Two men emerged on foot, both with scarves covering the lower halves of their faces, but I recognised them all the same.

The red-haired one grinned at us as they pulled their scarves down to their necks, but the black-haired one stood behind him with no emotion on his face. These two guards were cropping up an alarming amount now, first at Gallows Oak, then at Kainen's lair, now here.

"Are you safe, Your Highness?" The redhead asked in a rolling rumble of bass notes, his beard twitching.

Taz took a step forward. "Excuse me?"

The men exchanged a glance and both rolled back the sleeves covering their left arms. Taz's hand twitched in mine as he stared at the undersides of their left wrists, a white, glittering star tattooed onto each one.

"Who are you?" He sounded less sure this time.

"My name is Eldrich," the red-haired man said. "This is Sagar. We serve the Queen."

I shook my head. "You work for the Old King. You were in his service when we were at Gallows Oak. You were coming to catch us when we escaped. Then you were there as Kainen's guards the other day in the home of the Mage of Nightmares!"

Eldrich's beard twitched again, a definite smile. "We serve the Queen. Sometimes, she sends us to spy on our enemies. They believe we are loyal to them, and it is useful to her."

I flinched as Taz's head appeared beside mine.

"That white star is a sign of servitude to the Queen's court. If they'd betrayed her in any way, it would have turned red and all sorts of ugly things would have happened to them by now."

I wasn't convinced. "Are they Fae? Can they lie?"

"No, to have that mark they must be court Fae, so they're telling the truth."

Without warning me, he dropped my hand and stepped outside the warding. I gasped, trying to go after him, but Ace held me back. I glared at him and stood ready to send my gift out.

Both Eldrich and Sagar dropped to one knee, bowing their huge shaggy heads. I saw the distaste at their behaviour flash across Taz's face; he hated being part of the royal lineage. But this could work to our favour if they really were on our side.

"Do you swear not to harm or try to trick any of us?" I asked.

Eldrich lifted his head, amusement dancing in his eyes.

"Yes. While we are here, and as long as you remain loyal to the prince, I swear it. As we protect Prince Oakthorn in this realm, we will endeavour to protect you too." He nudged Sagar, stoic and silent beside him. "Won't we?"

Sagar nodded. "Yes, I swear it."

I sifted through the words, the 'while we are here' and 'endeavour to protect' reassuring me that, although they would put Taz's safety above anything else, they also weren't against the rest of us either.

And so that appeared to be that. I stepped out of the warding, which made the others extinguish it, and the two men clambered to their feet.

"Do you know much about the layout of the castle?" I asked. "We need to- Wait, should we get them to turn out their pockets? They might swear not to hurt us, but that doesn't mean they aren't spies. What if they've got an orb or some kind of listening device?"

Taz snorted. "Do either of you have any listening devices or orbs on your person?"

"No." Eldrich beamed, showing a row of perfect gleaming teeth. "I have a jar of Amaryl pickles, some Oia berry cream for rashes in inconvenient places, and two pieces of string, I think. Oh, and instructions from your aunt to guard you and keep you safe."

His aunt, not the Queen. I frowned. *Perhaps Queenie has her own plan in play here if all the rumours about the Queen losing the plot are true.*

I looked at Sagar next, who shrugged. "I have sixteen blades of varying sizes, and nothing else that would harm you. Unless you're allergic to cheese. But the Lady is wise to be suspicious. I trust you're here to free the princesses from the Old King's court?"

Taz nodded, but I beat him to it.

"You don't have to call me Lady or anything," I insisted. "But we need to find a way inside to the dungeons, then a way to get the princesses out. We crossed one of the Forgotten on the road, and she let slip that the Old King has them in a cell that can't be opened or broken by magic."

Sagar rubbed his beard, his eyes fixed on me.

"The Old King has used *metirin* iron previously for cells, gift-resistant. Only the Queen herself could break them most likely. You would need the right key, and I can only assume that the guard would be left in charge of that."

My mind started whirring and I began to pace.

"Could you get yourselves on guard duty?"

Sagar shook his head. "We have been called in to serve, but I doubt we could guarantee being given that role. We're more likely being expected to protect the Old King himself, no doubt why the Queen's council sent us. If all else fails, we have our orders."

A grim look passed between him and Eldrich.

I shivered. *Are they on a potential assassination mission in case we fail? Surely they'd never walk out alive, if they even managed it first.*

"Could we realm-skip into the cell?" I asked.

Eldrich shook his head. "That would count as magic. The only way is with the key."

"Okay." I tapped my hands against my thighs. "We creep in as soon as night falls, through the gardens and in by the side-door. If you know the way to the dungeons, great, if not, we'll have to search. Once we get to the dungeons, overpower the guards and open the cell with the key. Taz, you take your sisters home. We'll make our own way back to Arcanium."

Taz opened his mouth, presumably to say he didn't want to get separated from us, but I wasn't done.

"We'll also need to plan some kind of distraction for once we're inside the castle and grounds, in case we get caught. Some can be the diversion to get themselves caught, and the others can remain hidden and follow behind as we get thrown in the cells."

Sagar and Eldrich were nodding to each other. The Eastwicks were conferring in their three-person huddle. Ace and Milo were digging through the piles of books, I hoped to find a suitable diversion.

"They'll expect you to be with me," Taz muttered. "I get the feeling you're going to send me off with the others to be part of the hidden crew so I can skip my sisters back to my mother's court, but they'll know something's up if we're not together."

I had a slight inkling that wasn't the reason he wanted to be in the same group as me, but I decided not to call him on it. This would be tricky enough without causing little rifts between ourselves, so I faced the Eastwick sisters instead.

"Fine. Taz, Ace, Milo and I will sneak, if you three want to do a diversion? Or we can swap."

Cheryl grinned. "We can more than cause a diversion if it's needed, don't worry. So now we just have to wait until nightfall. We'll continue guard duty for a bit to plan."

We sat on the grass, Ace and Milo both absorbed in dusty old tomes. I caught the subtle hint of shared manners, Ace nudging Milo's leg with his knee, a coy smile returned, and Milo completely oblivious to Ace's personal space as he leaned over to point something out.

I grinned to myself, guessing shipping them was safer than eavesdropping on whatever the Eastwicks were muttering between themselves. I thought I heard the words 'explosion' and 'faucets', and decided not to get involved.

Eldrich sat cross-legged quite happily on the grass, taking out a couple of long needles and a ball of wool. I eyed the needles, expecting the noise to set off my misophonia, but almost as soon as he started knitting my tension dissipated like magic. Surrounded by birdsong and the rhythmic clack of the needles, I was starting to feel less anxious about what we had to do. We had luck on our side in Eldrich and Sagar, assuming they didn't betray us.

I reached a hand into my satchel to find where I'd squirreled away my packet of Jelly Babies, and my fingertip skimmed a familiar smooth warmth. I yanked the flap of the satchel open and gasped to see two beady black eyes blinking at me.

"How-" I couldn't even get the words out as Leo gave me a huge gummy grin.

He must have crawled in when I forgot it. Why didn't I bother to do a final check?!

Taz leaned over to peer inside. "Did you mean to bring him?"

"No! I left him in my room, and Petra's meant to be looking after him." I bit my lip.

She was probably going crazy thinking she'd lost my pet. Hell, Leo was pretty much the unofficial Arcanium mascot these days; most people loved stopping to say hello to him, and a couple of the mentees would even sneak him their lunch whenever he was hanging out in the library.

I pushed Leo's nose back into the satchel with a huff and went to my pocket for my orb, but stopped before I could bring it out.

"Queenie said that there was a traitor in Arcanium," I told Taz. "Someone who has links between this realm and home. This was Alannah's realm, and she was the reason I was sent here on my first assignment. What if she's somehow able to intercept the orb communications? I probably shouldn't orb Petra unless it's an emergency. She never trusted Alannah either, maybe because she's apparently related to Kainen and Diana."

Taz grimaced. "Technically so am I, related to her and them I mean. Actually, Alannah's side of the family were outcasted as Forgotten when my mother first took over, unlike the Hemlocks who wormed their way out of accusations. It wouldn't surprise me if Alannah were supporting the Old King though, hoping to reinstate her family's honour to favour."

"You mean Alannah Hazeldale?" Eldrich looked up from his knitting. "Her family were instrumental in the Old King's last war, ruthless and bent on power whatever the cost. They supported several of the draconian laws that were put in place all over Faerie, a policy the Old King wholeheartedly championed."

Sagar growled, his tone dark as he joined in. "He certainly doesn't shower his people with kindness and opportunity. He has always refused to put his people before his own ambition and should have no right to rule anyone."

"He is part of a time gone past," Eldrich continued. "Things have at least improved since those days thanks to our Queen. We do not entertain quite so many silly traditions now."

I saw Sagar's shoulders stiffen.

"Not all traditions are bad," he insisted.

Eldrich rolled his eyes, resuming his knitting at a furious pace. I got the distinct impression they'd had this argument many times before and didn't dare interrupt.

"I suppose you would choose to reinstate the sacrificial ceremonies?" Eldrich snapped. "Or perhaps it is the need to provide one chicken and a duck to the once-great warrior Obe every harvest season that would appeal to you, like they do in the inner realms?"

Sagar undid the roll of fabric that had been slung diagonally across his back, revealing an array of different blades, all shining lethal in the weak evening light.

"Traditions matter to the people," he insisted. "That is why true rulers endeavour to observe them."

"Would you have them keep doing the sacrifices in the old temples?" Taz joined in. "Slaughter our people to a belief, but not condemn a ruler who does the same? I can't see why we don't work for a day when we can all co-exist in peace with no need for sacrifice at all."

I wanted to applaud, but didn't think I could take the inflation of his ego that would probably follow.

"There will always be bad deeds," Sagar said. "Sometimes people need to see justice served. They need to know that the evil has been thwarted, otherwise what is there to hope for in darker times? What would you say is the most important matter a ruler must observe?"

Taz thought about this for a second. "Food. I'm starving."

That lightened the mood instantly, and Meryl delved into her bag for supplies. Ace and Milo took the next watch as the evening waned.

Meryl had several cereal bars, some apples and bags of crisps. We were moments away from tucking in, when Eldrich unpacked a large saucepan from his backpack and set up a small, contained fire.

Wooden tubs flew out of the backpack and a merry sizzling filled the air. He even had an apron, which turned out to be a good thing as he spattered what looked like weird mint green scrambled egg everywhere a few minutes later.

"I thought you said you only had pickles, cream for rashes and string?" I asked, my eyebrows raised.

He grinned. "You didn't ask what I had on me. You asked if I had any orbs or listening devices, to which I answered no. The rest was pure oversharing on my part to reassure you. Did it?"

"Um, yeah. I guess it did." I rubbed my forehead, embarrassed.

I should have thought of that, should have minded my words and his way more carefully.

I couldn't feel too guilty though, not with the amazing scent wafting over from Eldrich's corner. My stomach was growling by time he handed out bowls of delicious vegetable stew with slices of bread that he'd baked right there in the pan. It tasted like honey- no, vanilla and something else sweet. Tangerines maybe. The flavour reminded me somehow of Christmas.

We whiled away the evening hours with odd bits of conversation, but after a short while I started to pace, unable to keep still. Even after the sun disappeared, leaving us in moonlit shadows, I walked the same patch until Taz got up and wandered alongside me, back and forth without a word.

With each pass, I eyed the village below. I could just make out the tall stone wall surrounding the village and the turrets and battlements of the castle looming above.

"Okay." I took a deep breath. "We might as well give this our best shot. Got your diversion, girls?"

"Absolutely," Meryl whispered nearby. "You get the princesses, we'll bring the entertainment."

I nodded, even though they probably couldn't see me in the dark.

"Good. Milo, you ready to do what you do if all goes wrong?"

"Yes, of course." His anxious voice echoed somewhere nearby to my left.

"Sagar, Eldrich, still 100% in support of us and the Queen?" I added. "Ready to charge into town to keep their attention on the front of the castle, not the side?"

Eldrich chuckled and I heard Sagar's weary sigh. "Yes, but after that our main mission will have to be protecting the prince. We may not be able to step in to defend all of you."

Beryl snorted. "Charming."

I didn't need to ask Ace, knowing he'd have the smarts to go where he was needed without instruction. As for Taz, his fingers warm and firm around my hand were all the reassurance I needed.

As if blessed by Faerie itself, the clouds drifted just enough at that moment to let a glowing moon beam down on us, giving us enough light to see our foot clear all the way to the village boundary.

I took a deep breath. *We can do this.*

"Okay, let's go."

Sagar and Eldrich started down the hill toward the village, surprisingly noiseless for such big men. As we followed, I stumbled over long tufts but Taz stayed steady beside me. When we neared the wall surrounding the village, Sagar and Eldrich turned right toward the front gates, while we veered left to sneak in through the gardens at the back.

Meryl took the lead as we neared a wooden door in the stone wall and, in the dim light of the moon, I saw her bend down and press a fingertip to the keyhole.

"She's getting so much better at manipulating metal without getting carried away," Cheryl murmured, undisguised pride in her voice.

Moments later, a click echoed through the silent air and the door swung open. We crept on anxious tiptoes around the edge of the walled garden, keeping to the shadows. When we reached the archway to the castle, I led Taz past the others and we crossed the bridge first.

The village was quiet apart from a distant clanging that might have been from the forge. On my first journey here, I'd knocked over a tank of lizards and ended up with Leo stowing away in my satchel, but despite the upheaval I remembered the layout clearly.

A warm glow spilled across the courtyard from the forge's half-open door, and I recognised exactly where we were, from the forge to the sewage pit I'd accidentally knocked the realm's prince into.

Alannah told me the prince had met a sticky end a while back and I was curious. I shuddered. *I don't think I want to know what exactly happened to him now.*

None of that would help us, but I did have a few bits of knowledge I could share.

"Whatever you do, avoid that dark hole near the wall," I whispered. "You'll smell it before you see it, but so will everyone else for miles around if one of us falls in."

Ace sighed. "It's impossible to see around that far corner. How do we know there aren't guards in plain view of the door?"

He had a point. The courtyard was in full view of the L-shaped forge building, while the door we needed was just out of sight of it.

But last night, because I couldn't sleep thanks to Taz and Diana, I'd done some research on translocation gifts.

Time to test out what Old Tara gave me.

"Stay here," I told them. "I'm going to creep across and see if the coast is clear from the other side."

Before Taz could insist he was going with me, I shook my hand free of his and closed my eyes.

The books had said translocation was all in the visualisation and the belief in being able to move through the nether and fabric of Faerie. The few practice runs I'd done from my bedroom to the hall outside and back had exhausted me, but that was a place I knew better than anywhere.

I took a deep breath. With my focus strong, I visualised the castle wall and side door materialising in front of me, building the image brick by brick, wooden door panel and metal studs.

If it doesn't work... No. I believe I can do this. I do.

I focused my efforts on imagining the door I'd seen once before, the stones of the wall around it.

A moment later, a waft of warm air brushed my face.

I opened my eyes to see dark wood and gave myself a silent, weary cheer as fatigue swamped me. I looked back to see the forge doors open but no sign of anyone within viewing range of the courtyard.

With a sigh of relief, I pushed my fingers onto the metal door ring-pull and twisted with aching slowness in case it squeaked. As soon as I had the door open, I lifted my weary, gift-exhausted arm and beckoned the others over.

Taz was a blur of darkness, beside me in seconds. I blinked hard to ward off the temptation to fall asleep right there leaning against the door, and lifted my lids to find six shadowed faces sharing at me with almost identical expressions of awe.

I had a vague memory that I was supposed to stop Taz manhandling me for some reason, but the exhaustion was too strong and the arm he slid around my waist was so comforting. But I had to keep myself as sharp as I could.

I have an assignment to finish.

I lifted my head and eyed the courtyard.

Sure that we weren't being watched and that the hallway behind the door was clear, I waved everyone inside. Only once we were all on the other side with the door closed did I sag enough for Taz to take some of my weight.

"You can translocate?" he hissed. "Why didn't you tell me that?"

He's mad at me. I smiled. *Oh well.*

"Old Tara gave it to me and we haven't had much time for chatting lately. But it only works in places I've been before, and not from place to place or realm to realm. I'm okay."

"Wow." Taz wiped his face. "You just started fading in front of me. You're full of surprises, Sparky, but not sure I like that one. I bet it took a lot out of you."

I stuck my tongue out at him, even though my entire mouth felt laden down with lead, and we set off along the stone-walled corridor.

The décor was the same as the other hallways I'd seen when coming back to collect Leo, grey stone walls and rich blue carpet runners lined with silver. In the semi-darkness of the halls lit by firelight, shadows loomed like waiting guards.

As we tiptoed along, I checked my satchel but Leo was slumbering peacefully, looking like the titch lizard he was when he first stowed away in there. I frowned.

He shouldn't even be able to fit in the satchel properly

anymore, not since he had that huge growth spurt.

"I still say we're going to get caught," Beryl grumbled.

Cheryl rolled her eyes. "Well can you stop saying that? It's not something people say when they hope to blend in."

She wasn't exactly blending in either, walking with a jaunty swagger and a toothy smile. I dropped the flap of my satchel and focused my attention forward. I could deal with Leo's weird growth patterns, or what looked more like reverse-growth patterns, later.

When someone scurried toward us from an adjoining hall, head bowed low, Cheryl gave them a regal wave while the rest of us shoved Taz out of sight behind us.

"This is going to go horribly wrong, isn't it," Milo muttered.

I was starting to agree with him but didn't dare voice my fears. The most important thing, other than getting the princesses out of here, was keeping Taz safe.

"Can't you glamour?" I murmured to him. "You can, so you should glamour now. We can't let them recognise you. I should have thought of it before."

Taz shook his head. "No need. I have other ways of staying safe, don't worry."

"More stuff you've not told me?" I frowned back at him, lifting my head with effort.

He sighed. "I have told you, technically, but probably best I don't shout it out while we're here."

Irritated and weary, I wanted to halt everyone right there and demand that he stop being so infuriating.

Let him have his secrets. Once we get the princesses back to the Queen, I'm going back to Arcanium, then I'm going to transfer to the Quarantine level for a year and train frost cats to bite his knees or something.

Unable to actually do that until we'd rescued his sisters, I found a second wind of energy and powered forward away from him.

My pulse pounded loud in my ears as we continued on, determination and no small dose of pettiness toward Taz the only thing pushing me onward at speed.

We turned a corner into a wider corridor, decorated with hanging banners in the castle's standard royal blue and silver. Moments later, a maid came hurrying toward us, her arms piled high with laundry.

"Uh-oh," Ace said. "Taz, hide behind us. Demi, ask where the dungeons are."

I wobbled from side to side as the maid got closer, trying to catch her eye until she had to stop and face me.

"Hi, um, we've got to find the guards in the dungeons. Where are they?"

Instead of haranguing me or screaming for help, the maid nodded and glanced over her shoulder.

"They're on the east corridor," she said. "Go left at the end of the hall, then take a right, and the entrance is under the portrait of the new Queen. They've got some high profile people in those cells, so everyone has been sneaking up to get a good eyeful. But they had to call the many of the guards off this morning too."

I thanked her and stood aside. The moment she was out of sight, after a jerky, tell-tale bow in Taz's direction, I gave the others a hopeful look as Ace sagged. I remembered Elvira answering our questions before and complaining about being compelled. I caught his eye. He gave me a rueful smile, a confession almost, and I decided not to ask about his apparent ability for compulsions until he was ready to tell me.

"Not many guards left," I said. "That's got to be a good thing."

Taz huffed. "Did you hear her mention a new Queen? Wonder who that could be."

"Let's just keep pressing on for now," Meryl suggested. "Either way, we've come this far."

The Eastwicks steamed off as a united trio without waiting. The rest of us hurried after them, zigzagging through the halls.

"Oh look, there it is!" Taz shouted, louder than I ever could imagine his voice reaching.

It bounced off the walls like a beacon, no doubt summoning every guard and Fae in the entire castle. I'd have even put money on it being somehow magically magnified somehow, although why he was being such a colossal idiot I couldn't work out.

Everyone turned round, but I was the one right beside him. With my ears still ringing, I slapped his shoulder hard.

"Quiet!" I hissed. "Do you want to get us caught?"

He didn't answer, pointing instead to a tapestry, newly woven given the rich colour and fresh-fibred scent. I couldn't stop the growl escaping my throat as I stared at the hideous woman wearing a large golden tiara for a crown, Taz's blunder momentarily forgotten as rage thundered through me instead.

"Elvira is his new Queen?" I fought the urge to zap the tapestry to ashes. "Urgh, I should have guessed."

Taz rolled his eyes. "Come on, if there are no guards, we can find places to hide and jump them for the keys. Then we can get out of here."

I jostled behind him as he reached for the edge of the tapestry, but a tentative hand tapped my shoulder. I eyed the hand and up the arm to Milo's wide, worried eyes, then realised everyone else was staring down the hall.

"Oh, you won't be going anywhere."

CHAPTER FIFTEEN
Natural Gifts and Snotty Princesses

All of us threw up our protections while trying to get Taz safe behind us, difficult when he was fighting to do the same with me. We stood in a confused scrum of scrabbling boys and girls, all bashing into each other, unable to grow our wardings strong in such close quarters.

Elvira stepped forward with a cruel smile spreading across her face. Behind her, four guards loomed with crossbows nocked and pointed at us.

"It is so thoughtful of you to arrive promptly. It'll save us the task of trying to round you up. I did so hope you'd be here in time to see my coronation. Once the King and I are joined and I am crowned Queen, there will be little Faerie can do but accept us as the strongest regents to serve."

I thought of Old Tara.

Bet she wouldn't see what she does as serving.

"You're no Queen," I said, hating that my voice was shaking. "You only think of yourself and your own gain, but you're just one insignificant Fae. You've come up against us multiple times now, and you've failed each time. Nobody will remember you when you're dead, except as a cautionary tale or a joke to scare the kids."

Elvira probably wouldn't have noticed an earthquake nearby as she glowered at me, her mouth twisting like she was trying to itch a mosquito bite on her tongue.

"We'll see about that." She adopted her silkiest tone. "I wouldn't bother fighting or donning your silly protections, children. These guards are equipped with iron crossbows. I'm sure even you know that *metirin* iron is magic-resistant, and can pierce even the strongest of wardings."

I hadn't known about the piercing of wardings but stood firm. The others were giving me the dignity of not looking at me, but their silence told me it was down to me. This was my assignment, my responsibility.

"What, you'd shoot down a load of 'children' as you keep calling us?"

Elvira laughed. "Of course. I'm sure Prince Oakthorn won't let his companions die for him."

"No, I won't." Taz stepped forward. "I'll let you capture me, but I'll owe you and your supporters nothing after this. If you take me or my friends hostage now, any dues will be settled."

"Taz, don't," I muttered, thinking frantically.

Elvira cackled, like full-on witch-over-a-cauldron cackled. I clenched my jaw, resisting the urge to strike her down with every essence of zap I had left in me.

"Guards, escort them to the dungeons and lock them in cells. The Old King wants to ensure there are no last minute hitches, although perhaps I would like them to attend the ceremony and witness my triumph. Hmm. Something to ponder on. The cells, for now."

I couldn't let everyone get shot, and there were enough guards with crossbows to pick our warding and us to pieces. Perhaps this was the better way, get captured, taken to the cells and think of a plan from there. At least that way we could be in the same place as Taz's sisters, which was the initial plan to start with.

Except for any of this to work in our favour, we'd need to be on the right side of the bloody bars.

I held my nerves tight in my clenched gut as more guards filled the hall.

"Protections down," I muttered. "The wardings protect against people and gifts, but the arrows will sail straight through."

I lowered my hand and guards flanked us on either side.

As we passed Elvira, Beryl spat at her. It was loud, phlegmy and completely unladylike as it landed on Elvira's nose. Moments of shock subsided, and Elvira leaned toward Beryl until their faces were inches apart.

"If you were worth hurting, I would retaliate." She stepped back. "As it is, I do not have time for simple tortures. But when the time comes, you will be the first." She glanced at me, her lips curving. "You will be the last, and your pain will be the longest."

She turned away and pulled a handkerchief out of her cloak. Behind her, Sagar and Eldrich stood side by side, legs planted wide and hands clasped in front of them. Elvira barely gave them a second glance, sweeping away down the hall. Eldrich caught my eye and gave me the quickest of winks, so fleeting I wasn't sure it was real.

I couldn't rely on them getting word to anyone who could help us, or coming for us themselves. They were sworn to protect Taz, but it was Queenie who sent them, so they might have higher orders from the Queen to obey first.

Elvira must be feeling confident, I decided as we got jostled under the tapestry of her and along a dark, narrow tunnel lit with flaming torches. *She hasn't even bothered to follow us to the cells. If only we could find a way to turn that confidence against her.*

As we started down a staircase of stone, I heard one of the guards whisper a tiny apology to Taz. He nodded, wordlessly accepting.

A row of barred cells waited at the bottom of the stairs and the stone walls were stained dark in places by leaks. A melancholy *drip-drip-drip* echoed nearby and I wrinkled my nose at the overpowering stench of damp.

Of the four cells, only the cell furthest from the doorway was occupied. Four faces looked up at us, not in surprise but dismissive recognition. I recognised Taz's sister Belladonna with her dark hair and bright green eyes, after seeing her briefly at Taz's birthday party. She looked flawless despite having been locked in a cell for who knows how long. Beside her, Taz's other three sisters had varying degrees of lighter hair, but were otherwise carbon copies of Belladonna, and I couldn't remember their names. All had similar expressions of disgust pinned to their faces, probably permanently.

Ace and Milo were shoved into the cell at the end nearest the exit, the barred gate shut hurriedly behind them. Taz was guided with slightly more respect into the one next to his sisters, but he refused to let go of my hand. One step away from him pulling my fingers clean off, the guards pushed me in after him and slammed the gate.

Finally, the Eastwicks were manhandled into the cell between our cell and Milo and Ace's. Given the grunting noises and the scuffling of flailing limbs, they were putting up a pretty decent fight, but the guards outnumbered them. Soon their gate also clanged shut.

All of the guards disappeared up the stairs, but from my cell in the middle, I could see two of them remaining at the top.

"Traitors!" Cheryl shouted after them, rattling the bars.

Beryl threw her a dismissive look. "I told you it was all too easy. I said this wouldn't work."

I wanted to pace but Taz was already doing that, and the cell wasn't exactly roomy. I leaned against the stone wall at the back instead, closing my eyes.

"Well, little brother." Belladonna's voice was an eternal, mocking sing-song. "You've well and truly stuffed this up, haven't you?"

I could almost believe in that moment that she was Elvira's child, rather than the Queen's. I opened my eyes to glare at her, but Taz only shrugged.

"Lasted longer than you."

Belladonna sneered back at him, but that appeared to be it for their squabbling.

"Why did you have to go and shout like that?" I groaned.

Taz grimaced. "You'll just have to trust me."

"You mean you did that on purpose?! Why?"

He didn't respond, and made a huge effort to take an interest in the metal bars of the cell.

Screw him then, and whatever game he's playing. I'm getting out of here.

"Right, plan anyone?" I asked.

Ace and Milo stood with their heads close together in their cell, muttering to each other. Beryl tried to prise her gate open with pure force, while Meryl attempted her metal-wielding gift on the bars themselves, but nothing was working.

I let my brain whir.

Gifts and magic didn't work.

We didn't have any keys.

Force clearly hadn't helped Beryl, who was now so red-faced and out of puff she had to sit down on the grimy stone floor.

I peeked into my satchel at Leo, but he wouldn't be able to help if I let him loose.

What about natural gifts?

The idea lit like a firework in my brain. I strode to the bars and peered out.

"Does anyone know how Elvira would address the

servants?" I kept my voice low, just in case.

Taz snorted. "I reckon she'd call everyone, 'you', because she wouldn't care enough to remember their names."

Belladonna eyed her nails. "As much as I hate to agree with the half-breed, I have heard her call people 'you', on the two occasions she's been down here."

I nodded and took a deep breath. *I can do this.*

"You!" I threw my voice in a mimicry of Elvira's strident tone, making it boom through the dungeon as though it came from the upper hall. "Why are these pieces of filth still in cells? The King is waiting. They must witness my triumph! Let them out and escort them to the hall. Now!"

It took all of my effort to throw my voice past the guards at the top of the stairs so that it sounded like Elvira was shouting from behind the tapestry. I peered up the steps in time to see the guards jolt upright. One bashed the back of his head on the wall for his trouble. I doubled over, out of breath.

"Where'd she go?" one guard muttered.

"Does it matter?" The second one snapped back. "Get them out or she'll have us in there next!"

I stepped back as they appeared at the top of the stairs, trotting down with keys jangling in hand.

The guard approached our cell first, and Taz held his station by the gate.

"I do apologise, Your Highness," the guard mumbled. "I'm only doing my job. We're not all here by our own choices."

Taz nodded, impatient as the guard rifled through the ring of large black keys. The moment the right one turned in the lock, Taz shunted his shoulder into the bars and sent the guard flying to the floor. He grabbed the keys from the guard's unresisting hand. The second guard stood at the bottom of the stairs, baffled as Taz and I darted out of our cell and I threw up a protection around both of us.

"Where did you get that gift then?" Belladonna asked me.

I wondered if she couldn't help the natural sneer in her tone, but she and I would probably never be friends. I faced her as Taz rushed to free Ace and Milo first.

"That's the one thing about humans." I bit back. "Some of our gifts are totally natural from birth, like we're special or something. We don't have to smile pretty and wait for some relative to take pity on us. But you're welcome to stay in here and rot by all means."

The first guard scrambled to his feet but tumbled back to the floor as Milo and Ace stormed past him, vanishing a second later.

Taz grabbed me, one hand on my wrist and the other reaching toward my hip as if he meant to pull me under his arm. I twisted away and waved my hand in the furthest cell's direction.

"Assignment first. Get your sisters out and home. Milo will come back for me."

I didn't look back at him as I grabbed the keys out of his hand and opened the gate for the Eastwicks. Almost on cue, Milo reappeared as Beryl, Meryl and Cheryl gathered around him.

"I'm going to try taking all three of you," he said.

"Oooh, you're brave." Beryl clamped a hand on his shoulder as he took Cheryl's hand on one side and Meryl's on the other. "Get on with it then."

It was almost worth the delay to see Milo go bright red.

"Demi, I'll be back for you in a second." He grimaced as the air around him wavered and the four of them disappeared.

I threw the keys back to Taz and stood tense as he unlocked his sisters' cell door.

They burst out like fireworks and he dropped the keys so that he could clamp his hands on two of their wrists, the two youngest girls if I had to guess.

As the others jostled to hold his shoulders, Belladonna's nose wrinkling even as he was essentially saving her butt, someone else stampeded down the stairs.

"What's all this noise?!"

CHAPTER SIXTEEN
Demi Faces the Old King and Can't Quite Keep Her Mouth Shut

Elvira appeared framed in the archway at the top of the steps as the air shivered around Taz and his sisters. His mouth got caught in an anguished shout as he disappeared, leaving me on my own.

I raised a hand to strengthen my warding, but a wave of blistering heat blasted against it and knocked me back into the cell door. I tried to visualise a different part of the castle to translocate into, but Elvira charged down the stairs and lunged forward to grab a handful of my hair. All thought of visualisation vanished as I screamed in pain. She shoved a clawed hand on my shoulder, fingers biting into the skin.

I yelped as she pushed me back into the cell with such force that I stumbled and fell backwards. My bones rattled with the impact but I struggled to my feet as she slammed the gate shut. Even as I surged forward, she locked it with the bunch of keys Taz had dropped before disappearing.

"Filthy vermin," she spat. "I don't have time for you now, but the King will no doubt let me torture you at a later date."

She stormed away and up the stairs in a swirl of white, the keys clutched tight in her hand.

I sagged against the stone wall at the back of the cell, my mind rioting through endless possibilities, all of which were useless to me.

I had to hope that Milo would come back, but then what could he possibly do without the keys to unlock the gate? Taz could realm-skip between Arcanium and his mother's court, but he wouldn't be able to get back here without Milo, and what could he do anyway now that Elvira had the keys?

I could only hope that Taz would drop his sisters off, skip back to Arcanium and find Milo so they could both come back for me, or alert Queenie and hopefully find a way to get past the *metirin* iron.

I closed my eyes and visualised the hallway upstairs, piecing together the grey stone, the blue runners and banners, the suits of armour. A responding tingle filled my limbs and I dared to hope.

BANG.

I was thrown back against the wall, a quiet ringing coming from the cell bars.

I reached behind me and rubbed my back as best I could, glaring at the gate.

Worth a try. I sighed, pressing a hand into my pocket. My fingertips skimmed something cool and my heart leapt. *Looks like the human way wins again.*

Petra had taught me to pick locks without magic, and I pulled my penknife out of my pocket, looking for a suitable extension. I reached tentatively through the bars, growing bolder when no shock sent me reeling.

Typical Fae, so arrogant they assume everything is only fixable with gifts and magic.

I grabbed the padlock in one hand, penknife poised in the other.

"There is someone here who I would have you extract answers from."

The sound of a deep, masculine voice entering the dungeon made me jump. I veered backwards and slid the knife into my pocket again. With any luck, whoever it was would do what they needed to do and leave so I could get myself out.

I retreated to the back wall and pressed my shoulders against it, as far away from anyone trying to reach in through the bars as possible.

Hopefully Milo knows better than to reappear when danger's about.

I eyed the two men who entered the dungeon, one pausing at the bottom of the steps and the other striding with innate, entitled grace toward my cell.

The Old King stood in front of my gate, peering in with a gleeful smirk, but I only had eyes for Kainen. He stared back at me in shock, his bottom lip dropping.

The last time I'd seen him was unconscious in his mausoleum of a home. Anger flickered inside me, burning like acid in my gut, but at least Taz hadn't killed him.

"I have discovered why the young princeling is so taken with you," the Old King announced.

I transferred my gaze to him, glad I was at the back of the cell already so I didn't have to show my fear by stepping away.

His golden hair fluffed around his face, shining more beautifully than was natural or normal, his face a perfect build of smooth lines and flawless skin. But his eyes were green and cold, the ancient well of viciousness easily visible for me to fear.

I forced myself to stare back at him and feign nonchalance when my pulse was threatening to gallop out of my chest.

"Well done, gold star for you."

The Old King sighed. "Hostile attitude aside, Prince Oakthorn has shown a great intrigue in the negative. It forms nothing more than a desire for rebellion, cleaving to the unsavoury in the hopes of shocking and angering those who actually matter to him."

I folded my arms. "If you think that's hurtful, you should hear my sisters berate me. I've got a busy day ahead and I'm sure you have too. Why not just do what you have to do and get on with it?"

The Old King stepped back and waved a hand to Kainen without looking at him.

"*I* don't have to do anything. The blessing of being pure power is having people to do that for you. Kainen here is going to interrogate you. If he is prudent, he will extract the answers I need quickly and leave most of the fun for Elvira."

Kainen bowed low as the Old King swept past him and back up the stairs. He stared after the Old King for several seconds, as if to make sure he was actually leaving.

Might as well beat the poor boy to it and save all the dancing around. With any luck, Taz will somehow psychically assume I'm smiling at him and come charging back to stop us.

"We both know you can't compel me to tell you anything," I said. "We've been here before. I might not have access to gifts now, but I know your power, and I know my friends. You can't compel me, and there isn't a single vision you can create that would make me doubt them now."

Kainen inched toward my cell as if afraid I might bite. The shift of the power balance made me feel stronger and I walked to meet him there, staying just out of reaching distance.

"The King wishes to know what the Queen has planned," he said.

I snorted. "You think she'd tell me? Or, knowing I was coming here to rescue her kids, you think she'd tell Taz, knowing he'd tell me? I haven't seen the Queen in ages."

"But you could give us something, anything."

"Why should I?" I started pacing a slow arc back and forth with my arms folded. "I know you think you've been nice to me before, but you tried to lock me up and use your powers to torment me, like a spoilt brat throwing a tantrum because I wouldn't do things the way you wanted. The Old King is the last person I'd tell anything to, and you're like the second last."

Kainen's face twisted, but I forced my mind away from thoughts of pity at the pure, panicked anguish in his smoky grey eyes. The Old King would likely punish him if he didn't succeed in getting anything from me, but Kainen wasn't my main concern right now.

"At least tell me this, is there something special about you after all?" he begged. "Anything at all?"

Is there anything special about me? His idea of special and mine probably weren't the same. *Do I think there's anything special about me?*

Before Arcanium, meeting Taz and making friends, I wouldn't have said so. But since then?

I smiled wide. "Yes."

Not a lie. The special things about me were my friends, and the place I got to call home. My ability to love my Arcanium family and want them to be okay was the biggest power I had. It made me strong.

That or my sheer stubbornness, but still.

Kainen leaned closer, his lips parted and his eyes taking on a hungry gleam.

"Well? What is it? What's so special about you?"

I leaned closer, almost enough to reach through the bars and touch him, holding his gaze. My natural instinct was to look away, the sheer fix of his eyes on mine feeling so invasive. When I couldn't stand the tension anymore, I lunged forward and snapped my teeth in a mimicry of biting.

Kainen stumbled back, almost falling flat on the stone tiles. He glared at me, his eyes sparking. I saw the glitter massing in the darkness growing around him and resigned myself to whatever came next. If his gift could get through the iron somehow, I was probably done for.

It's not real. Until I get back to Arcanium, whatever torment he puts on me is not real. He can't possibly recreate the whole of Arcanium in a vision, and even he wouldn't bother with that just to spite me.

"Well, Kainen." The Old King's voice filled the room. "What have you learned?"

I eyed the smoke now receding fast.

It didn't have time to get to me, or is this part of the vision?

"I-" Kainen froze.

The Old King tutted. "You learned nothing. How disappointing. I have heard there are boys with their heads turned by this girl, for reasons I cannot comprehend, but I didn't expect you to be one of them."

I took several steps back just in time, and made it back to the wall before the Old King turned to face me.

"I take a close interest in all my inner circle subjects," he said. "I had hoped the rumours weren't true, that Kainen wasn't as doe-eyed over you as his family feared. But here he is, not even able to bring himself to compel you to answer."

I flicked a glance at Kainen, who stood with his head bowed in disgrace.

Whether for my safety or his own reputation, he hasn't mentioned the whole not being able to compel me thing.

"Still, subjects must learn their place."

The Old King flicked out a hand without so much as a look back, holding my gaze. I fixed mine on his shoulder as Kainen's eyes widened. His hands went to his throat, fingers clawing at nothing as his face started going red.

"I can do whatever I like, girl." The Old King threw Kainen across the room with a mere twitch of his fingers.

I winced as Kainen hit the wall and slumped over with a quiet groan. He lifted his head, but made no attempt to stand.

"Ruthless strength is the only power. Weakness comes with emotion, failure comes from feeling. When you have power, you have everything. I could easily give Kainen the Mage of Nightmares role he covets so dearly." The Old King clicked his fingers, cloaking Kainen in roiling darkness. "And I can take it away just as easily."

I kept my expression neutral, but I couldn't stop the wave of pity as Kainen's eyes widened at the mention of the role, then fell into listless resignation as the Old King's taunt landed.

"Leave us."

At the command, Kainen gave me one last look and used the wall to clamber to his feet. He walked toward the stairs, limping slightly, and left without any hesitation, a minion following a master's command.

He still chose his side in the end.

I shook all thought of Kainen away and faced the Old King.

"Now, you have caused some trouble," he said. "I admit this piques my curiosity. I could of course bewitch you, crush you, and all sorts of other delights, but the young princeling will be back for you. Best let him think there's something to come back for first, or this will have all been for nothing. I do believe that the Queen, in some misguided mania, thinks he is the most special of all her children. Her only son. Perhaps there will be no need to recapture the princesses after all."

A loud tapping echoed from the corridor above, then drummed on the stairs. Elvira burst into the dungeon dressed in a monstrosity of white feathers and lace, her eyes narrowed and her cheeks flushed. She looked at the Old King, then me, like a dodo coveting its last egg.

"Ah, Elvira, my sweet." The Old King looked less than impressed with this interruption but covered it with vague pleasantry. "This one will be instrumental as an example of the new regime. Of course, she will need to be our lure for the prince, but after that, we shall use her as a device to cement the traditional ways. I think it has been a long time since a true sacrifice was bled on the altar, and what better way to celebrate my future rule."

Elvira smiled, a horrific visage of sickly sweetness stretched across her garish face.

"Our rule, love," she cooed.

The Old King stilled for a moment. "You are precious. The time is near and we cannot rule out another attempt to recapture our little sacrifice by the enemy. Bring her along to the ceremony."

He disappeared up the stairs, leaving me with heaving sickness in my gut and panic pounding through every inch of me. Memories swarmed of Sagar talking about sacrifices with Taz, the old, 'traditional' ways.

I need to think of something, but what?

If I could fight long enough to get free and cast a warding, that'd give me some extra time, but I wouldn't be able to hold anything against powerful Fae like Elvira or the Old King for long.

Elvira unlocked my cell and advanced. I couldn't use my gifts inside the bars, but neither could she. The moment she made a grab for me, I swung sideways and landed a punch on her shoulder.

A backhanded slap slammed into my cheek before I could right myself, her speed and vehemence making my attempt laughable. She gripped my arms behind my back and shoved me along ahead of her out of the cell.

I struggled as she pushed me up the stairs, but I couldn't find the right angle to try fighting her off, and with her holding me tight I couldn't summon a protection warding against her either.

"Oh, you think you're so clever," Elvira snarled. "But your pesky friends are of no consequence and you're all alone now, little runt. Even if the supposedly dashing prince comes back to save you, neither of you will be able to take on the might of the King."

I decided it was best not to answer as she rammed me along the halls and through two huge wooden doors. I knew the main hall, in that it was a huge room I'd been in once before, but I barely recognised it with the renovation job.

The entire hall was blue. Blue tablecloths, blue runners and blue ribbons hung from every available ledge and crevice. Bright blue water bubbled up from a huge stone fountain that was carved in a scarily accurate likeness of Elvira and the Old King, although I noticed that only he had been given a crown. Looking around, I saw even the servants wore blue suits with silver buttons.

I turned my attention to the crowds crammed into the hall, all gawping at our grand entrance. One lady stood with a tiny handbag dog, its fur dyed blue of course, clutched in her arms and another peering out over the brim of her feathered hat. One elderly man sat in a peacock green suit, clashing with the decorations and trying to trip servants with his cane, cackling the whole time. A younger man drifted by with coat-tails trailing on the floor and two monocles, one over each eye.

Up at the front of the hall on a raised platform sat the Old King. He lounged on his throne, now decked in regal blue fur robes. In the pale gleam of the blue and white room, his honey-coloured hair looked almost silver. Either side of him, stood Sagar and Eldrich, 'guarding' their king.

Elvira jostled me forward as all eyes lit on us. The Old King rose out of his chair, his eyes narrowing.

"You are familiar to me," he said, his tone deceptively rich and warm, as if he'd not just been taunting me in his dungeon. "Where do I know you from?"

But if he was going to feign ignorance, I wasn't going to appease him by playing along.

"You don't recognise me from two minutes ago? Ouch. How rude. Typical Fae behaviour, I suppose."

Instead of the anger, he smiled wide and dazzling. Dangerous. Of course, this was always going to be a performance to the death in front of his people. He tilted his head, pretending to think.

"Oh yes, the Puzzle Tower at Gallows Oak. You were in training no doubt for your royal debut. For, you are here as the entertainment, yes? Fitting for someone of your kind."

Raucous laughter filled the room. I raised an eyebrow and pushed past the fear thundering through me. Even if I was shaking, Elvira was gripping me so firmly in place that nobody would be able to see it.

"My kind? What, women?" I tutted. "Didn't take Fae for overly sexist, but you learn something new every day. Is that why you're the only one that's wearing a crown on that fountain over there?"

The Old King moved so fast I couldn't do anything to defend myself. A surprisingly bony fingertip pierced the skin under my chin, forcing my head back a painful amount.

"Such foolish fire," he murmured. "Too much time with the young princeling perhaps, or maybe this is just you. Some of my subjects inform me that there is something 'other' about you. The prince's chosen toy, Arcanium's star errand girl, and Queenie's pet champion. Is this true?"

His breath smelled like berries and late summertime, the sweet scent of hay just before the leaves begin to turn and crinkle. I got the feeling that if he tried a compulsion or anything on me, I'd be completely powerless to resist, blessing or no blessing.

I pushed my shoulders up into a jerky shrug and refrained from answering.

"Perhaps we should send you back to him in pieces, or better yet, hold you here forever," he crooned. "I could have any of my court seduce you in front of him. Tell me, fairy, what should I do?"

Elvira still had her fingers gripping my shoulder. The Old King had his hand under my chin and his face so close I could practically headbutt him, but I knew if I did that it would be the last move I ever made.

Think smart. I caught sight of Sagar and Eldrich still a few paces behind him. Eldrich's nose twitched. *Keep him distracted enough for them to get close and strike.*

"You could do the sensible thing," I said, my voice wavering.

He forced my head back that little bit further. "And what is that?"

I took a strangled breath, my neck feeling like it was about to snap. If I was going out then I'd go out swinging and make sure the whole crowd gathered knew exactly what side I was on as I went.

"Stand down." I lifted my voice as best I could. "Admit defeat. Slink away. That's what you do best, right? Like last time, when Arcanium was attacked? What kind of coward has their minions do battle but doesn't lead the fight? That will be the rhyme they'll sing in the evenings from now on, to make little Fae *and fairy* children laugh in their beds. Here comes the Cowardly King."

It wasn't my best creative attempt, but as his finger disappeared from underneath my chin, I could at least straighten my head. Something dropped onto my hoodie and I tipped my head down to see a circle of dark blood soaking through the blue.

If I ever wanted a piercing, I guess this will leave enough of a puncture wound to be my first.

I ignored the panicked dizziness heating my cheeks and swelling in my chest. The Old King stalked away and turned to face me again, his face sharp with malice.

"Your prince will be given a special role as payment for your insolent treachery. He will become my fool, made to endure pain and humiliation for the rest of his pathetic life."

I froze as the Old King strode back toward me, but he didn't touch, didn't come close enough to be tainted by me again.

"Every day he will be forced to look at you," he spat. "We'll also find a suitable punishment for you, a slow, agonising one. Then I will make him stare each morning at your decaying head once you're dead."

Yuck. I wrinkled my nose.

"Nice rhyming, but are you sure he'd see that as a punishment?" I asked. "As you suggested, I'm pretty troublesome."

Without being able to lie, questions and word-tangling were my only way of playing this game now. Not that I was ever going to win, I knew that, but false bravado was the only part of me I had left. With Elvira's hand clamped to my shoulder, a hefty chunk of my hair under her fingers, and my arm pinned tight behind my back, I couldn't even try to fight her off.

"You are determined to make things worse for yourself, why?" The Old King frowned, his watchful court momentarily forgotten. "Is this some human self-destruct instinct?"

I snorted. "Oh please. I just know that if you kill me, Taz will become crueller, more vicious, and so much more wickedly Fae than you can ever hope to be."

The King stilled, his eyes flicking over my face.

A-ha. He's afraid of what Taz might become.

I should have considered that. Even with his ego and his over-confidence, the Old King must have been somewhat smart. He would have considered that in toppling the Queen, there might be one that Faerie would choose or champion to succeed her over him.

This is what it's all about. Taz has always been intended as the Queen's successor, her favourite 'project', and the child who has enough humanity to do it right. Now that he's old enough to be trained for ruling, the Forgotten are making their move to stop it.

So caught in my own revelations as the Old King stared back at me, curiosity scrawled across his face, I didn't see the danger coming.

Elvira twisted me, my arm wrenching. I howled with pain as she tossed me to the hard floor like a doll.

"How dare you speak to the King that way, like you're an equal!"

The memory of what Taz had said earlier on in the forest echoed in my head. As I looked up at Elvira, I found a wicked smile and repeated it.

"Jealous?" I flicked my gaze to the statue. "I might not have a crown, but neither do you."

When Elvira kicked out, she didn't hold back. Her foot, while encased in a slipper-shoe as part of her soon-to-be-fake-Queen garb, found my gut. I grunted but held the scream inside, clenching my nails into my palms.

"Stop the wedding!"

The voice filtered through my agony and I groaned in disbelief. With everything I had left, I lifted my head and looked for the absolute idiot who'd just interrupted my beating.

CHAPTER SEVENTEEN
The One With All The Fighting

"Oh wow, what is this even meant to be?" Taz's strident voice blasted through the air, reducing my bones to anxious but relieved jelly. "A wedding? Or a coronation? Whatever it is, it's a total monstrosity."

My breath tumbled out in punctured anguish. As I noticed Milo flicker in and out, the realisation hit me. Taz was planning to do this alone.

Elvira pulled me up, no doubt to use me as a hostage or a shield, and I'm betting she wasn't fussy about which. I stayed still, knowing struggling now might lose me an opportunity to catch her off guard at a later point if something distracted her.

Taz held himself tall like a true prince, chin up and eyes blazing with fury. The effect was no less powerful for his 'I Don't Give a Duck' t-shirt with the *Demolition Ducks* logo on the back, or the fact his jeans were torn on one knee.

The Old King raised a hand, but Taz swiped his through the air. A moment of utter stillness passed, before one of the banners burst into flame.

"Your time will never come again." Taz raised his voice above the murmur of the crowd. "My sisters are back and my mother is regaining strength. Take me if you like, it'll make little difference, but I'll warn you of this: make one more wrong move toward my future queen, and I will end you."

Tense silence filled the hall, the air sizzling with uneasiness. A couple of Fae were already disappearing, a few creeping out of the open doors at the far end of the hall, while one or two others discreetly vanished into thin air.

Future queen? My insides flipped. *Was it just a taunt to rile up the Old King, to pretend that Taz might go for the crown after all? But... he can't lie.*

Baffled, I had to bring my focus back to Elvira. Her attention was on Taz and the Old King as they faced each other down, but I knew she'd still delight in killing me quick if she didn't get a chance to make it last instead.

The Old King took the tiniest step back to his chair and his guards. Sagar stood completely still, but Eldrich's hand was sneaking toward the pack hanging on Sagar's back.

I bit my lip and tried to think of a way to shake Elvira off, but she was gripping me like a hawk. I made out Kainen and Diana now near the front of the crowd, with Jack Harmony and Alannah.

All my least favourite people, great.

I almost missed the person walking directly toward us, but as Elvira shifted her grip, I caught the eye of the most unlikely man I ever thought I'd see in the enemy camp. For once there was no boiler suit to be seen, and the black suit looked so weird on him I had to blink and take a moment to get over the shock.

"Watch her," Elvira told him. "I should be seen to stand beside the King."

Emil clamped his hand to my shoulder where Elvira's had just been, the other tight around my upper arm.

"What's going on?" I whispered. "Are you here to get us out?"

Emil said nothing, until the silence unnerved me and I had to ask again. Elvira's instruction suggested Emil was acting as one of them, like Sagar and Eldrich were.

How did Elvira know where we were in the forest?

I sucked in a startled breath and gulped at the same time, spluttering on the damning truth.

It would make sense, Emil had control of the Arcanium orb-waves, the mentees, the FDPs...

But I had to ask, had to be sure.

"Are you- did Queenie send you?" I whispered.

Emil started to laugh, but still he didn't say a word as Taz squared up to the Old King, walking toward him.

A traitor. Someone with access.

The scenes flooded back to me as if Kainen's nightmare gift was holding court in my head. Emil sending me for my first assignment despite Queenie's hesitation. Emil always being exactly where he needed to be when Elvira had been inside Arcanium posing as Sandra. I couldn't remember seeing him fight when they invaded the atrium either.

He managed the orb-waves, he coordinated who went where. He might well have known it was Alannah's orb that sent that first realm-wide warning after my first assignment. Was she really warning the enemy about something, not us about them?

The thoughts swarmed, so many that I couldn't make head nor tail of the specifics, but they left me with the one excruciating truth.

Emil was a traitor.

I didn't fancy my chances against him, but if I could get free of him, I could throw up a warding. If Taz and I could get to each other, he could skip us home or to his mother's court.

"You know, I can vanish as easily as breathing," Taz distracted me momentarily from Emil.

Could he? Why hadn't he told me that?

"Oh, really." The Old King faced him down from atop the platform.

Taz nodded, cocky, confident and oh so stubborn.

"Yep, good luck catching me."

I saw his fingers flex, Emil recognising the movement too

and loosening his grip on me. I twisted, kicked out against his shin and bit the nearest finger on my shoulder.

Emil yelped and released me, but that was all I needed. I threw up my warding and drove him back with it. If Taz could disappear, that would leave me stuck here alone again.

"If you vanish, I will torment your "future queen" over there," the Old King yelled. I stopped dead. *Oh hell.* "I will blast her to pieces limb by limb, in bone-crunching agony. She will die knowing it was you that caused it. Every single day her death will be on your head, and I will make her beg for death before I end her."

Taz actually snickered. "Oh please, have you ever tried so much as arguing with her? Good luck with that then, she's impossible."

I glared at him, indignation firing through me, just in time to see him vanish.

A couple of seconds passed in silence.

Then all eyes turned to me.

I put all my effort and gift into my warding as room attacked, focusing all my will behind it, but each blast from all directions shook me to the bone. I gritted my teeth, but with my warding up I had no hope of translocating anywhere, and no way of splitting my focus to summon my energy gift either.

I thought I heard a voice shouting my name, but I couldn't risk it being a trick, couldn't do anything other than put every essence of myself into holding my warding.

A flash of blue caught my eye through the onslaught, moving fast. I could barely see for all the attacks exploding against my protection in multicoloured sparks and clouds and flames of dust, but I was sure I'd seen it. Even with my protection failing around me, I twisted my hips so I could bend one knee and bounce my satchel against my thigh.

Empty.

"Oh god, Leo," I groaned.

Shouts of glee at causing pain turned to screams of agony. I managed to squint through the mayhem in time to see Leo, but he wasn't my Leo, not like I knew him.

A chameleon the size of an elephant charged through the room, scales rippling various shades of blue like a huge weirdo Chameleophant wave.

Kainen surged toward him and just as quickly went flying, slamming through the nearest window and shattering glass everywhere.

Emil raised a hand but Giant-Leo already had him clamped in his jaw and threw him toward the Old King, who raised a hand and sent Emil crashing sideways into the drinks table.

As if the whole thing was personal, Leo was charging against my enemies.

I gawped even as my protection began to fracture around me, realising that Leo could clearly change size at will.

That explains the growth spurt yet him still being able to fit in the satchel.

He rounded the chaos of broken chairs, his gaze fixing on the Old King next. I opened my mouth but the scream didn't burst out in time.

A flash of brilliant purple light shot from the Old King's mouth across the room, hitting Leo square between the eyes.

Leo blinked. I tried to run forward but crowds were still fleeing in panic, crashing all over each other in a bid to get out.

As Leo started to shrink and wobble, I dropped my breaking protection and dragged the very last ounce of my power up from the depths. I visualised Leo in front of me, the soft scales of his head under my hand and the floor beneath my knees.

The scales materialised beneath my fingertips, but softer than

I knew was normal. I opened my eyes to see him now human-sized with his scales fading, grey-green lizard hues turning a tanned pink.

The entire room lit purple, and I slumped forward as a human shield without caring what happened to me.

I barely even noticed the air shivering around us and the floor turning from grey stone to light wood as the tears flowed free.

But the absence of scales and the sudden blur of honey-brown hair under my fingertips… I would never get that nightmare out of my head.

CHAPTER EIGHTEEN
Premonitions and a Chat With the Queen of Faerie

"Demerara, look at me."

The command was so full of compulsion, I didn't even try to fight it. I blinked through a face full of tears to find a blurry-looking Queen in front of me.

Taz must have used the last of his strength to get us back to his mother's court.

"He used his changeling gift." I sobbed. "He pretended to be Leo so he could rescue me. Save him, do something, please."

Already kneeling, I bent over Taz's chest again, wishing he was conscious so I could smack him halfway across Faerie instead of grieving for him. The fact that he'd turned himself into a mutant Leo to take on everyone who was firing at me was absurd, and dangerous, and so like him. Then I realised the real Leo was unaccounted for and a distraught whimper tore out of me.

"He sacrificed himself for you," the Queen said.

Where the hell is her emotion? Why isn't she screaming? Why doesn't she care?

"Up now, Lady." Another voice surrounded me. "Let me have a look at him."

I refused to move so Marthe, the housekeeper, used my shoulder for support as she groaned her way down to kneel beside me, her wrinkled hands tracing over his forehead and through his hair.

"Oh now that's not right. Someone's unravelled his mind. All this purple, not good."

I glared up at the Queen. "Why don't you do something? What the hell is the point of all your supposed power if you do nothing?"

"There is nothing I can do. Royal Fae and those sworn to their court can't interfere with family, or it would be too weighted an advantage. It's built into the very laws and fabric of Faerie."

I rose to my feet, aware of Marthe muttering things as she continued to feel Taz's face.

"You don't give a damn about him," I shouted, not caring who I was talking to now. "Not one single catch in your voice, and you do nothing. You've done nothing since your daughters were taken, sulking here like a child! You don't deserve to be Queen."

I ignored Marthe's sharp intake of breath and leaned further forward as the Queen grabbed my right wrist, her fingers pinching hard. I looked down to see the skin going blue and flinched as the Queen laid a savage kiss on my forehead with burning lips.

"I give you the gift of foresight," she hissed. "Make it choke some sense into you."

The world dissolved around me. All I could see was darkness, and all I could feel was the Queen's grip on my wrist beginning to zing with a metallic pain.

Before I could free myself, the grip disappeared. I looked down to see a bruise blossoming on the inside of my wrist, in the exact same spot as Sagar and Eldrich had their signs of service to the Queen. The grey-blue turned purple and brown as a scene began to materialise around me.

I recognised the atrium in Arcanium but brushed aside a deep yearning in my gut. I would never be able to walk any of those halls ever again without breaking, not without Taz beside me.

Someone dashed past me and a flash of yellow lightning lifted them off their feet. I looked further and saw Elvira with rage on her face. Beside her stood the Old King and further back, Kainen and Diana were talking in frantic whispers. Kainen had the remnants of a thousand cuts on every visible piece of skin, some still plastered over.

He went through the window earlier. Foresight, is this meant to be a premonition?

I looked down at the bruise on my wrist, put there by the Queen's hand. If this was a premonition then the attack Elvira had mentioned in the forest, the one they'd called all the Old King's guards away for, was going to come soon, before my bruise had time to fade. Something flickered beside me. I saw Taz, whole and alive, mouthing frantically at me although I couldn't hear the words. If this were a premonition, then he could still be saved.

"I get it now," I called out.

The bruise started throbbing and I closed my eyes to the sight of Arcanium under attack. The sensation of a hand around my wrist materialised, but let go just as quickly, dropping me to my knees.

I looked up at the Queen, wanting to ask why. Her expression was impassive, a mask, as she stared down at me.

"The Old King has cursed him with dark, ancient malice. His brain will continue to unravel unless a sacrifice is given."

I thought back to what Eldrich and Sagar had said about the old ways, about sacrifices to old Gods.

"A life?" I asked.

Would I sacrifice my life for his mind? Could I?

"A gift." The Queen's voice was pure iron.

I didn't hesitate. "Take it."

"Take what?"

"My gift, take the premonition one, is that enough? Does it need more to bring him back as he was, no lasting damage? Take all of them if you have to, even the natural one, my voice mimicking. Will he be the Taz we know again?"

The Queen dropped to one knee opposite me, Taz motionless between us. I flinched but held myself in place as she stroked a finger down my nose and one along Taz's at the same time.

I looked down, praying although I had no idea who I was praying to. Beyond frantic, I could only think of Old Tara, but praying to her would probably do me as good as any other.

Please let him be okay, please.

Moments passed.

Then, a twitch.

A shudder of his ribcage, barely there.

Taz opened his eyes, blinked a couple of times and looked around. I held my breath.

What if it wasn't enough? What if he doesn't recognise me? What if-

Taz noticed me and a weary smile started to spread across his face. He tried to get up with a groan, but settled for balancing himself back on his elbows.

I wasn't having that.

A strangled sob tore from my throat as I lunged forward and threw my arms around his neck, knocking him backwards again. He started to laugh, breathless as he wrapped a hand tight around my waist and snarled the other in tangles of my hair.

"If you ever do anything like that again, I'll do something awful and beyond painful to you," I murmured. "Do you understand me?"

Definitely just a saying. Faerie knows I could never hurt him.

He continued his hoarse chuckling. "If you say so. Orbs alive, Dem, I thought you'd use my distraction to translocate out of there, not try and face them!"

I clambered to my feet and helped him sit up, aware of Marthe hovering nearby with two cups on a tray.

"What about Leo?" I asked, guilt pouring in that I hadn't thought of him before now. "He disappeared from my satchel."

Taz managed a guilty grin. "I may have lifted him from your bag when I brought my sisters back. I knew you'd want him safe and that we'd run into trouble, plus I couldn't risk him seeing me impersonating him and trying to join in the fight. I had Marthe put him in the conservatory and skipped back to Arcanium to find Milo and come get you."

Him trying to hug me in the dungeons. He wasn't saving me, he was taking Leo with him. As if he knew Leo was more important to me. As if he trusted me to handle myself until he got back.

"He was playing merry hell with the cushions last I looked." Marthe butted in, pressing a cup into Taz's hands then turning on me. "Drink this, Master Oakthorn, and you too, Mistress."

I wasn't sure about her calling me mistress, but when she patted my shoulder with a newfound fondness shining in her eyes, I decided not to make waves.

"There are things that need to be ascertained," the Queen said, her tone calmer now. "Where does your allegiance lie, Demerara? Will you pledge it to my rule?"

I glanced at Taz but he mimed buttoning his lip. I was on my own for this one and chose my words as carefully as I could considering my mind was completely frazzled.

"As much as my conscience and free will allow. But in the whole you versus the Old King thing, you have my loyalty against him because I want him very, *very* dead."

The Queen's expression cleared and she smiled like fresh, sweet meadow hay smells on a spring morning.

"That will be sufficient for me. Thank you, Demerara, and be welcome as a member of my court." She paused and nodded to my tonic. I took a huge sip to keep the peace. "You may now fairly be considered among us, take up various court positions, marry into the royal line, things like that."

How I managed not to spit half the tonic at her in alarm, I don't know. I gulped instead and spluttered for several seconds. Taz however seemed to be regaining his composure super quick now that he had a chance to laugh at me again. He even stood up under his own steam and gave me a wink.

"I'm going to fetch the last of my stuff to take back. I assume we're going straight back to Arcanium?"

The Queen nodded. "Yes, go find your belongings, and do say farewell to your sisters. You may find they're less than delighted to be in your debt, but such is life, so make the most of it while you have the opportunity. Demi and I will converse a while."

I froze. *What on earth can she want to chat to me about?*

I sipped my tonic super slow, hoping that would keep me looking busy. Taz gave us a both a doubtful look before fleeing the room and leaving me to my fate.

"Give me your wrist."

The command came out of nowhere, but the Queen wasn't using any compulsion this time. I bit down the urge to remind her that a please wasn't unheard of. I'd basically insulted her, shouted at her and called her a bad mother who was also unfit to be Queen. I'd apparently been given a free pass for that, but she was still my regent. She could still pulverise me.

I held out my bruised wrist. She swiped a thumb over the mark there and turned my arm wrist down, letting go so it dropped to my side.

"There will always be a mark there, once the bruising fades

naturally. I'm sor-, I a-ap-, I *apologise* for the necessity of causing you pain."

I blinked. The idea of having to say sorry was so alien to her that she physically struggled to get the words out.

"I apologise for everything I said in anger," I said much more easily.

The Queen smiled. "We'll say no more about it then. Every member of my court bears a symbol there, a mark of their loyalty. For your kindness and sacrifice to my son, I will allow you to choose your own mark."

I eyed the bruise, the choice coming instantly. "Leo, a tiny chameleon. Oh, can you make it change colours? No, that's silly."

Her laughter filled the air like bird-song in springtime rain.

"I can, if you wish it."

I nodded and held out my right arm with my eyes closed. I expected pain, or at least a touch, but I opened my eyes some moments later when nothing came.

"Oh." She smiled wider. "Were you expecting some kind of ritual? A chant perhaps, some drumming?"

Fae. I shook my head. *Bloody impossible.*

"There will be discomfort for a few days," she continued. "Nothing is without its payment, but at least you can forgo the blood. It looks as though you've had your share of that already."

I peered at the inside of my wrist as it started to prickle with a searing sort of burn, beaming in delight at the small curling lizard now tattooed on the skin amid the circular bruise. It looked exactly like Leo, and I could see the shimmer of it flickering different colours like the oil-slick effect of my hair did.

The Queen didn't seem to notice my attention had wandered.

"I'm very pleased we have your allegiance. I have worried

about Oakthorn for a long while now, not making many friends, content to sequester himself in Arcanium without reaching out into the wider realms for any kind of adventure. You've woken him up, and for that you have my gratitude."

I knew if there was ever a time to be blunt and step out of my place, it would probably be now.

"Old Tara said that Taz could be king whenever you retire, or whatever Faerie regents end up doing when they're not ruling anymore." I left it floating there.

The Queen raised an eyebrow. "Did she now?"

Ah, so the Queen knows who Old Tara is, which means Old Tara is important.

"Yes." I bit my lip. "I'm wondering though. If I've pledged my loyalty to you, insofar as defeating the Old King goes, does that mean I can't then pledge to someone else afterwards?"

"You're wishing to change sides already?"

"No, not that but, well-" I hesitated. "Look, Taz doesn't want to be king, so it's irrelevant I'm guessing. But just in case…"

I couldn't say it. The Queen let me hang there in mortification for a few seconds before shaking her head with a wry laugh.

"No, you are not sworn to my court, only a member who is pledging to be loyal to it against a common enemy. Should Oakthorn ever choose to embrace the future, rather than hide away from it, I would be relieved to know he has you at his side."

I would normally have brushed that off, blushed, insisted that 'no, we're just friends'. But we weren't just friends, not now, and we weren't exactly together either. I'd rather take Taz's friendship over all the fiery romance in the world, but now I sort of hoped I wouldn't have to choose one or the other.

"Old Tara also said I'm Taz's anchor." I pressed on. "She

said yours used to be Faerie but that you've not been bonding as much, and I'm Taz's, which I'm thinking is probably why he's been a total idiot about throwing himself into danger lately."

The Queen sighed. "She's right of course. I have neglected my duties in favour of my personal life. That allowed the Old King to leech his way in without my knowing. Losing my children, and regaining them, helped me realise that."

"Is there anything we can help you strengthen the bond with Faerie?" I asked.

"No, dear one. The last time I did that, Oakthorn was born."

"Oh." I hesitated. "We don't discuss it much, but he has mentioned that he never knew his father, or who he was. We have that in common."

The Queen raised one eyebrow, turning her head to stare at a vine creeping up the side of one wall.

"Once I took a walk in Faerie and lost myself in wonder. All the while I wandered, I wondered what missing wonder I was wandering for."

I let my brain skip through the fluff for a moment.

"So, he has no actual father? Or rather, he's born of Faerie and royalty?"

Her lips twitched. "I wandered. When I returned home, I had Oakthorn growing inside of me. I believe Faerie has its ways of balancing its own equilibrium."

So a load of cryptic crap to say basically Taz's "father" is Faerie itself. It took all my effort not to pull a face. *But then how does that solve the whole Queen's anchor needing to be Faerie again thing?*

It also wasn't exactly my business, something I should remember before the Queen got tired of the questions and eviscerated me despite my status as Taz's whatever-I-ended-up-being.

"Fair enough." I hesitated. "Maybe wander but ask for no more kids?"

The Queen chuckled, the room lightening several shades and flowers bursting into bloom around the walls at the mere sound.

"You haven't asked," she said after a moment of silence.

"Asked what?"

She frowned. "You haven't asked which gifts you sacrificed."

Oh.

I rubbed my forehead. "Um, I hadn't even thought to be honest. Which ones?"

The Queen cocked her head to one side, regarding me with confused curiosity.

"I took the premonition one only. You were willing to sacrifice them all, so I only took the one you would miss the least. But you honestly think less about your gifts than you do about people, don't you?"

"Um, yes?" That baffled me. "I mean, gifts are great, really great, but if I can't use them to help people, or save people, what's the point? Besides, I grew up surviving without them, so I know I can do it again if I have to. I guess that's the difference between Fae being given token gifts by family and fairies having to earn them."

Taz came in before the Queen could answer and found us frowning at each other like wary cats, not entirely sure we understood each other at all.

"All okay?" he asked.

I nodded. "Yeah, fine. Got everything you need?"

He reached an arm back to tap the bottom of a large rucksack.

"Everything including Leo. Ready to go?"

I wondered if I should tell him about his mother's supposed Virgin Mary status, or keep it for later.

He still hasn't told me what he and Diana were so secretive about. Perhaps I'll keep this as payback until he tells me the truth.

"Do I need to escort you?" the Queen asked.

Taz shook his head, Marthe's tonic clearly working wonders for him. I couldn't shake the weariness trying to close my eyelids, but I clenched my jaw against the yawn that threatened to break free.

Taz appeared beside me, one arm sweeping around my waist. At that point I barely even noticed, settling my head on his shoulder. For someone who had the ability to make me see red on a regular basis, he was astonishingly comfortable to slump against.

Over his shoulder, I could see Leo blinking out at me from beneath the flap of his rucksack. Reassured, I closed my eyes against the brief brush of air and opened them again as I struggled to stand upright.

I didn't even say goodbye to the Queen or Marthe.

The familiar walls of the Arcanium residents' floor gave me the last remnants of strength to take a step back. We'd succeeded, and I needed to report in before I crashed.

"Can you take Leo back to my room for me?" I asked. "I'll report in to Queenie. I should probably find Petra too and let her know she hasn't lost my pet."

Taz nodded but picked up my hand in his, holding it out so we could both see the bruise and tattoo the Queen had left on my wrist.

"She did this?" he asked, a low growl catching in his throat.

I nodded. "It's Leo, look. She also gave me premonitions with it, I think."

"You have premonitions?"

"No, I gave them up to bring you back. Can't miss what I've

never had, and could you imagine having to see things all the time? No thanks, once was enough for me."

I ignored the thought of how useful it could be, convinced I was better off without. Taz searched my face for several moments.

"I owe you," he said.

"No, you don't. I've lost count, but it's meant to be you and me, right?" I asked. He nodded, so I plunged in before I could back out. "Are you going to tell me what the whole Diana thing was about now?"

Taz grimaced then, and I had my answer before he even spoke.

"It's not- I can't- it's not something you need to worry about, okay?"

I folded my arms. "You keep telling me to trust you, but how can I when you're keeping secrets?"

He bit his lip. "I can't say, I'm sorry. Look, you go do what you need to do, and we'll talk later, okay? You should definitely go and have a chat with Petra first. I'll drop Leo off, then I'm going to the Ogle to make sure the mentors are okay, what with Emil gone. I still can't believe he would turn traitor."

I struggled with the urge to insist he tell me, but he and Emil had known each other and worked together for a while now. Taz and the other mentors would no doubt carry that betrayal for a long time.

I stiffened as he gave me a one-armed hug and watched him stride off in the direction of the bedrooms. I didn't hang around for him to come back, stepping into the lift and wondering where Petra would be. I needed someone encouraging before I faced Queenie and told her about Emil's betrayal.

CHAPTER NINETEEN
Demi Goes Savage and Taz Finds it Hilarious

I found Petra in the library, a pair of glasses nestled on top of her head and a furious frown stamped on her face. I almost backed out of approaching her, but she looked up and saw me.

"Demi!" She got up, her expression panicked. "I'm so sorry, I-"

I held up a hand. "He snuck into my bag and ended up in the realm with me. I had no idea and I was going to orb you, but I figured the waves might be being tracked by the enemy. There's a lot to unravel still, and people have turned traitor, but we got the assignment done."

Petra thumped into her seat with a tumbling sigh.

"Well, at least I haven't lost him I guess." She rubbed her forehead. "I was watching on the Ogle but it was a really skewed view. I don't know how they get those visuals but someone needs to do some serious upgrading. All I saw was a load of blue, you getting thrown about a fair bit, then flashes of purple, a giant blue animal and you were gone. The Old King went into a rage and started picking off people in the crowd, actually really frightening to watch. The rest of the court started fleeing and he vanished with Elvira. And Emil."

Her face fell at the mention of Emil, and I understood it. She, Taz and the other mentors had all worked closely with him. I took the seat next to her and explained everything, about Emil, the assignment, the whole issue that was Taz. Petra smirked at that.

"Well, he is very fond of you."

I snorted. "Yeah, so fond of me he's keeping secrets. I saw him and Diana Hemlock, sworn enemies, whispering together the night of the revel and he refuses to tell me what that was about."

Petra sat back in silence. I eyed her for a moment before getting nervous.

"What?"

"Taz came to me that night and asked my advice," she said. "Diana caught and goaded him after the revel to 'enjoy you' while you last. Apparently, she'd been tasked with killing you by the Old King. I think the plan was to make Taz go wild with grief and send him charging into the enemy lair. Of course, Queenie pre-empted that and turned it, and you, to our advantage. But Taz made his own deal with Diana - go to the King's court and get himself captured. In return, Diana can't directly or indirectly harm or attack you ever again."

I stood up, my chair flying back and crashing to the floor. Petra grinned.

"Come on." she laughed. "The boy has complete idiot brain whenever you're involved. You're like his biggest trigger."

I ignored that and set off toward the lift. When I slammed the grill back and stormed inside, Petra was right beside me. I looked at her as I pressed the button for the Ogle and she winked at me.

"I've missed most of your dramas one way or another," she said. "I sure as hell won't miss this one. Are you going to start zapping his bits off?"

I tapped my foot, but that wasn't enough to contain my fury so I stood clenching and unfurling my fists as the lift shot downwards.

Taz has the whole of Faerie and the royal line to think about, whether he likes it or not, and he's getting tricked into stupid deals to save me. And how difficult would it have been to say, 'hey, have a quick word with Petra, she has something to tell you' before we left?

Several people looked up in alarm as I threw the gate open the moment we reached the Ogle and burst out like an irate monster.

Taz stood in a circle of mentors near the first row of screens. The moment he saw me, his eyes lit up, but the elation froze halfway across his face when he recognised how furious I was. Mindless of everyone else around him, I stormed up and jabbed a finger against his chest, driving him backwards.

"Is it true? You made a deal with her to give yourself up to the Forgotten?"

I expected surprise or unease, but he sagged with relief and gave me a sheepish grin.

"Oh thank Faerie. It took you long enough! She passed me in the hall right after the revel and made some comment about you, so I compelled her to tell me what she meant. She was tasked with hurting you to drive me over the edge if Kainen failed to catch me, but I offered to let myself get captured once we got to the Old King's court if she never made another move to harm you ever again."

"What is wrong with you?!" I stared at him, fury rising. "Is that how Elvira found us on the road? Did you tell Diana where we'd be?"

I wasn't thinking straight because Taz couldn't have known where I'd tell Trevor to drop us, and nobody would have told Diana our side of the plan for her to know when my assignment would be. I kept my finger pressed against Taz's chest to the point of hurting my joints, anger eclipsing all else.

Taz ignored my questions.

"It worked surprisingly well, I thought. I said if Diana never made any move to harm or attack you ever again, I'd 'get myself captured', so that's exactly what I did. I don't think she liked the idea of having to destroy you though, because she seemed relieved that I was agreeing to it. Didn't even think it through or hesitate."

"Is that why you were yelling like an idiot in the middle of the castle when we found the tapestry?"

Taz nodded, his guilty grin widening. "Yeah. I told Ace and Milo before we left that they were to keep everyone safe and let me get taken, but it didn't work out so well. Didn't expect them to have actual iron weapons, should have thought of that. It's considered really unsporting, but then I guess this is a war."

"Why couldn't you just tell me?" I raged, aware of everyone hovering nearby whispering and not caring one bit. "I've been worrying for nothing that you- that she-."

I couldn't admit it, that deep down I'd been petrified that perhaps there was something going on between them. Mortification burned my cheeks, and anger felt so much better than embarrassment so I continued glaring at him. But my finger was hurting so I stopped prodding him and dropped my arms to my side with my fists clenched instead.

"Diana added a caveat to the deal," he explained, his smile widening as he noticed my fists. "I couldn't tell you about it. Luckily, she said I couldn't tell *you*, not I couldn't tell anyone, so I went straight to Petra. To be honest, all I was thinking about was making sure you were safe. It's been hell keeping it from you, knowing you don't trust me."

I skipped over all that, still raging after coming so close to losing him for good.

"You were almost killed."

He folded his arms, his grin becoming the most annoying, know-it-all smirk.

"And if I hadn't done what I did, you may have been actually killed by her somehow, so I've got no regrets."

So desperate to summon my gift and zap that stupid, superior look off his face, I did the only other thing I could think of to properly shock him without actually hurting him.

I lunged forward, grabbed his cheeks between both hands and pressed my mouth to his.

His lips were soft beneath the frozen shock, and he tasted like cherry bubble juice. I dropped my hands to his shoulders for support, meaning to step away, but his arms wound tight around my back and all thoughts of stopping evaporated.

Where did he learn to kiss like this? A brief flash of jealousy swept through me. *Who with?*

Then every part of me was fizzling over, the jitters in my limbs exhilarating for once instead of anxious, and hope leapt at how right it felt.

When Taz broke the kiss and pressed his forehead against mine, we stood for a moment, silent and breathless.

"We need to work on not keeping secrets," I murmured. "You can't go offering yourself up as a trade to save me all the time either, not when I keep having to rescue you afterwards, I'm exhausted."

Taz straightened up with a shaky laugh. "Agreed. We work best as a team, and it's always been you and me, but is this okay? I know you said you weren't ready for anything more at the revel, but I really want to kiss you again."

I gave him a look. "What do you mean, 'again'? It was me that kissed you. Both times."

He rolled his eyes to the sound of people nearby finally getting bored of the show and moving on with their lives.

"Technicality, but fine, can I go first this time then? Is that okay?"

I nodded, my insides *boinging* off in all directions. It was more than okay, that at least was one thing I could be completely sure of.

CHAPTER TWENTY
Battle Plans Are Made and Demi's Getting a Reputation

Sleep + shower + two helpings of breakfast from the Braunees = feeling awesome.

The morning after the battle, I walked from the canteen to the library with Taz, Ace and Milo, astonished that people kept smiling in passing or stopping to congratulate us on saving the princesses.

"News definitely gets around fast," I said. "It's mad that classes are just going on as normal."

Taz seemed content to go back to our normal routine, but occasionally he'd squeeze my hand or bump my shoulder. Each time, Ace and Milo would grin at each other which made me blush, and that was really starting to annoy me now.

I tried not to groan as Petra came trotting toward us, long dark hair flying in a braid that looked only half-plaited.

"Queenie's summoned you, Demi," she said.

I still hadn't had a chance to go up to Queenie and report in, but Taz and Petra had both reassured me last night that Petra would handle it for me.

"Trouble?" I asked.

Petra rolled her eyes. "Always, but nothing specific. I think she just wants to talk to you. If she offers you any more assignments though, feign illness or something, my nerves can't take it."

She was joking, but knowing Queenie another assignment was a high possibility.

As Petra disappeared down the corridor and Ace followed

Milo off toward the library, Taz started toward the lift. I followed, wondering with a surprising amount of amusement whether Queenie would refuse him entry to her office again.

"Is there anything you haven't mentioned?" Taz asked.

I gave him a look. "Anything *you* haven't mentioned?"

"No." He stuck his tongue out. "I'm an open book now. Come on, I said I'm sorry, and I knew if I told Petra about Diana, she'd tell you eventually."

I sighed. I'd already decided to let that go and renewed my efforts.

"Okay, that was unfair of me. I'm trying to think back about what I might have missed." I skipped over any mention of Emil being a traitor, knowing I'd have to confirm it for Queenie all the same. "All I know now is that the attack is coming soon, if the premonition is anything to go by. My bruise was still there in the vision, so it has to be coming."

We stepped out of the lift and strode down the hall toward Queenie's office. One of her doors stood open, but I hesitated to knock all the same. Taz didn't have the same manners and steamed straight in.

"Ah, I should have expected both of you." Queenie's lips twitched as I sidled in behind him. "Hardly possible to separate you nowadays. Still, I've been updated by Petra, the Queen, Ace, Milo, the Eastwick sisters and just about everyone involved who wanted to give their side of the story. They seemed to think that given your past precedent for rule-breaking, you'd be in some kind of trouble."

I blinked. "Oh. Am I?"

"No." She flicked a weary look at me. "The assignment itself was a success, but I hear we have a war to prepare for."

I nodded. "I don't know how they can get inside the walls this time, unless they're already here under glamours, but it's what I saw. The atrium was being attacked and it'll be soon, in days. The Queen gave me premonitions and that's what I saw."

Queenie pressed her fingers into a steeple, her elbows wedged on her desk as she held my gaze.

"Do you still have these premonitions?"

"No, I sacrificed them for him." I jerked my thumb in Taz's direction.

Queenie was silent for a long moment. "You're a very odd girl."

"Um, thanks?"

I could almost sense Taz beside me trying not to laugh, but didn't descend to giving him a sharp elbow to the ribs just yet.

Queenie stood in one sharp movement, making me jump. She gave me a withering look and swept out from behind the desk.

"I've called a meeting of all staff and trainees in the atrium," she announced. "Petra confirmed what you told her, but I wanted to hear the warning about the battle from you direct. I've also long suspected about Emil's treachery, and he knows many of Arcanium's secrets, but perhaps not all of them. We must decide our strategies and arrange for anyone who wishes to leave. I'll see you down there."

She vanished, no doubt using her translocation gift. Desire for payback leapt into my head and I took a step away from Taz, closing my eyes with a grin. I imagined the atrium forming itself around me, the tall red pillars and the marble walls, the reception desk. It was a big ask for a gift I'd only used a handful of times, if that, but I was feeling bold and this was my home. I could visualise every inch of each place I used daily.

The subtle brush of air suggested I'd achieved something at least, and I opened my eyes.

Several open mouths gawped at me, including Queenie's, as the atrium filled with buzzing crowd noise.

I tried to take a step and stumbled to my knees, the sweep of flu-like weakness swamping me.

Okay, maybe that was pushing it a bit.

I managed to stagger to my feet, breathing hard, and searched the faces until I found Ace and Milo trying to push through the crowd to get to me. I nodded to them but stayed where I was near the lifts to catch my breath. A minute later, Taz shot out of one, his cheeks flushed. When he caught sight of me, he gave me a furious look.

"Don't do that!" he muttered. "You're going to send me to an early grave."

I might have scowled at the mention of him dying, especially after yesterday, but I was too busy enjoying the sensation of being home safe and generally not under fire from Fae or Faerie or some other threat.

My devilish urge seemed determined to stick around, so I dropped a kiss on his cheek in front of everyone and ambled over to Ace and Milo with way more pretend strength than I actually had inside me. It only took a few steps before I was wobbling on unsteady legs and Taz was beside me with a huff and a wordless arm around my waist.

"So, what's the plan?" Ace asked.

I shrugged, hoping it would cover a shiver that wriggled through me. Taz flicked a glance up and down at my t-shirt and pulled his hoodie off, holding it out. I hesitated until he started physically trying to put it over my head.

"Dunno." I mumbled, pulling the hoodie over me and shrinking into its warmth. "I'm sure Queenie has one. We're prepping for a fight, but I don't know the actual strategies or anything. I'm quite happy being a minion trainee for a while."

Ace snorted. "Oh please. You've already got a reputation. Might as well own it."

"What reputation?"

He turned his head away, looking far too innocent for that revelation to be a good thing. I sought out Milo but he was already nose-deep in a book, and I wouldn't get out unscathed if I interrupted his reading for something as trivial as reassuring my ego.

"What reputation?" I muttered to Taz.

He put a finger to his lips and shushed me as Queenie climbed on top of the reception desk.

I eyed Call-Me-Henry, Head Receptionist and Stationery Organisation Director. Rumours said that he'd apparently once installed an item of stationery somewhere unpleasant on someone who had in fact dared call him Henry. I stuck to Sir whenever I had to speak to him and, given the arctic look he was giving Queenie's heels on the polished surface of his desk, I could easily believe the rumours were true.

"We are aware of a threat to Arcanium." Queenie's magnified voice reverberated around the atrium. "We have information that the Forgotten plan to invade, and soon. Provisions will be made for anyone that wants to leave. If you are in that number, please liaise with Avril about getting yourself home. For anyone that wishes to stay, we now need to organise a plan of defence."

"I say we lockdown, station patrols at the exits and wait them out!" Gnat called.

"Forever?" Petra asked. "They won't mind waiting, and they have intel on all the different routes in from traitors."

As the crowd descended into arguing groups, I groaned.

"They're going to do this all day, aren't they?" I asked.

Gnat and Petra were now in a frantic discussion. Avril was being overwhelmed with people wanting to get out while they still could. Queenie was trying to be heard above the din and

Call-Me-Henry was starting a frenzied count of the stationery being scattered across his desk by Queenie's heels.

As the Eastwick sisters strolled up to us, I noticed several of the mentees and younger FDPs were looking our way. It gave me an idea.

"Milo, can you make a list of every known entry or exit in the library, skip-ways and normal doors?" I asked.

He nodded. "Of course, I'm almost done with one actually."

"Good. We'll need to find people to go down and help you defend it. Ace? Can you go to the Braunees and find out how secure the canteen is? I know you used that way in during the last battle, but are there any more? After that, find a couple of people willing to be responsible for holding it and you can support Milo in the library."

I knew they'd want to be together and Ace shot me a grateful look. I ignored the faces that seemed to be turning toward us more and more now, my adrenalin beginning to pound as I looked at Taz.

"We need to find some way of getting the atrium protected, but also the despatch. I reckon they'll try coming through the quartz wall if they can."

Before he could answer, another voice piped up.

"We can help there."

I looked over my shoulder to see Trevor with what looked like the entire group of realm-skippers crowding behind him. It also meant most of the atrium was now focused on us. I didn't dare look in Queenie's direction.

The troll Governor stood beside Trevor and nodded his agreement.

"We can fling them back through the wall quick enough," he said. "But we might need some hands to help hold them while we move them. Perhaps we can use a holding location, trap them where we keep the old, broken rickshaws."

I nodded. "That would work great if you can please. Any volunteers to help up top?"

Beryl raised her hand. "That'll be us."

Before anyone could answer, Harvey Hutchinson appeared towering over the crowd, his hair a shock of bright purple.

"I will be wherever my beloved Beryl is." He pretended to swoon and blew her a kiss.

Taz snorted beside me, but I was too busy trying not to grin as Beryl went bright red and gave him the kind of gesture that I usually only saw from my sisters.

Realising that our collective group essentially had the whole atrium's attention, I decided now wasn't the time to be coy. I strode up to the reception desk, Taz hurrying along beside me as I faced down Call Me Henry.

"Henr- I mean Cal- Si- Look, could you please man the fort here? They will likely try the lift trick like last time, and we need to be ready, to try and keep the flow from getting further into the halls."

I waited for the stationery to start flying discus-style at my head.

Call-Me-Henry eyed me for a moment. "Of course. Leave it to me."

"It sounds like you have everything covered."

I flinched as the Queen appeared in the middle of the atrium. Sagar and Eldrich flanked either side of her, but when I caught Eldrich's eye, he gave me a tiny wink.

The Queen should have looked out of place with her regal blush-pink gown of velvet, belted with flowers carved from gold, but the atrium seemed to glow brighter from her mere presence.

As she glided toward us, everyone dropped in a massive

kneeling wave. I did the same, pulling Taz down beside me and ignoring his grumbling.

"We stand together in times of trouble." The Queen's words flew across the crowd like a full Aragorn-style battle cry. "We are strong, and the unity we hold between us will keep us resolute long after they have fractured and become memory. Now, is there anything I can do?"

I clamped a hand over Taz's mouth, pre-empting whatever he'd opened it to say. But the sight of the Queen did remind me of something I'd not thought of for a long time.

"There are paintings, portraits and mirrors all over Arcanium," I said, struggling to my feet. "Some of them are skip-ways, like the one outside Emil's office and the one on the second floor of the library. Is there any way to disable them, take them down or like at least cover them in case? Someone once told me they keep reappearing if they're taken down."

As Queenie moved to stand beside her sister, I couldn't see much family resemblance between them. I wondered if her appearance was a permanent glamour, but it wasn't my place to ask. Especially as she gave me one of her most unimpressed looks.

"I think we should be able to manage that," she said drily.

"What about a space for the injured if we can't reach the medical hall?" Marvin, the head healer, asked.

I'd never been to the medical hall, weird considering how many scrapes we'd been in since I started here, but I'd been most other places and knew exactly what would work.

"Use the study floor," I suggested. "There should be minimal danger there hopefully, and there's a skip-way in Avril's classroom that leads to the residents' hall, so you can use beds for emergencies." I faced the crowd and lifted my voice loud. "Anyone who's willing to let their room be used for emergency patients once the battle starts, put a circle on your door. Paint, pen, lipstick, whatever. Although, if you end up in mine please don't feed Leo, he's getting huge."

A smattering of laughter filled the hall.

As collective discussions started up, Taz nudged me with a broad grin.

"You asked about your reputation," he murmured in my ear. "I think several people are waiting for you to challenge my aunt for her job next."

I glared at him and gave him a rough shove, snorting with laughter when he almost fell over.

"What if people glamour?" someone asked. "Is there a way to block that in here? Otherwise, how will we know who to trust?"

Ace held up his arm, his finger plucking at a white rubber band around his wrist.

"What about these? We could get tons if there's time, they wouldn't figure that out as our way of identifying each other."

"I'm sure I can facilitate those," Call-Me-Henry said.

"We will take volunteers for each team." Queenie lifted her voice across the crowd as she regained control. "Individual teams will decide their own strategies. A warning alarm will be sounded should the invasion occur, so please be prepared."

Her gaze swept the atrium and the compulsion tingled right through my bones as she issued her final warning.

"Nothing that has been discussed here today, or that is being prepared for the upcoming attack, or anything that might help the Forgotten, or any enemy to Arcanium, is to be spoken of to outsiders, or shared with anyone outside our walls. Now, until the battle comes, you should all have training and tasks to be busy with."

The crowd dispersed toward the lifts like a puff of air into dust, revealing a face I didn't expect to see.

Xavio, my mentor from fairy classes when I was younger, strolled over like he was out for a Sunday walk. I noticed that he'd French-plaited his long grey beard for the occasion and had his hands shoved in the pockets of his khaki shorts.

Seeing him approaching, even Taz deserted me.

"Ah, Demi." Xavio stopped in front of me with a smile. "I knew you had it in you. Proud of you. I always had high hopes for you, my dear, more so than any other fairy I mentored."

"Um, thanks. We're not going to have a 'Luke, I'm your father' moment, are we?"

He frowned for a moment. "Oh, I see, movie trivia. No, I never had biological children, but I like to think of those I train as a big family. It's not your fairy side that makes you the person you are, who you're born to or your blood. It's what you've been through, how you've survived. Focus on who people are, not what they are or where they're from. If I've taught you that, then I've done okay."

I blinked back at him, trying to assess whether he was trying to tell me something important or just happened to be here and fancied hearing himself talk. With Xavio, either could be possible.

Without another word, he wandered off toward Call-Me-Henry, who seemed to be trying extra hard to look busy all of a sudden.

Taz reappeared and tugged on my hand as I was beginning to feel the waves of overwhelm lapping at me.

"It's going to be complete chaos, but I'll fight wherever you do, Sparky." He gave me a cheeky grin. "Until then, *Demolition Ducks* catch-up?"

I groaned. "Trust me I'd love to, but we have Beasts and Baronies class this afternoon."

His grin widened and he slid his hands into the front pocket of his hoodie, despite the fact I was still wearing it.

Mine now. I decided with a smile.

"I got my mother to get Queenie to let you off all your classes today," he announced. "*And* training with Petra, which you know is near impossible to avoid."

I laughed then, beyond relieved.

We should have been training all hours and preparing for the inevitable, but we'd had so little time to rest lately, the idea of not doing anything was beyond blissful.

"What, like a date?" I teased. "With popcorn and cherry bubble juice? Are you actually going to be a gentleman this time or are you still going to sulk when I do better duck impressions?"

Taz released the hoodie, along with any chance of him getting it back, and threw an arm around my shoulders as he guided me to the lift.

"Whatever you want, Sparky. Whatever you want."

CHAPTER TWENTY ONE
The Forgotten Return

Three days passed with everyone on high alert, but no sign of the Forgotten. I went to classes and tried to learn all I could without dwelling on the fact the topics taught had shifted to pure defence and attack practice. We were in training for the war without knowing when exactly it was coming.

I checked my wrist more often than not, trying to remember exactly what the bruising had looked like in my premonition, until Taz turned up with a thick bit of white ribbon. He tied it around my arm to hide the mark and my tattoo, which was itching like crazy.

"You're just obsessing over things you can't control," he'd said.

Everyone who had remained at Arcanium, the FDPs and most of the mentees, were put on patrol duty. I don't know how he managed it, by stropping most likely, but Taz wangled it so that we had to do patrols together like a buddy system. Whether he didn't trust me to go flitting off after adventure, or he just wanted any excuse to hang out with me, I was secretly glad.

As we kept watch on the despatch platform with the sky a dusky hue of blue through the glass ceiling above us, Taz held my hand on his knee, his fingers fidgeting with mine.

"I wish they'd attack already," he grumbled. "Waiting is the worst."

I grinned. "You're just obsessing over things you can't control. Come on, think about what you want to do after. Any life goals?"

He frowned, his expression turning furtive.

"I wanted to be a mentor, but now I'm not so sure. After getting thrown into FDP adventures with you, I don't think I'd like to be left behind all the time. It's weird, isn't it?"

"Hmm?" I eyed Cheryl stepping out of the lift.

"I never felt at home at my mother's court, but the moment I came here, it was like I belonged. This is home, but is it weird to find home so early in life, like where you want to stay forever?"

I shrugged. "I think home is more about the people than the place a lot of the time, but Arcanium is cool. Who wouldn't want to call it home?"

We both looked up as Cheryl flopped to sit down cross-legged on my other side.

"I'm here to relieve you of patrol," she said. "Also, Taz, Queenie wants to see you."

Taz stood up, looking down when I didn't move to join him.

"Go on, I won't do anything rash without you," I said.

At least, I won't go out of my way to do anything rash without you.

Taz frowned. "Okay, I'll come find you when I'm done. Or meet in the canteen?"

"Canteen sounds good." I nodded as my stomach growled at the mere thought of food.

He disappeared along the walkway and into the lift, leaving Cheryl and I sitting in silence.

"He certainly seems smitten." Cheryl broke the still air with a smile.

I blushed. "He's beyond protective. It'd be suffocating if he wasn't so sweet about it."

"I envy you sometimes," she said. "Famous as a mentee, known among most of the FDPs and tutors, dating the prince-"

"I dunno if we'd call it dating." I interrupted. "I mean I guess so, but we haven't put a label on it."

"-not-officially-dating the prince of Faerie then. But I reckon it's scary too. How do you do it?"

I blinked, unnerved. This was beginning to sound like one of those scenes in the thriller where the previously unassuming character starts talking all sinister and turns out to be the bad guy. I glanced at Cheryl, but she was staring off into the air in front of us.

"Do what?"

"Be yourself." She tugged at the hem of her sleeve with a heavy sigh. "You don't seem to care what anyone thinks about you, and you crash through everything but it somehow turns out okay every single time."

I pushed my hands in my lap, sliding my thumb back and forth over my fingertips. Unnerved at having to have this discussion, especially as we didn't know each other that well, I shrugged and let the whole truth tumble out.

"I grew up trying to avoid my sisters picking on me all the time. Then I struggled to make friends at school because nobody wanted to get on the wrong side of them, so I tried extra hard when I got here, I guess. I'm definitely nothing special, and I screw it up most of the time. But I have good friends, people I can rely on. Why all the questions?"

Cheryl's shoulders slumped. I thought for a moment she would change the subject or tell me not to pry, even though she was the one technically questioning me.

"Beryl got gifted when she was eight," she explained, her tone flat. "Meryl a while ago now. Beryl was always the outgoing fun sister. Meryl was always the kind-hearted one who people liked." She took a deep breath. "I was just the sister that accidentally got born as a boy."

She glanced at me and I shrugged with a hesitant smile.

I knew there were some people out there who had a problem with stuff like that, my sisters being among them. But Xavio, in all his bonkers philosophies had got one thing right – it was who the people were, not what they were or where they were from. And Cheryl was her own kind of awesome.

"Fair enough. What gift would you have wanted?" I asked.

She blinked, as if surprised I wasn't bombarding her with questions. Or worse.

"I'd love to be able to shift appearances at will. It's hard to keep holding my glamour until I'm where I need to be for real."

I bit my lip, trying not to worry for all the people who didn't have the option to glamour themselves into who they really were.

"Ah, you shouldn't have to hold a glamour, but I get it. Society can be so stupid. You're a great friend and that's what matters. I hope. I mean I hope we're friends, not that I hope you're a great one, because you are, but-"

Cheryl sighed, barely hearing me. "A memory gift would be great too, like being able to read something and it's just in there, that'd be cool. I wondered if Milo had something like that, he's so brainy."

"Milo is just bonkers about books," I laughed, relaxing when she joined in.

"And we are friends," she added. "All of us. Arcanium's the only place I've felt like I can maybe belong, where people accept me mostly for who I am. But I think you of all people understand that."

I nodded. Arcanium was my home, and Cheryl's. It was Ace's and Milo's. Taz's. But before I could tell her that, a buzzing noise filled the air.

Cheryl and I exchanged a look and scrambled to our feet as Queenie's face burst into ghostly grey clarity, magnified under the glass dome ceiling.

"BREACH IN THE ATRIUM, TO YOUR POSTS."

Down below, figures swarmed like an ant colony escaping a fire.

The Forgotten had arrived.

We'd discussed use of the lifts and the creation of extra sets of stairs, but although Cheryl was staying here to help the trolls, it might take me a while to get down to the atrium. Trolls started to appear and Trevor nodded to me through the massing crowd.

"Ready as we'll ever be," he said.

He'd changed his normal uniform of shirt and slacks for jogging bottoms and a t-shirt, and had a bandana tied around his forehead beneath his huge, batlike ears.

Other trolls had taken to putting war paint on their cheeks, and most of them were beaming in anticipation.

"I think you might actually have some fun here," I muttered.

Cheryl grinned, nervousness dancing in her eyes.

"It'll take you a long while to get the lift in this chaos," she said. "I've been given permission for what I'm about to do from Taz, so don't curse me or anything."

"What?"

I faced Cheryl just in time for her to land a savage shove against my shoulders. I shrieked and my arms flailed as I stumbled backwards, until there was nothing left to stumble on.

Air rushed past me, not the gentle brushing of realm-skipping but the utterly terrifying blast of freefalling from a great height. Shock stole any hope of screaming and I clenched my eyes shut.

Storeroom, lots of buckets and tubs. Old sofas. Yellowing walls. Floor under my feet.

I visualised the scene as best I could, panic clawing at my chest and stealing my breathing.

Solid ground slammed against the soles of my feet. The wind died away.

I staggered forward and opened my eyes as I slammed to my hands and knees.

The storeroom at the back of the atrium swarmed around me, and I breathed a sigh of relief.

What on earth was Cheryl thinking?! Taz gave her permission? Why? Who the hell does he think he is?

The shock and use of my translocation gift zapped at my energy, but I was buoyed up with enough indignant rage to make it irrelevant. I pulled my protection warding around me and threw open the storeroom door. The whole atrium was in chaos already, gifts flying back and forth while others fought in hand-to-hand combat or with weapons.

I ducked out of someone's way and dodged two women fighting. I vaguely recognised the FDP as someone who was almost always on assignment, but she looked like she was holding her own fine without any help.

One of the mentees, Teri, rushed past with two grown-up Fae chasing her. I glared at them and sent a bolt of energy through my warding to catch their shins, enough for the 'smacked sunburn' sensation. They started hopping in agony and Teri shot me a grateful glance as she threw up her own protection.

I twisted around as Taz came skidding out of one of the lifts. He surveyed the crowd, found me and charged. I barely got my warding parted for him in time.

"You know you could be someone glamouring as you and I just let you in?" I shouted over the din.

He hesitated. "Oh, true."

He pulled a rucksack off his back and dropped it to the floor, bending down to unzip the main pouch.

"Are you really Taz?" I asked, just in case. "The real original one?"

"Yeah, of course."

Phew. "Okay then. Wait, what are you doing?!"

I gawped in horror as he pulled a disgruntled Leo out of the rucksack. My anger gave me a prod and reminded me he'd also apparently told Cheryl she could push me off the despatch platform.

Taz gave me a sheepish grin as he handed Leo over. I settled him on my shoulder.

"What did you bring him into this for?" I glared at Taz. "And why in the name of Faerie did you tell Cheryl to push me off the despatch platform?"

Taz twisted and threw out a hand just in time to turn the strip of black marble on the floor to water as three Fae spotted us and charged.

Their screams filled the air around us as they sank into the water and Taz re-solidified the floor around their middles.

"Will that hurt them?" I asked.

He shook his head. "Not unless I start doing the same to their bones. Quick explanation. I went to speak to you in your room when you got captured by Douchebag of Darkness, but you weren't there."

"Obviously."

He gave me an impatient frown. "I went in anyway and Leo must have thought I was doing something dodgy because he grew."

Didn't I know it. I shifted Leo's hefty bulk on my shoulder, his tail clenching around my ribs to keep him balanced.

"Yeah, he's put on a few pounds the last couple of months."

Taz shook his head. "No, I mean he literally expanded in front of my eyes, from normal Leo to huge mutant Leo in a few seconds. I panicked and shut the door, but it gave me the idea for transforming when we were in the Old King's court. If Leo can do that, I figured he'd want to protect you now, like I do."

"And the whole pushing me off the platform?"

Taz grinned. "We mentioned not knowing what would happen a few days ago, didn't we, before leaving for the realm. So I asked Queenie. Apparently, if you fall you bounce, kind of like an invisible bungee. I figured people should know in case it came in handy, so I told Ace, Cheryl, Petra, anyone I could think of. Most of them knew already to be honest."

"I don't know if to kiss you or strangle you," I muttered.

Taz might have said something smart, for once in his life, but the lift to the human world was yawning open and more Fae were spilling out. I recognised several of them now, a wave of fury hitting me in the chest. Given Taz's sudden scowl, he felt exactly the same.

A flash of yellow light tore the atrium in two for a second, and I saw the vision the Queen had given me made real.

Kainen and Diana were keeping back, but Elvira, Alannah and Emil charged forward without hesitating, swiping their gifts at people as they passed. Behind Elvira, two familiar scaled beasts prowled, snapping their enormous jaws.

"Oh great, she's brought the kids," I groaned.

I didn't have fond memories of the last time we'd met Luchia and Draven, the two Oricadae that Elvira kept as pets. They darted straight after a girl who looked vaguely familiar and seemed to be heading straight for us.

"Um, little help here!" the girl shouted.

I recognised her then as Sarah, Ace's little sister. Given that she'd once thrown an apple at Draven's head during the last battle, I kind of understood their instant vendetta, but she was one of ours.

Horrified that they'd have invited families from outside into this mess, I summoned my energy.

Before I could aim for the Oricadae, Leo's tail disappeared from my middle and he dropped to the ground.

"Wait, no!" I screeched.

He shuddered and made a disagreeable grumbling noise, his limbs lengthening and his tail elongating. I stepped out of the way, Taz right beside me as Leo grew until he was built like a hippo and twice the size.

With a feral roar, Leo shook the very foundations of the atrium. Several people fighting hesitated and turned to look. Luchia and Draven snapped their heads up, wary eyes fixing on him. They took flight on their leathery wings, but Leo twisted and lashed his tail upward with lethal precision, pulling one back down to the ground.

"He'll be fine," Taz said, taking my hand. "The grown-ups are holding things here, but look."

He pointed to one of the internal lifts where Diana and Kainen were disappearing. Behind them, I saw the Queen unleash a swarm of butterflies at the Old King, turning them to iron shards that pierced his protection. She had things here, but I had my own score to settle and turned toward the lift Kainen and Diana had entered.

"Payback?" I asked.

Taz's eyes glinted. In that moment, I could see every particle of his Fae blood glowing with eagerness.

"Payback."

CHAPTER TWENTY TWO
Demi's Kidnapping is Avenged and Nobody Mess With Petra

We zigzagged through the hordes fighting, Taz holding our warding with me pushing ahead to shove people out of our way.

As we tumbled into a waiting lift, he jabbed a complicated series of buttons. I could feel the hum of his warding around us, the bars of the lift pressing against it as we shuttled upward.

"Queenie put in a weaving that makes the lift take you to the last floor it stopped on," he said. "Need to know basis only for royal safety. Whatever happens from now on, don't do anything dangerous."

I flicked a warning glare at him. "Likewise."

The lift stopped on the library floor and I had the grill open before he could reply. A couple of people had clearly spilled in from elsewhere, battling FDPs along the circular platform. I eyed their wrists of those I didn't recognise but couldn't see the white band that all Arcanium people were wearing.

A girl burst out from behind one of the statues as we dodged the fighting, her attack bouncing our protection so savagely that we rebounded into the wall. Taz's hand slithered from mine and I could feel his protection lift away from me. He reached out, but the girl turned quicker and sent a hand flying out toward me.

A shockwave pulsed through my chest. I gasped, but the air didn't travel into my lungs like it should have done. Focused on me, no doubt thinking me the weaker one, the girl didn't notice Taz rush her bodily from the side.

She crashed against the nearest bookcase stack and all the fight left her as she crumpled, her head in her hands.

"Is she-" I huffed, unable to draw a breath. "Okay?"

Taz scowled at me. "Who cares? I know her, she has an energy drain gift. You'll feel cruddy for a while yet so let me take the lead in here."

I straightened up, my cheeks flushing from the effort. Sweat beaded on my forehead but Taz reclaimed my hand, even though it was now disgustingly clammy.

Unable to waste energy on disagreeing with him, I followed him instead. As we strode toward the main desk, I felt him firm the warding secure around us.

"I told you, not the collectables!" Milo's shrillest screech filled the air.

My head was drooping from exertion, but I lifted it in time to see him holding protection over the main desk with both hands raised and waving in irate alarm, while Ace threw dusty old books frisbee-style with lethal accuracy at a group of Fae.

Kainen stood at the head of the opposing group, Diana close beside him with Alannah and Jack Harmony, the boy who had tried to curse me with my energy gift at Diana's request.

They turned to face us, a satisfied grin spreading across Kainen's face. Perhaps he saw how out of breath I was, or the fact that we were on our own. Perhaps he was simply having fun.

Diana however looked on edge at the sight of us, and I guessed it was because she would be powerless to attack me if she had to, if her deal she'd made with Taz held firm.

"My issue with you is personal, Kainen." Taz's voice carried strong across the library.

Ace had stopped throwing books. Milo's arms stilled in the air mid-wave.

Kainen cocked his head. "Yeah? What issue do we have then, other than my family's attempt to trap you for the wider Fae war?”

“You kidnapped my girlfriend. You tried to ruin our relationship. Oh, yeah, and the family stuff I guess. You’ve dishonoured me and mine.”

“Now is not the time to start sounding like a cheesy mafia film,” I muttered, more to hide how flustered I was by the whole ‘my girlfriend’ thing.

In front of everyone, Taz turned his head and kissed me, a quick brush of his lips over mine. I blinked in surprise.

Was that some kind of Fae claim or something? Or is he thinking it might be the last?

“When I let you go and step away, put your warding up,” he said, keeping his voice low.

I nodded. His hand slithered away from mine before I could find my connection. I sought for it, sluggish from whatever the girl in the hall had hit me with. As Taz walked forward, I managed to get enough energy tingling through me and raised a hand to support a warding.

Something slammed into my side, jolting me to the ground. My connection fractured. Even as I scrambled to claw it back, I was defenceless and at the mercy of the cruel laughter surrounding me.

The tightness in my chest eased enough for me to take a loud rattling breath, and I guessed the energy drain the random girl put on me had worn off.

I clambered to my feet on shaking limbs and found my connection, throwing up a weak warding.

“You can stop the charade now, Taz,” Diana said. “Tormenting the poor girl is fun, but there’s no need for it any longer.”

Taz walked right up to her, closer than I’d ever want to see him to anyone now. He was almost chest to chest with her. I gasped, a tiny, pathetic breath, as he turned back and stepped alongside her.

My insides twisted and anxiety began to knead its itching claws into my skin. Diana put a hand on his shoulder, leaning in, her victorious grin for me alone.

No, no no no. I came one step short of shaking my head.

A smile spread across Taz's face, one that mirrored Diana's, confident, gleeful. Cruel.

"Ah, Dem, did you really think this was real?" he asked, speaking words I couldn't comprehend. "I know Queenie picked you as her pet project, but I thought you'd have some inkling by now that this was all too good to be true?"

I straightened up, my adrenalin returning some of my strength to me. I eyed Ace and Milo, both safe and still behind the main desk and looking concerned.

They don't understand it either.

When I didn't answer, Taz shook his head with a barking laugh.

"How could you possibly think I'd like someone like you, when I could have anyone? I'll admit, the deception has been fun, but honestly, the only purpose behind my little 'friendship' with you was self-interest. I'm the prince of Faerie, not some doe-eyed fairy boy. And one day soon, I'll be king."

"What?" I couldn't control my own horror.

This has to be some kind of trick. He's going to slip the act in a minute and give me some sign of what he's playing at.

Taz wound his arm around Diana's shoulders, the action like a knife to my gut. I tried not to react but nobody could have missed me wincing.

"We knew Queenie was picking some idiot to send on missions, fodder for spying on Alannah in the first assignment, then the Old King's visit in the second. I thought it would be half a challenge, but you were depressingly easy to befriend, to seduce."

I had to believe that this was still some kind of ruse he was going through with, a double bluff.

This has to be a trick still, it has to be. Doesn't it? But he can't lie.

The enormity of it crept in like a wrecking ball. Demi Darcy, outcasted by her sisters, nobody's first choice for a friend at school or fairy classes. Nobody had made any effort to be as kind to me as Taz had been.

And I'm the world's biggest idiot who fell for it, just like I did with Jack and Kainen.

I tried to fight the doubt, but the reality was too depressingly obvious, unfolding right in front of me.

I wanted to run back to the lift, but I didn't trust my legs to keep moving. There was still a battle going on and, while this would likely ruin my ability to trust anyone again ever, I couldn't let the others down. The Queen, Queenie, the Eastwick sisters, Ace and Milo, at least one of them couldn't be aware of this.

I glanced over to the reception desk just in time to see Ace and Milo vanish.

Milo's getting Ace out to safety.

I should have been relieved, but the loneliness stuck in me like lie shards.

I swallowed against the sour taste in my mouth.

Sour. Like earwax or bitter lemons. Where have I tasted this before?

My mind swam back to a hall of dark marble, a cage of smoky bars.

The effect of the energy drain had vanished like magic when Taz turned traitor. I glanced down at my wrist and pulled aside the ribbon Taz had tied there.

Kainen didn't know I'd been attacked by that girl, so he wouldn't have known to create my weariness when casting his visions either. And he didn't know about my bruise, so it was possible…

The bruise was gone and so was the Leo tattoo, the skin on my wrist whole and unmarked. Kainen hadn't seen me with it and clearly hadn't managed to dredge that little detail up from whatever part of my mind he was trying to manipulate. He must have attacked me with his nightmare mind control when I was knocked over.

The thieving little bastard.

My connection flared near my elbow, rippling through me. Righteous anger felt so much better than heartache, so powered by sheer relief that I managed to smile.

"You know, Kainen, if you really aren't like your family, why are you fighting for them?"

He'd been quiet during the performance, letting Taz do the talking, but I could see a subtle pinch around his eyes now, as if he were concentrating very hard.

"What?"

"I mean, if you really want to be the future Mage of Nightmares, like you said before, why are you fighting against the winning side?"

Kainen was quiet for a moment. When he responded, his laugh sounded strained.

"Oh, Demi, don't turn this on me. I know his betrayal hurts, but you had your chance to assist me. You refused. You could have been one of us."

Oh yeah, sure, like the elite Fae would accept a 'dirty-blooded fairy' as one of them.

I visualised the strongest warding I could muster, in case it did any good at all, then forced my legs to take a step toward him. And another.

"Oh please," I scoffed. "If Taz was only pretending to be friends with me, why did he almost die for me? Dedication to the cause? Even your psycho sister wouldn't go that far, would she?"

Diana snarled at the taunt but I noticed Taz was suspiciously expressionless now that Kainen wasn't focused on him.

I would have to drop my protection to do what I had to do next, but I only needed a moment. I saw the wave of glittering smoke in the air flying toward me and let go of my warding.

I visualised our favourite reading nook nearby, nestled between bookcases. In moments I built the image of it around me and air brushed my face. I held my breath as I opened my eyes. It would either be the bookshelf I saw, which meant I was free, or another manipulation of Kainen's design.

Familiar books stared back at me. I sagged and dragged a warding back around me. Once protected, I peered through the shelves. Jack Harmony held a struggling Taz with his arms pinned behind his back while Diana held her golden penknife to his throat. Kainen was twisting left and right, his face a tantalising picture of horror.

He didn't know I could translocate either.

I inched my hand through the gap and sent my energy gift crackling across the library. The jolt hit Kainen square in the chest and he grunted in pain. No warning shot for him, but I wouldn't leave any lasting damage.

Guilt trickled in as he dropped to his knees, and from nowhere I remembered a huge bag of Skittles and disappointment in his tone, as well as the sheer anguish on his face back in the Old King's dungeon.

It's not what they are, but who they are. Xavio's words

danced back to me. *Is he really a complete monster, or is there something redeemable in there? If I keep attacking, what am I?*

"What's going on here?" Alannah asked. "Where did she go?"

I was seriously outnumbered and Taz was in trouble, so I had to make this work.

"Darcy's got a translocation power, I saw her materialise earlier in the atrium," Diana said. "She zapped Kainen just now, so she can't be far, unless she's already translocated somewhere else."

That was what I should do, I knew that. Translocate into the lift, go for help. But I wouldn't leave Taz here on his own.

"Oh, Demi," Alannah sang. "Come out, come out."

A wave of yearning occurred to me, like a thought someone else had put in my head because I'd heard them but wasn't really paying attention. I ignored her attempt at what I assumed was a sloppy compulsion.

When I didn't reappear, she glowered and took a deep breath like the big bad wolf in front of a straw house. She breathed out in one long stream, but it wasn't just air. Small, round items like nuts or big seeds shot from her lips, pinging and plinking against various surfaces. One almost struck Taz in the face.

Okay, wow. Where does she keep them, like does she just kind of pop them in ready, or have to swallow them? Eww, does she have to generate them like eggs and reverse-lay?

I almost missed someone else stepping out of the lift, but she was hard to mistake.

In a bright blue strappy dress with a flowery white t-shirt on underneath, Petra looked fit for a poetry reading.

Without a word, she raised a hand.

I watched for several moments, until Alannah started to cough, her eyes going wide. For a moment, I thought Petra was long-distance choking her, but then Alannah's nose began to bleed.

Not bleed… sprout.

A small green shoot edged its way out of Alannah's nostril and she opened her mouth to gasp for air. A second one curled out of her nose, growing fast. I watched, morbidly fascinated, and decided not to get on Petra's wrong side in training any more just in case.

"I've wanted to try that for ages." Petra's voice was a soft, taunting song. "Taz, I'm assuming if you're here then Demi's somewhere nearby?"

I didn't see him nod or hear him speak, but with Alannah occupied, it gave me an idea.

"Do you think the Old King would have favoured your family if you had blood like mine?" I asked Kainen.

I threw my voice to a different location with each sentence, upping the confusion.

"Of course not.
You didn't earn your fortune, you inherited it.
You once told me you wanted to earn your title separate from your father's successes.
Do it.
Join us and earn your place.
Or take your sister and run away if you must, but don't bother fighting against us.
We learned how to win the hard way and we're so much stronger for it."

Kainen stood still for several moments, his brow furrowed as he looked left and right, still seeking me out.

I bit my lip, hesitating as Taz managed to get a leg around Jack's and pull him to his knees. The two of them toppled to the ground, grappling as Taz tried to roll free enough to protect himself.

"Diana, I know you can't attack or harm me," I called out. "If you want, you can come looking for me though, be brave. Otherwise, I'm going to continue giving your brother reasons to leave."

Diana scowled, fists clenching but she stayed put. Kainen gave her an incredulous look.

She hasn't told him.

I grinned. "She didn't see fit to tell you that, Kainen? She made a silly deal with Taz to make the task of killing me that was given to her easier, and it backfired. She can never harm me now. This is the kind of effort my side learns the hard way, and that's what will always make us the winners."

I paused, exhausted from the sheer concentration it took to throw my voice around.

Alannah was still struggling against Petra's hold despite having to huff breaths through her mouth. Even though I had to focus on Kainen, I wondered if the shoots up her nose could be removed after, or maybe at least pruned a bit.

"What do you suggest?" Kainen asked.

I shrugged, although nobody could see me. "Fight alongside us. If you can't bring yourself to do that then walk away, but if you stand against us, we'll continue tearing you down."

Taz managed to land a savage kick to Jack's gut, winding him enough to get free. He threw up a hand to no doubt cast a protection around himself, a sure sign he was exhausted or in pain. Or both.

"Demi, where are you," he shouted. It wasn't a question, or a compulsion. It was a frantic command powered by anxiety.

"Safe." I forgot to throw my voice. "You stay there."

Of course, Taz ignored me. Hearing where I was, he started toward me. With my hiding place outed, I reinforced my own warding and emerged, eyes only for Kainen as I gave him a dismissive look.

. "People are possibly dying while you're dithering. What's your choice?"

Kainen looked me up and down for several long moments, long enough for Taz to reach me.

"Let me in," he hissed.

I nodded, parting my warding just for him and reaching out a hand. He grabbed it and I pulled him in, sealing the protection around us both.

"We'll meet again sometime, Demi," Kainen announced. "I'm not sure yet in what capacity."

I wasn't sure yet what he was going on about, but he turned on his heel and strode toward the stairs leading down to the second floor without a single glance back.

Diana stared after him, her mouth open, then surveyed the group. Alannah's narrowed eyes beamed hostile threats along the lines of 'don't even think about it', and Jack Harmony was still clutching his gut and groaning.

With a venomous look at me, Diana left her companions behind and followed her brother. I sagged with a weary groan as Taz slung an arm around my shoulders.

"I thought you'd believed him there for a second," he said.

"For a second, so did I."

I almost burst into tears when someone else shot into the library, tumbling out of the lift in a tangle of limbs.

"The atrium is overwhelmed," Cheryl panted.

She had Hutch Hutchinson with her, and even with everything going on, I noticed the subtle link of his little finger curled around hers. Then Ace and Milo appeared behind her and my heart lifted that final amount.

They didn't abandon me, they went for help.

"Are the trolls okay?" I asked.

Cheryl grimaced. "Er, yeah. Let's just say, I'm glad they're on our side. We were only getting in their way in the end, so we went down to the atrium to help there, but the Forgotten are swarming like flies."

I noticed Jack getting to his feet, but Taz turned a nearby metal trolley to liquid. As it washed over Jack's legs, he turned it back to a metal plinth, sealing Jack's feet inside it.

I managed to stop myself saying that he was lucky it didn't have books on it or Milo would have slaughtered him.

"You think these little tricks mean you can win?" Jack sneered despite being breathless. "The other Fae will destroy you."

I loved my energy gift now, but the way he'd tricked me so easily into warming to him and falling for it still rankled. He froze as I left Taz's side and walked up toward him. I kept a dome of my protection around me, just in case, but weakened it enough so that I could reach through and touch him.

The Queen welcomed me as one of her court. At least if this doesn't work, it might still scare some sense into him.

I leaned down and pressed a featherlight kiss to his forehead, like he had once done to me. He cringed away but the damage was done, and I promised myself I'd never wield my power in anger or vengeance ever again. Just this once.

"I give you the gift of guilt for every mean deed you have done or ever will do," I whispered.

As I stepped back, Jack's eyes widened. Seconds later, he pressed his hands to his forehead.

"What? What is this? Oh orbs alive…" he murmured.

I grinned. *Okay, sounds like I can gift people. Officially court Fae. Cool.*

"I'll keep watch in here with Ace and Milo," Petra offered. "Cheryl, Hutch, you can hang around and help."

"Thanks, all of you." I gave them a weak smile and set off toward the lift.

I didn't even look back or hesitate to see if Taz was following, knowing he wouldn't be leaving my side.

The lift was waiting for us and I tapped the button for the atrium while Taz closed the grill. As the lift shuttled downwards, I wondered if I was in for some kind of telling off, given his folded arms and glowering face.

"I suppose you had to kiss him for that," he grumbled.

A huge splash of something scarily more than 'like' jolted through me, and I grinned. We were about to go into an even worse situation in the atrium than we'd faced in the library. We had no guarantees, but there was one thing I could be sure of. I didn't want any regrets. I turned to face Taz and grabbed his arm.

"Yeah, but never like this."

I pulled him against me and pressed my mouth to his, not bothering with coy or hesitant. Taz froze for a second before his arms wound around me, clutching me tight. I didn't care that I looked a mess, or that his hands drifted down to rest in my back pockets so he could pull me closer. All I knew in those short moments was the adrenalin pounding through my veins and the intoxicating feel of him pressed up close.

The lift stopped and I forced myself to pull back. Taz grinned, his mouth all smiley and his eyes hazy like he was drunk on *Beast*. He grabbed my hand and hauled the grill open.

"Best girlfriend ever."

He yanked me out into the mayhem before I could pretend to

be indignant that this was the second time he'd defined our relationship without asking me first.

CHAPTER TWENTY THREE
A Fleeting Meeting and an Unwanted Gift

We threw out a joint warding to protect us, but the crowd was near impossible to push through. Gifts and fighting exploded around us, and a surprising amount of random snakes were hissing in self-defence as people stampeded past them.

"Watch the snakes!" I yelled, like an idiot.

"What do you think I'm trying to do?!" Taz shot back, stepping high over one.

"Well do better, you almost stepped on that one."

"Do better!? It almost bit me!"

Near the reception desk, two Oricadae bodies were flat on the floor, not moving. I bit my lip, searching around and finding Leo, still enormous enough to part the crowd wherever he went. I gasped as he leaned his head down and picked up a young man by the back of the shirt with his teeth. Beside him, Marvin was navigating a large pallet cart with people either sitting or lying on it in various states of injury.

"Look." Taz nudged me and pointed to a group near the far wall. "They're protecting him."

The group of mentees, my classmates and people I'd barely spoken to along with those I only nodded hi to in passing, were all focused on Leo, keeping a huge warding over him as he helped Marvin collect the injured. I remembered what Cheryl had said to me earlier about finally belonging and pride filled my heart with determination.

This is my home. Leo's home. Taz's home. We defend it with whatever we've got.

I saw three Fae ganged up in a fight against Avril, who was

holding them back with a fearsome display of water and ice, but she was outnumbered and looked exhausted.

"I can thin Avril's enemy," I squinted. "Can you take out that pillar, turn it into air or something so I can get a clear shot?"

Taz flicked a finger and turned the pillar to a waterfall. Summoning my energy gift, I sent a bolt through the water stream. It hit one of the Fae in the hip, and he convulsed a couple of times before dropping to the floor in a foetal crouch.

"Oh, crud, do you think I've electrocuted him?"

Taz shrugged. "Does it matter? Oh, no look, he's moving. Do the other one. She should be able to manage the last."

I did as he suggested, although the guilt flared up inside me when I saw the man fall. Avril glanced over her shoulder, and a strain of gratitude passed over her face before she wheeled herself back into the fray and renewed her attack.

A subtle chill rippled against my left leg, enough to draw my attention down. I flinched but the dark eyes that blinked back up at me had no malice in them amid the chilly icicle fur. As far as I knew, we didn't have any frost cats at Arcanium after the Forgotten had stolen them, yet here one was. The subtle tinkling of the fur was lost in the roar of the battle, but I could see a small patch of its tail missing, identical to the frost cat we'd freed a while back at Gallows Oak.

If I needed any more confirmation, I didn't have to look far. Taz pulled me out of the way as a woman with a bright blue bandana tied around her head ran past, roaring loud enough to rival even the most feral of beasts. I recognised her as Mrs Paget, team leader of the housekeepers at Gallows Oak, with what looked like dinner knives glinting in her hand.

"She's not going to-" I froze as she plucked one knife with her free hand and threw. "She is going to. Wow, look at that accuracy!"

The frost cat darted after her with a snarl, bowling over a man who dared to try and bring her down.

"Dem, concentrate on us for a second, yeah?" Taz shouted.

I made a mental note to find out how Gallows Oak was doing and turned to see Elvira emerging from the crowd. She loomed in front of us with a long, thin blade in one hand, and a collection of thin vials clinking in her fingers. She'd tried to use potions on us before, but I could feel Taz's protection pulsing alongside mine.

I flicked a glance at Taz in time to see his expression change, from wide-eyed, watchful wariness to a twist of pure fury.

"You," he hissed, his voice almost lost in the chaos.

Emil stepped out from behind Elvira, passing her to approach us. I sent out a warning jolt of energy, singeing the toes of his boots until smoke curled up from them. He stopped.

"Stand aside," he said. "Or I will hurt you."

"Don't reason with them!" Elvira growled.

I flicked another warning shot toward her hand, catching one of the vials. A red one exploded, sending a thick plume of russet dust spiralling into the air. Elvira waved it away but her face was contorted, as if she was having to fight off some effect.

"Why are you doing this?" I asked.

Emil smiled, a wicked gleam crossing his lips that I hadn't seen before. I was used to the idea of Fae being manipulative, wearing masks to hide their real selves. But I'd never imagined Emil being one of them.

"I am bound to protect my king," he said. "When all is as it should be, I will serve alongside him."

Elvira stiffened at the mention of 'alongside' rather than beneath. But apparently the shocks of the day were destined to keep on rolling.

"Oh, I wouldn't count on that."

I almost passed out as Xavio popped up, tapping both hands on Emil's shoulders with a grin as if they were having a matey chat in the street. Emil whirled around but Xavio was already twiddling his fingers in the air.

Elvira froze, a strangled scream contorting her face. A loud pop filled the air, attracting the attention of several others battling nearby. I stared in morbidly delighted horror.

Where Elvira had been standing, all decked out in her fancy white suit, there was now a large white chicken.

"That's for threatening my pupil," Xavio said cheerfully. "It will wear off eventually, but every time you step foot in Arcanium from now until your dying day, you will revert to your chicken form. Now, Emil. We need to have a chat about your priorities."

The force of Emil's invisible attack exploded so violently that it pushed against mine and Taz's warding. Elvira went flying across the atrium, her high-pitched squawking sounding out over the entire clash of the battle.

Xavio withstood the onslaught and flicked his hand out. A whip of flames lashed through the air, coming within inches of Emil's face.

"He must have lost his warding," Taz murmured, transfixed.

Emil grimaced and raised one hand high, the other one sending out a wave of dirt. The earth domed, marking out Xavio's protection. Emil dropped his hand and summoned a crossbow from thin air.

"No!" I screamed.

Part of Xavio's warding became clear, his face just visible surrounded by the soil bubble. The loud twang of the crossbow caught me like a string had been snapped in my chest along with it. The arrow sailed through the air, straight toward Xavio's warding.

I started forward but Taz was right there holding me back, clinging on with all his might as I fought him. I don't think either of us had any protection of our own at that point, but I didn't care.

Xavio's expression froze. He blinked and looked down at the arrow now floating in mid-air through the dirt covering his protection. A scream tore from me, and even Emil looked unnerved at what he'd just done. Perhaps he hadn't meant to hit Xavio, just pierce the warding, but then what was his plan if not to kill in the name of his chosen king and queen?

Taz grunted as I elbowed him in the gut. He grappled to hold me but I slithered free. I didn't care that Emil had turned to me next, or that Taz was throwing a protection over me and himself, splitting his ability in two.

I burst through the dirt falling like muddy snowflakes. Xavio dropped to his knees, so I joined him on the floor.

"Don't fret, Demi," he said, his voice laboured. A vicious wheezing escaped with the bubbling blood around his chest wound. "Don't bother taking out the arrow until I'm done either."

"We can fix you!"

"No, dear one, you can't. Even I can tell his arrows are tipped with poison. He always meant to kill. Be careful."

I couldn't help it. Even as I steadied him to the floor and laid him on his back, I glanced back for Taz. He stood strong and determined, not a shred of hesitation as he faced his old mentor.

"Demi." Xavio closed his eyes. "Don't carry my death with you. I'll be becoming part of Faerie, and there is no higher honour than to return to that which made you."

I wiped at the tears streaming down my cheeks with a savage hand and sniffed.

"I'm sorry if I-"

What could I say?

Sorry I didn't make more of an effort to get to know you?

Sorry I have absolutely no idea if you even have any family who'll miss you?

Sorry I couldn't save you?

He patted my hand then with cold, shaking fingers, as if he knew.

"I pass to you my natural gift, in the hope it'll lighten your life as it has lightened mine. It's not what we get in life, but what we *give* to those who deserve it, and even more to those who don't."

His breath rasped as he beckoned me closer. When I leaned forward an inch, he lifted his hand to my shoulder with a wince and pulled me down. I froze as he pressed a ragged kiss to my forehead, fleeting as his hand fell onto his chest and I reeled back.

"I gift you my natural gift," he confirmed. "Use it well."

I expected something to drift out of him and into me at that point, but there was no great moment of passing, no shiver or tingle. I wiped my eyes with my sleeve, looking around for someone, anyone that might help save him. Legs dashed back and forth, feet kicking inert bodies nearby, unconscious or dead I couldn't even tell.

"Let me go, Demi," Xavio murmured. "Be brave, but don't worry for me. Faerie's calling."

I sniffed loudly. "Tell it I say hi then."

"Her." Xavio said with a smile. "And she's already very fond of you."

He managed to hum a few bars of *Vivaldi's Winter* before his head lolled. I wish I could say I felt the life leave him, or saw his soul sail to be at peace with Faerie, but it was all I could do to let go of his hand.

Something big pushed against me, but it was a gentle nudge. I looked up, blinking through the blur of grief, to see scales. "Leo." I held up my hands to him.

He made a soft crooning noise and passed his mouth over Xavio's chest. I hoped as I never had before in that moment, but Leo picked up Xavio's body with his teeth and carried him over to Marvin's cart. There were other bodies there too, whether unconscious or dead I couldn't tell.

As I watched the first person who had taken a proper interest in me get wheeled away, I found the strength to stand. The anger prickled like white hot pins. If being tattooed over your whole body at once was possible, I imagined it felt something like this. Only the heavy weight hanging in the pit of my gut remained motionless. The pain cleaved through my emotions, hardening me, giving me the clarity to focus and drawing up a wave of retribution from deep inside me.

Taz was breaking down the ground around Emil quicker than Emil could send attacks. While Taz held his warding easily, Emil seemed to be struggling to keep up.

Someone dropped a sword the exact dark grey of the cell bars in the Old King's dungeon, one of the enemy. I would have put money on that blade being forged from *metirin* iron.

I visualised myself behind them, building the picture with frantic intent. They didn't even see me as I translocated behind them and snatched up the blade.

"Taz, here!" I threw it to him.

He caught it and used it to pierce holes in Emil's protection, driving him back.

"You chose the wrong side," he taunted. "Your Queen is a chicken and your oh so faithful Forgotten families, like the Hemlocks, have turned tail and fled already. Admit it."

Emil winced under the sheer power of Taz's attacks, but he

wouldn't back down.

"I know where the truth of Faerie should sit," Emil bit back. "Old days, old ways. We weren't meant to be hidden underground, scratching through Faerie to build a 'civilisation'. We're power and beauty, malice and delight."

Taz snorted. "Very lofty. What did they offer you then? This isn't about the Faerie of old, it's personal, it's about you serving your own ends. No sense keeping them secret now, as if I don't kill you, my mother or my aunt will."

"The King gave me a promise," Emil insisted, almost on his knees as Taz drove against him again and again. "He said the human world is to be mine, under their rule, while he and the Queen have dominion over all of Faerie."

I looked around for the wannabe queen of Faerie. Chicken-Elvira was almost right behind Emil now. I didn't even feel bad for hoping he stepped on her, or that she pecked his eyeballs clean out.

Taz laughed, sharp and humourless. "Pretty tales, but he said he'd crown Elvira, and was he really going to? Surely, he would have told you the truth, his most trusted lieutenant, the snake in our grass? Was he going to crown her?"

Discomfort passed across Emil's face that was nothing to do with Taz's onslaught. Taz paused, giving him a chance to answer.

Silence.

"As I thought." Taz renewed his attack. "He had no intention of crowning her, so why would he give you what he promised? Did he call you special? Flatter you with pretty words? You've chosen the wrong side."

Behind Emil, Chicken-Elvira squawked indignantly. She drew my gaze past the fight and on to a bigger problem, a crowd of Forgotten penned together, backs to each other to create a circle. It looked as though they'd originally been captured and corralled, but now they were using their united strength to fight back.

"You good here?" I shouted to Taz.

"More than. Don't do anything I wouldn't do."

"That leaves literally everything!"

I darted off without waiting for his answer and grabbed Meryl's arm as I ran past at speed.

"Can you do your metal thing with a couple of the pillars, or whatever you can grab?"

"Sure." Meryl nodded. "What's the plan?"

I pointed to the Forgotten group as we dashed toward them, both throwing up a warding as someone came rushing at us. They bounced and I didn't bother checking to see where they landed, forging on.

"If you can create a metal circle, I think I can get my energy to form a pen around them. I don't know how long I'll be able to hold it, but it might be enough for Queenie to get most of them through into the holding area."

Meryl pulled me to a halt some metres away from the mayhem.

"Keep the protection while I move a few bits then."

I held my warding over both of us, only able to watch in awe as she severed parts of the metal beams from high above.

I expected some kind of kickback from someone official, but even Call-Me-Henry had taken to the chaos surprisingly well. He stood on his reception desk with his tie knotted around his head, throwing hefty pieces of stationery with a deadly aim. He flinched as a couple of his staplers zoomed past him, but when he saw us, he returned to his task.

"Okay, all done." Meryl sagged beside me. "Quick, before they figure it out and start kicking stuff away."

She took over holding the protection as I called my connection and my energy to me.

Okay little gifty thing. I know we haven't done this before, but I need to try it now. Please.

Talking to my gifts always seemed bonkers, but I swear sometimes it felt like the connection grew stronger when I acknowledged it as a living entity rather than a thing.

I focused on the tingling seeping into my shoulders and down both arms, sending it out through my hands to be safe.

Please split and find the metal.

I grunted as the energy tore from my hands, the effort of focusing to keep it split and moving in two separate streams draining me in an instant.

The power surged toward the metal items Meryl had gathered, a collection of bits of steel from above and clumps of random stationery from the main desk.

I winced as my gift latched on and gobbled across the metal, leaping from thing to thing. The Forgotten started to panic, but I held the two streams from meeting at the other side of the metal circle, just enough of a gap for Queenie to pull people out.

What if they stampede her?

Queenie looked up, found me and her face grew thin.

I've done completely the wrong thing, I know it.

Queenie clapped her hands, bringing several FDPs scurrying to her. Before I could fathom what she intended to do, she put her fingers to her mouth and let out a harsh whistle that almost pierced my eardrums.

I concentrated on holding my makeshift energy pen until thuds began to shake the ground nearby.

CHAPTER TWENTY FOUR
Iron Arrows Need To Be Banned

Trolls landed in the middle of the crowd, dropping with a thump on one knee and rising, surging toward Queenie. Without any hesitation, they started grabbing people from the makeshift pen and disappearing with them. Trevor grabbed two of the Forgotten and vanished, but I couldn't see the Governor anywhere. When Trevor returned for another two, I noticed a purple armband on his arm.

I tried not to think about whether that meant he'd just been made acting Governor of his team, or something worse had happened. I couldn't even tear my gaze away from the pen to look for Taz or the whole thing would collapse.

But the enemy crowd was thinning. The trolls worked fearlessly and fast, until I felt safe enough to let my gift return to me. I dropped to my knees, aware of Meryl panting nearby.

"I have to take five," she said. "I urge you to do the same."

"Taz." I tried to struggle to my feet.

Meryl looked back before I could. "He's fine, holding his own better than most of us. Oh, crap."

I twisted in time to see someone I didn't recognise running toward Taz and Emil, who both looked exhausted. Taz hadn't seen the person coming up behind him with two vine-like whips, one in each hand. The first attack cracked against his protection and he flinched.

I managed to get to my feet, but my wobbling legs wouldn't get me to him in time.

Think Demi, come on, idiot! I stumbled forward.

I couldn't use my gifts any more, drained to the point of

fainting.

Queenie was ferrying the last of the cornered Forgotten away.

Taz was under attack.

To my left, the Queen was engaged in a fierce duel with the Old King.

An idea almost knocked me over, distracting enough that I almost lost my footing. I halted and threw up the weakest warding I could manage, conserving my strength. This next idea was likely to get me slaughtered.

"FLEE." I sent the sound of the Old King's voice into the hall. "RETREAT. BACK TO THE COURT."

Fighting ceased around me and I almost passed out with relief. A few of the Forgotten started moving toward the lifts. They didn't need to be told twice.

"Stop!" The Old King's real voice filled the air.

Most of the Forgotten hesitated, but I saw others still taking the opportunity to disappear while they could claim confusion as an excuse. Several of the lifts vanished, full of Forgotten fleeing back to wherever they entered from. I hoped the hall and floor teams could cope with them.

"I SAID RETREAT!" I tried one last time. "I'M COMMANDING YOU, DON'T FALL FOR THESE CHEAP TRICKS TO KEEP YOU CORRALLED HERE."

I choked over the last word as the Old King's gaze found me. He snarled, his face torn with fury. He sent out a wave of something at me but I held my ground just about, my protection laughably weak against his power.

I turned to look at Taz, whether to implore him not to get involved and stay safe, or to save me, I wasn't even sure. I found him in the crowd, just in time to see Emil raise the crossbow behind his back.

I screamed. Taz whirled around to face me. The arrow whistled past, missed him by millimetres.

They weren't far away at all, only a few metres. I didn't even have time to flinch as the arrow whistled through my warding.

I grunted as the tip sliced into my side, whipping a savage chunk of skin with it.

Taz roared and sank the iron sword into Emil's shoulder, driving him to the ground.

I looked down to see blood beginning to trickle from a gaping wound under my ribs, like someone had used a spoon to carve out a lump of flesh around the arrow. I shuddered, my vision blurring. Taz appeared in front of me and I could smell him somehow, all apple-fresh. His hands held me as I dropped to my knees, their touch familiar and comforting.

Taz laid me on my good side and Marvin's face swam beside him, grimacing at the wound. My head flopped back but from this angle I could see the Queen renewing her attack on the Old King with a fervour I hadn't seen before.

She knows Taz will be lost to grief if I die.

The thought both comforted and frightened me. I didn't want him to be left alone. I didn't want to die.

"Arrow's poisoned," Marvin muttered.

Taz's hand clenched mine painfully, anchoring me.

Because of course, he's my anchor too. Probably has been since the first time he smiled at me.

"Fix it." His voice was pure menace.

"I don't think I can." Marvin sounded far away now. "There's only one known antidote to this poison, and getting it will be near impossible before she-"

"DO IT."

I clung onto Taz's hand, my fuzzy brain watching the whirl of the Queen fighting the Old King.

Most of the crowd had stopped to watch, and it was beautiful, in a savage, Fae way. The monarchs whirled and danced around each other at great speed like frenzied butterflies, almost equally matched although the Queen seemed to be the more furious of the two.

I'm going to die. Might as well make some good on my way out. Perhaps that's what I'm here for.

While Taz and Marvin verbally circled each other, I found the length of the arrow. If Emil had soaked the whole thing in poison, I didn't want anyone else touching it. My card was already marked, although I'd never understood what that saying really meant.

Won't get to find out now either.

With my teeth gritted, I pulled hard and wrenched the arrow out of my side. I shook Taz's hand away from mine and ignored his voice, now just a muffled string of frantic notes.

Dredging up the last of my dying gifts, I visualised myself standing tall and strong with the Old King's back in front of me. I'd only have a moment before reality made me crumple again, but I only needed one.

The hazy image of the Old King's back and shoulders, cloaked still in royal blue, appeared in front of me. With the last of my strength, I lifted the arrow and stabbed the Old King under his right shoulder blade with all my failing might.

He froze, but I couldn't hang around to see him die. I was dying faster, my limbs crashing to the floor in an undignified heap.

Can a dying person still be considered undignified?

With my eyes closed, I threw my last hope into the air for all to hear.

"Watch. Listen. Learn." I spoke the Arcanium motto as loud as I could, then added my own. "Faerie remembers and Faerie always chooses in the end."

I thought I saw the haze of a rainbow drifting around me, a protection perhaps.

Then I realised my eyes were closed and imagined a smile on my face, thinking of what Xavio had said.

Faerie was calling me home.

CHAPTER TWENTY FIVE
Demi Dies (Again), and Old Tara is Definitely NOT Impressed

Tutting. So much tutting.

The vague awareness of 'being' surrounded me, which was weird. I didn't know why it was weird, but the vagueness felt familiar, which was also comforting.

"Am I dead yet?" I found the words easily.

"No, dear."

The voice sounded familiar too, and given the disapproval in the tone, I wasn't endearing myself by hanging about.

"I should probably get up then, shouldn't I."

"That would be wise. Most of the Forgotten will flee after your little reminder, but the Old King will remain to the bitter end."

The battle. How does she know about my reminder?

I sat up and squealed as pain blossomed across my side. My eyes snapped open to an abundance of green, and I looked up to find Old Tara had parted her willowy branches. Peering further, I could see that the knots in her trunk were all scrunchy. She was seriously not impressed.

"Sit still," she insisted. "This may sting."

A plump, ominous-looking brown root extended along the ground toward me. I clenched my fists and tried to hold still, but as the root slid over my wound, I couldn't look away. It seemed to be leaking some kind of pearlescent substance which coated the injury. A radiating heat seared the skin and the end of the root began to shrivel.

Emil poisoned me, but he was aiming for Taz.

Panic slammed into me and I lifted wide eyes to Tara's trunk "I need to get back."

The root's substance seemed to be knitting the wound together, and I silently willed it to hurry.

"Yes," Old Tara's branches rustled. "You do. We can't have the prince and potential future king threatening to tear Faerie down every time you get yourself killed. It's a very bad look. Now, another minute or so and you should be fit to go back."

"You can heal me?" I asked without thinking, earning me an indignant rustle.

"I've told you before, dear, I am Faerie. I can do, and access, almost anything. There are laws of course, but luckily the Queen is not as airy-fairy as she often appears."

She hadn't told me that she was actually Faerie itself before, not technically. Only that she was formed from it. I also couldn't ever remember the Queen ever being airy-fairy, but decided it wasn't the best time to comment as Tara continued.

"I believe some of your humans have given me many names in their mythologies, but Old Tara is what my family call me, my friends."

As I sat there staring at my quickly healing skin, my mind played puzzle with the pieces of information.

The Queen said that the last time she wandered in Faerie, Taz was born. Xavio said Faerie was a 'she'.

Old Tara had mentioned her kin last time I'd died here, and how she would be happy for me to be part of it. Deep in the recesses of memory, I recalled that the code names for Taz and the Queen were acorn and oak.

I can't possibly ask her if she's somehow one of Taz's parents, can I? I mean, this is Faerie- she is Faerie. Stranger things must have happened before.

I had to play the next question very carefully, although sitting here in the gentle balmy air amid the endless greenery, I could think of worse ways to go if I overstepped the mark and she pulverised me.

"So, as Faerie, you pretty much see everything, right? I mean, you're a willow as well. Don't willow trees sometimes see the future, or is that just a myth?"

Silence. Then, a distant rustling that grew louder as Old Tara's laughter trickled down around me.

"Oh, my dear, are you suggesting that I've somehow orchestrated everything that's come to be? Pulled on various branches, tweaked various roots?"

Seduced various queens and birthed various future kings of Faerie to oppose the enemy more like.

I took a deep breath. Nothing like being my blunt self to seal the deal with my future in-laws.

Orbs alive. I swallowed wrong and started to splutter. *Why on earth am I thinking that?!*

I really hoped Tara couldn't read my thoughts as her branches rustled with laughter above me. I threw everything into the ring as the burn in my side started to ebb into a tingle.

"Taz always said he could never be king because of his blood," I pressed. "But I reckon he's more Fae than even his sisters are, more Faerie than anyone, except perhaps Faerie itself. Or yourself, if that makes any sense at all. Almost like an heir apparent, kind of thing."

There it was. I would either get more laughter, or a branch would probably send me flying down the hill never to be seen again.

"If you like." Old Tara sighed, a soft breeze whispering through the clearing and wiping away old secrets. "He doesn't know, of course. As for the suggestion I have brought all this about, I am honour-bound not to meddle in the affairs of Fae."

I thought this through with my smile growing all the while.

"But what about the affairs of fairies, or family?"

Old Tara whipped out a branch and tapped me gently on the nose.

"Too smart, dear, but I do like you. You bear the mark of the queen on your wrist, the anchor of the prince in your heart, and the imprint of several earned loyalties from your friends. This will be my final gift to you. May you forever be free of compulsions, with or without your mentor's blessing, and may his natural gift forge the path you will take."

I had no idea if blessings only hung around while the giver was alive or not, but it sounded like Old Tara was securing it for me just in case. Still, my heart plummeted at the thought of Xavio.

"He is at peace," Old Tara said softly. "If there is an 'after', he will have earned the best version of it."

"He gave me his natural gift, but I don't think it worked." I sniffed. "I have no idea what it was so I can't even test it to find out."

"A gift such as his will take time to grow with you. It may manifest in ways individual to you, but in short his was the gift of giving."

I thought back to all of the little things Xavio used to do during fairy lessons, and the time we'd been interrupted by an elderly Fae woman who he'd gone out of his way to help. The extra tuition he'd offer to anyone struggling, and the way he immediately noticed if a student was going without a warm meal at home, or missing a coat on a chilly day.

"That sounds like him."

"And it sounds much like you, my dear. But remember, learning to accept help and love, even the occasional gift, is as important as learning to give them."

I frowned, letting that sink in. Old Tara gave me all of a few seconds before her branches tutted.

"Now, I am unfortunately not as gifted as the Queen, so you will always bear a scar on your side, and I cannot fashion it into pretty imagery like your lizard. But scars are like the weathered bark of a trunk, a badge of growth and strength."

I shrugged. I could think of way worse badges to bear.

The heat from the root had almost subsided now and the substance was soaked into the wound. Whether it had actually formed itself into shiny new scarred skin to cover the gap, or simply encouraged my body to create new cells super-fast, I didn't know. I filed away the knowledge about Old Tara's roots having healing properties to tell Marvin later though.

As I stood on shaking legs, Old Tara sighed again.

"Do come and visit soon, dear, with your young man if you will. One day the tree you planted will sprout but occasional company would be lovely all the same, so I can see all my little acorns grow. Be prepared on your return, and thank you for reminding the right side that Faerie is worth fighting for."

I glanced at the patch of earth I'd planted the acorn in, now showing the tiniest tip of a green shoot.

'All my little acorns grow'. I wonder if I should tell Taz or at least give the Queen a chance to do it first.

I took a deep breath as the realm around me wavered. Moments after being able to smell the freshness of Faerie, I was thrown back into the sweaty, panic-ridden atrium without even having a chance to close my eyes, the brush of nether a strange, deep hue of purple amid grey.

Sound flooded in, the crowds standing in horrified silence as they watched the fight before them. Clashing blades filled the air and the sizzle of gifts.

Above it all, the unmistakeable sound of Taz throwing out

every single swearword known to man, mingled with some that I'd never even heard of before but were definitely not complimentary.

The Queen hovered nearby but even as she stepped forward, Taz reached out without looking to shove her away. He swung his iron sword at the Old King's protection, piercing, stabbing and hacking with one arm while his free hand was waving about, no doubt trying every gift he could dredge up to blast the barrier down. Even his wings seemed to bear his anger, flickering with actual flames that seared against the Old King's warding.

Okay, my boyfriend can be kind of cool sometimes.

The Old King looked like he was tiring. He wasn't old, at least not in terms of looks, but Taz fought with inhuman fury. I had to remind myself that the Old King had fought the Queen long ago, so his appearance was deceptive, but where he had experience, Taz apparently had an unending well of incandescent anger.

"Oakthorn, please." The Queen's tone was desperate. "*Taz*, this isn't your kill to bear. It won't bring her back."

No, but Faerie will.

Several people fighting nearby had noticed me now, some beginning to mutter their shock to others. I also had no idea how the Old King was still standing after I'd stabbed him, but perhaps he was immune to *metirin* iron, or maybe I didn't stab him hard enough to incapacitate him.

My side was throbbing with unending tenderness now, but a quick glance down showed the fresh scarring still holding firm.

I'll last long enough to calm Taz down.

I hobbled forward as quick as I could and raised my voice against the dry burn in my throat.

"Listen to your mother." I ignored the ill-timed temptation to burst into a *Tangled* song. "She's right."

Taz froze. He looked around, his eyes narrowing. Perhaps he suspected me of being a glamour trick, either by his mother to lure him to safety or the Old King to unhinge him.

"Oi." I clicked my fingers. "I'm not kidding."

I barely saw him move. He dropped the sword and loomed in front of me as I choked over an unexpected whimper of relief. He looked at my side, his mouth dropping open. I flinched as the Old King moved behind him, but Taz must have heard. He threw up a hand and cast a warding over both of us as the Queen took his place in the fight.

With his hands on my shoulders, he peered at my newly-healed wound.

"How?" he asked. "Are you really Demi?"

I nodded. "I am really me. It was Old Tara. I don't know how, or why, and I didn't have one of those nut things this time, but she thanked me for reminding people that she- that Faerie is worth fighting for. And some other stuff I won't go into now."

A loud echo drew us together, Taz's arms winding around my shoulders to avoid my side.

The Queen had the Old King backed against the wall, but he seemed to be taking strength from the fact Taz was occupied. He roared an order and his forces rallied, charging against the FDPs nearest and renewing their effort. I saw Petra bleeding nearby with Avril trying to support her toward Marvin. Ace was protecting as many people as he could while Milo zipped in and out, ferrying them to somewhere safe.

How can we be losing now? This is our home. The Old King stood taller, the Queen now straining under his renewed onslaught. *It's as if Taz had some kind of strength here nobody else does.*

I remembered what Kainen had said then, about Arcanium being linked to Taz's will.

Hell, Taz isn't just half Fae or half royalty, he's half Faerie.

"We should get you to the medical hall," Taz said, turning back to face me. "Marvin needs to check you over."

I frowned, distracted. "There's like a literal battle for the whole realm going on."

"So?"

I pressed myself against him, nestling into his chest. His arms tightened around me. I don't think he would have refused me anything right then, or been able to see where he was leading me given the tears that started soaking my hair a moment later. I let him hold me for a long moment, needing to take what comfort I could before we started fighting again.

Words floated back to me, Sagar's insistence that people needed to know when the evil had been thwarted, otherwise what was there to hope for in darker times.

"We stay," I murmured. "Sometimes everyone needs to see the evil vanquished and the demon slain."

Taz choked over a laugh. "Where did you hear that?"

"It's only the foundation of every Faerie tale ever. You need to wear him down though, before your mum finishes him off. He's gaining power but against you he was weakening. I-someone once told me that Arcanium is linked to your will, that it was the Queen's doing to keep you safe. You need to fight-Look out!"

I pulled Taz aside as Emil came at us from nowhere, his shirt torn enough to show a barely-healed stab wound in his shoulder. Even though we were protected, I knew he could still summon his crossbow, and the Queen had Taz's iron sword.

Fury massed across Taz's face, his shoulders bunching.

"I'll take this one for you, and Xavio," he growled. "If what you say is true, if Arcanium has ever responded to me in any way, then it will obey you now."

I opened my mouth to protest, but Taz stepped in front of me and threw out his transmutation power, turning the floor to liquid under Emil's feet.

Trusting his skill completely, I faced the Queen and Old King, locked in battle. He was her fight, as Emil should have been mine. Retribution on all accounts, but Taz was shouldering my fight so I could help his mother win hers.

For Faerie.

For our home.

I can do this.

I pulled my connection into every part of me and focused on the ivy strewn around the walls, the cherry trees in their huge pots either side of the reception desk. They would be rooted in the earth, I was sure of that now. They would be eternal, everlasting and linked to Old Tara. Wily as she was, she would have her ways of seeing all. If Arcanium was linked to Taz, then Old Tara would be sure it linked to her as well. She would hear me.

"Well, Arcanium, if you're listening, our enemy is right there," I whispered. "We just need to contain him, so the Queen can make her final stand. For Faerie and for our home."

I visualised the words leaking down my body, through my feet and across the marble in rivulets that reached the cracks beneath the cherry tree pots and down into Faerie. Old Tara might not be allowed to interfere, but if Taz did have any control over Arcanium, then she would lend me her part of it to defend ourselves this once.

A strand of ivy jerked away from the wall. It lashed out so fast several people had to leap out of the way. The end of it lassoed around the Old King's wrist. He shook it, but another vine was around his neck before he could free himself.

"Force him to face the crowd," I called out.

The Queen swept around and saw me as the ivy obeyed. She stared into my eyes while the ivy continued restraining the Old King, twisting him to face the atrium. An imperceptible nod of her head, the slightest dip of her chin. A regal thank you, and perhaps an understanding of how much I now knew.

I dropped the connection to Arcanium and turned to find Taz had not only felled Emil to the floor, but somehow trapped him underneath a mound of stationery. I saw Meryl nearby and she mouthed 'you're welcome'. I couldn't help but smile.

Silence fell across the atrium as the crowd realised the winds of fate had changed again. But looking out over the sea of expectant eyes, I realised they were not on the Queen, or the Old King. They were pointing squarely at me. Even though the Queen stood with one eye on the Old King, the rest of her attention was fixed on me. Waiting.

I died and returned. I realised. *Even if they don't know what happened at Kainen's the first time I went to Old Tara, they probably think I'm a phantom spirit or something, or secretly some super powerful Fae entity like Kainen did. No harm turning that to our favour now.*

"Faerie chose today." I winced to hear my voice wobble. "And it chose wisely. It honours those who value effort and kindness over meaningless power and unearned gifts. My Queen." I hesitated and gave her a rueful look. "I'd kneel but um, I'm kind of incapacitated and really, really knackered."

The Queen's lips twitched. She didn't reply as several around me took the hint and dropped to one knee. Nearby, FDPs were renewing the attack and chasing off any who were fleeing or still trying to resurrect the battle. The Queen picked up the iron sword Taz had dropped in his rush to get to me and approached the Old King.

I flinched as something snared my shoulders, but it was Taz.

I looked past him to find the Eastwick sisters standing guard over Emil and Chicken-Elvira.

No forgiveness for the traitors. No mercy. Only the vengeance of the grieving.

The Queen turned so that she could keep the Old King in view but face the crowd also. Her voice rang out across the atrium as a radiant golden-white glow engulfed her.

"A new era begins today. There will be a conditional day of forgiveness tomorrow, when any Forgotten may approach my court and plead their allegiance, which will be judged accordingly. Those that remain traitorous to me or mine will be punished by the laws of Faerie themselves. To those who have fought, died and lost for us today, we will mourn, and we will rejoice in their bravery of the fallen. Leave in peace."

I blinked. *She's letting them go?*

"Ah, she's going for the benevolent act," Taz muttered. "Fae love the chase, so her crew will have great fun hunting down any that don't turn tail and pledge allegiance. I wouldn't watch the next bit."

Despite the warning, I couldn't turn my gaze away as the Queen faced the Old King once more. He looked up at her, hatred narrowing his eyes amid the ivy still clinging to him.

Sometimes, we need to see the deed done and the evil slain.

Without hesitation, no sign of guilt or doubt, the Queen raised the blade and swiped the Old King's head clean from his shoulders.

"Hey!" A shout turned us all around.

I gasped, unable to move as two winged beasts shot through the air. A couple of FDPs tried to ensnare and block them with gifts, but Luchia and Draven were dodging every attempt.

I saw their bodies earlier and assumed they were dead.

A foolish mistake.

Dangling beneath them, Emil's wrists were clamped in Draven's talons and a large white chicken was hanging by one leg from Luchia's claws.

Before any of us could do anything, the two Oricadae, Emil and Chicken-Elvira were disappearing into the lift shaft to the human world and whooshing out of sight. I scanned the atrium and found the mound of metal Meryl had built smoking, but other than Harvey clutching his arm to his chest and a very red-faced Beryl, they looked unharmed.

I started to shake.

"Should I bother asking if you're okay?" Taz asked.

I lifted my head with monumental effort, peering into his swimming turquoise eyes.

"I've died twice in the last week. I thought you were a traitor at one point. I've been using my gifts so long I don't know if I can even move now it's over. Xavio's dead, and I've seen things." I burst into tears. "Of course I'm not bloody okay! Where's Leo?"

"Ace has him, don't worry. The moment you keeled over, Leo went mental. The only way your body wasn't carted off as a spoil of war by the Old King's inner circle was because Leo basically took out half of the Forgotten watching the show with one smack of his tail. He shrank moments after the Old King was killed, while the Queen was harping on. I knew you'd be worried about him, but I saw Ace pick him up and disappear with Milo."

If I knew my friends at all, they'd be going to check on the library, one of Leo's favourite places. So I let Taz press his fingertips to my temple, guide my head onto his shoulder and lead me forward.

With hesitant steps, we started a slow shuffle through the crowd. I watched the atrium pass by at an angle, wondering what the distorted roaring noise was. When I lifted my head again, I realised it was raucous clapping from those still gathered, aimed at us as we walked past.

The Queen met us at the lifts, along with Queenie, who put out a hand to stop us.

"We need to-"

"No." Taz shook his head. "We don't need to. Demi's going to get checked out, then we're going to kick back and rest. We've more than earned it."

Queenie's lips twitched, and I wondered how her make-up could possibly still be perfectly applied across her face. Again I wondered if she wore a permanent glamour, but I was too exhausted to care either way.

"I was going to suggest that we discuss your actions at a later date," she said. "I think taking the FDP trials a year early for both of you would be sufficient reward for your efforts, and your loyalty? Taz, you petitioned to leave mentoring and join the FDP ranks, which you're still welcome to do if you so choose, but I'm sure Demi at least will be pleased with the offer?"

I tried to nod but my head wouldn't cooperate.

"Yeah, I'd love that."

"Then so do I," Taz admitted after a pause. "Um, cheers."

I grinned, so relieved at seeing him both uneasy and unharmed that it took all my willpower not to burst into snotting, honking tears again.

"Unfortunately, Elvira and Emil have escaped into the human world. No doubt they'll find their way back into Faerie with no problems, but there will be no mercy once they are found."

The Queen's voice echoed loud over the atrium, a calming measure to reassure the crowd and warn any remaining members of the Forgotten who might try to re-establish their rebellion.

I had serious doubts about how easy Emil and Elvira would be to find, but Queenie stepped aside as Taz hustled me into the lift and jabbed a button before I could say anything.

"Emil and Elvira escaped," I mumbled as the lift shot upwards.

Taz shrugged. "They'll go into hiding for a while. We can only hope the round-up crews will find them and do something awful. The whole time he was a traitor, getting me to trust him, spying on us. He had no remorse about kil- let's not worry about him now."

I wished I hadn't asked. Thinking of Emil made me think of Xavio, and I didn't have the brain space for any more exhaustion or grief.

I let Taz support my weight as the lift came to a stop and we shuffled down the hall toward my room. Signs of fighting seemed less drastic here, the odd singe on the wall and several red marks on the doors we passed for anyone needing a sick-bed.

"Do you want me to-" Taz stopped outside my bedroom door. "Do you want me to leave you to sleep a bit? Or I can find Petra and ask her to stay with you?"

I pushed open the door and all but fell toward the bed. Curling up on my good side, relieved I could at least face the room this way, I gave Taz a wicked smile. Despite all the horrors, and the war, a little flicker of devilry reminded me that I was still part-fairy.

This was my home and I belonged here.

As he hovered in the doorway, I held out a hand.

"Why? Scared I'll bite?"

CHAPTER TWENTY SIX
A Meeting With the In-Laws and a Potential New Nickname

It took me three days to recover enough to leave my room. Nobody seemed to bat an eyelid that Taz refused to leave my side, although we managed to get a mattress set up on the floor for him. Despite everything we'd been through, and how much I trusted him with my life and everything else that came with it, that particular milestone was one adventure I intended to take in my own time, when I was ready.

On the fourth day following the battle, Queenie called us to her office, said thanks, then unceremoniously told us we were taking the FDP trials a year early and what did we want, a medal?

Ace, Milo, the Eastwick sisters and several other mentees and FDPs insisted on throwing us a celebration party, although the revel to celebrate the battle and honour the three FDPs who had died went on for a week anyway, so it got absorbed in the general chaos.

One thing that did bring me a huge amount of joy was Ace and Milo having too many cherry bubble juices one evening and announcing their relationship to everyone while hyped up on sugar. I think they were secretly disappointed that nobody was in the least bit surprised, or as Beryl put it, "yeah whatever, we all knew. What do you want, applause?" I just about managed to stop myself suggesting that she'd make a very good Queenie one day.

It was also a bit hypocritical considering she went bright red and made mumbling noises whenever anyone teased her about her new relationship with Harvey. Apparently by most trusted accounts, she'd given him a punch on the arm mid-battle and said, "oh, go on then", and he had to have a little sit down.

I also found out that Trevor had been promoted to Head Realm-Skipper, which was a completely different thing to the Governor's role (who turned out to be fine). There was apparently some discussion, but the trolls insisted, unions were mentioned and Queenie swiftly backed down.

Now that I was mending, I had an inkling that I should tell Taz it was time he started sleeping in his own room again, but so far I'd found excuse after excuse. So, as we sat in the canteen with a huge pile of cheesy Bolognese nachos between us, I tried to think of a way to bring it up without having to actually ask him.

"I-"

My words disappeared as Petra ambled up, the wound on her leg still not fully healed yet.

"Taz, your mother's here so Queenie's demanded your presence. Both of you."

Taz rolled his eyes and got up, holding out a hand to me. I eyed the nachos sadly and wrapped my fingers in his, letting him pull me to my feet.

"One day, we'll be able to get through a meal without my family invading," he grumbled.

We waved goodbye to Petra as she happily took over nacho-duty and set off toward the lift.

"Any idea?" I asked.

Taz shook his head. "Either another congratulations, or a trap. Probably the first hiding the second."

Before we reached the lift, I glanced sideways and saw Cheryl sitting with her head bent over a book, a frown on her face.

I remembered what she'd said to me moments before the battle raged. She and her sisters had helped me so many times in their own ways. I wanted to thank all of them, but perhaps the best thing I could do for them as a trio was level their sibling playing field.

She looked up with alarm as I swooped in beside her. A smile froze on her face as I ducked and swept the briefest kiss on her forehead.

I gift you with the ability to remember anything you read whenever you choose to or need to.

"Er… No offense, Demi, but you're not my type. Also, Hutch will probably want to fight you because he's an arse, and Taz looks like he's trying not to pee himself laughing. What's going on?"

I grinned and, because fairies like to make a bit of mischief while they can, I winked for good measure.

"Try reading a book."

As I walked away, I kept my paces slow until I heard "hey, cool!" echo behind me.

I had thought briefly about giving her the other thing she'd wanted, but that was a journey she had to make on her own.

Taz slid an arm around my waist as we stepped into the lift.

"Very smooth, Sparky," he said with a grin.

I'd told him everything Old Tara had said, especially about Xavio's gift of giving being mine now. But Xavio was right; those little things that I could do for other people were what mattered. I brushed the seriousness aside, smirking back at him.

"Okay, but if Hutch does want to fight me, you'll have to take it on for me. I'm still injured."

Taz chuckled as the lift shot upward and I fell silent, bracing myself for the inevitable. If I broached the sleeping arrangements subject now, he wouldn't have any time to react.

"I'm probably going to be okay from now on," I said, not meeting his gaze. "At night, I mean."

He was silent for a long moment. "If that's what you want. I know it wasn't going to be forever or anything, but I like being able to keep an eye on you."

I pecked him on the cheek then, glad he wasn't more upset. *And perhaps a tiny bit indignant as well.*

"Yeah, plenty of time for all that," I mumbled. "Besides, you snore."

"I do not!"

The grin crept back over my face. "You do a bit."

He opened his mouth to retaliate, but luckily the lift came to a stop and I pushed open the grill with a grunt, my side still twinging.

Taz said nothing as he guided me along the hall, but I could almost see the potential payback weaving in his head for me teasing him about the snoring.

I didn't even bother trying to slow him down as he swept us right through the open doorway to Queenie's office.

Queenie and the Queen both looked up, sitting with identical postures, cups of tea and saucers in hand.

"I won't bother with pleasantries," the Queen announced. Taz snorted. "We all know Emil and Elvira have escaped. Although we have defeated the Old King, they won't take the sleight and stay away for long."

"No doubt your crew will hunt them down," Taz said.

She eyed him for a moment. "It won't be the end. Emil has shown his hand but we shouldn't underestimate Elvira's power, as she was likely the one to raise the Old King in the first place."

I bit my lip. "Do we know how?"

"I could feel the Old King hadn't been risen long, maybe sixteen years or so." The Queen set her cup and saucer on the desk. "I admit that I wandered in Faerie for some time, a handful of years ago now. That may have given her the space to make it possible magically for the Old King to return."

Although her countenance didn't change, I thought I could see a slight flicker of shame amid the stubbornness in her eyes. As she looked back at me, I realised she was sending me a silent message, along the lines of: you're a smart girl, and you know how and when Taz was born already.

I wondered then if that was why Taz was able to best the Old King easier than anyone else, because he was born as the balance, but I kept that information to myself.

Although I'd told Taz about Old Tara's link to him already, he'd resolutely backed away from any mention of it since, so that was a conversation he could have with his mother on his own time.

"Perhaps a little less wandering and a bit more leading might be best in future," Taz suggested, his tone acidic.

I gave him a withering look. "Not helping."

"What?" He frowned back.

I ignored the attitude and focused instead on the issue, already worn out from having to be up since breakfast.

"If Elvira is still a threat, then we hunt them down, Elvira and *him*." I couldn't say Emil's name out loud, not after what he'd done, who he'd taken.

Queenie raised one perfectly pencilled eyebrow at me.

"There will be a regrouping period first," she said. "But all FDPs and mentees will need to keep their wits and training honed, especially if you two are taking your FDP trials a year early. Until then, best you enjoy yourselves while you can."

I took that as the dismissal it was and sagged into Taz's side as he put his arm around my shoulders. We walked toward the door, but a throat clearing stopped us both.

"You two are officially courting now?" The Queen asked.

I went bright red as Taz turned us around. Given the sharp edge to the Queen's voice, this was what she'd really summoned us about.

"Yeah, and?" he asked, his tone gruff. "If this is about Demi not being court Fae-"

"You might want to trim your hair a little." The Queen caught my eye with a haughty sniff as she set down her teacup. "If you're to be *involved* with the prince of Faerie, there are certain standards to be adhered to."

I stared at her, sure I saw the faintest tinge in her cheeks. Then she vanished. One moment she was in the chair, then both she and the chair were gone. Unnerved at the not-so-veiled sleight, I continued staring at the space she'd occupied.

Queenie's lips twitched as she slunk down behind a copy of *Faeshionista* magazine, wordlessly suggesting we get out of her office.

I let Taz tow me toward the lift, my cheeks burning with embarrassment and a big splash of indignation.

"Is my hair really that bad?" I asked.

Taz hesitated until we stood in the hallway waiting for the lift to arrive.

"No, I think it's lovely. A bit wild, I mean, my fingers tend to get tangled if I touch it, but-" He caught my expression. "But don't you see what that means though? She accepts you, likes you even. Normally if someone royal said they were dating a fairy, not even someone who's court Fae, it would be stopped immediately. There would be interventions. Arranged marriages would be discussed. Parties would be hosted by every possible eligible family in Faerie."

I frowned, unsettled. "That's... I'm not sure how to take that."

I had a frightening theory the 'involved' part the Queen mentioned was referring to the whole marrying into the royal line thing, but obviously Taz and I were nowhere near that stage.

"Don't take it at all then." Taz shrugged. "In Fae circles it's a huge accolade that she's even acknowledging you. In normal people circles, she actually kind of insulted you. Either way, Queenie said we should enjoy ourselves and you're still healing. You know what that means."

I would no doubt have to face the whole 'being accepted into the royal family' thing eventually, but it didn't have to be today. I found a smile as the lift finally arrived.

"We finally get to finish *Demolition Ducks*?" I asked.

We walked into the lift and I grinned as Taz stuck his tongue out at me.

"Exactly, a girl after my own heart. But I have to ask, what exactly did you do to my dear second cousin Jack, or whatever he is to me? And Cheryl, what did you give her?"

I pressed the button for the residents' floor and told him both gifts.

"That's a kind thing to do for Cheryl," he said, taking my hands. "Although I would have given Jack boils on his bits or something for eternity, but guilt works too."

I wrinkled my nose at the thought.

"Eww. The being able to gift people came in pretty handy though. Ooh, if your mother has accepted me or whatever now, does that mean I get to plan your birthday celebrations instead of her next year? I'm thinking a bigger party, two days, with events. Mandatory court Fae attendance. *Party games*."

He groaned. "I'm regretting this already, but no, no birthday parties, I beg you. It means you're now officially dating a prince of Faerie."

"We're dating?" I raised one eyebrow, pushing down the

wild fluttering inside my chest.

He grinned at me, wrapping one arm around my waist and brushing a kiss to my lips.

"Yes, we are." He opened the grill and guided me into the lift. "That basically makes you royalty too in many circles. You'll have to make your peace with that as well, because after the last week I'm never letting you out of my sight ever again. I'm even thinking a new nickname. My wicked princess sounds perfect for you."

I gaped at him as the lift set off. I also had to dwell on him calling me his future queen and turning out to be surprisingly possessive. But those issues didn't have to be dealt with today.

All the more reason to enjoy the silly things while we can.

I found my fiercest glare and faced Taz with my arms folded as we stopped at the residents' floor.

"Oh no. You are *not* calling me princess. Stop that right now."

He grinned and pulled open the gate for me, bowing low with a devilishly Fae smile.

"Make me."

As he darted out of the lift in an effort to escape, I tried to rein in my inane beaming.

There were still horrors lurking in Faerie, and no doubt the Forgotten would be out for revenge soon enough. But as I sucked in a breath and chased him down the residents' hall, I strangely felt no fear at the thought.

I have things to protect now. People I love. If they think they're taking any of this from me, they're going to wish they'd never been born.

ACKNOWLEDGEMENTS

Huge thanks go to my family and also my loveliest writing family as always, your support means everything to me – Anna Britton, Debbie Roxburgh, Samantha Williams, Sally Doherty, Marisa Noelle, Emma Finlayson-Palmer, Katina Wright, writing Twitter, Rebecca Kenney for the stunning covers, everyone who joins #ukteenchat, the WriteMentor crew, all the ARC readers, libraries and schools who took a chance on books 1 and 2, shops that are still stocking these books and giving this indie author a chance to reach more readers, and so many more!

ABOUT THE AUTHOR

While always convinced that there has to be something out there beyond the everyday, Emma focuses on weaving magic realms with words (the real world can wait a while). The idea of other worlds fascinates her and she's determined to find her own entrance to an alternate realm one day.

Raised in London, she now lives on the UK south coast with her husband and a very lazy black Labrador who occasionally condescends to take her out for a walk.

Aside from creative writing studies, an addiction to cake and spending far too much time procrastinating on social media, Emma is still waiting for the arrival of her unicorn. Or a tank, she's not fussy.

For the latest new and updates, check the website or come say hi on social media:

www.emmaebradley.com
@EmmaEBradley